BY LIV CONSTANTINE

Don't Open Your Eyes

The Next Mrs. Parrish

The Senator's Wife

The First Shot

The Stranger in the Mirror

The Wife Stalker

The Last Time I Saw You

The Last Mrs. Parrish

DON'T OPEN YOUR EYES

DON'T OPEN YOUR EYES

A NOVEL

LIV CONSTANTINE

BANTAM
NEW YORK

Bantam Books
An imprint of Random House
A division of Penguin Random House LLC
1745 Broadway, New York, NY 10019
randomhousebooks.com
penguinrandomhouse.com

Hardback ISBN 978-0-593-87520-9
Ebook ISBN 978-0-593-87521-6

Printed in the United States of America on acid-free paper

2 4 6 8 9 7 5 3 1

First Edition

BOOK TEAM: Production editor: Cindy Berman
• Managing editor: Saige Francis • Production manager: Jennifer Backe

Book design by Susan Turner

The authorized representative in the EU for product safety and compliance is
Penguin Random House Ireland, Morrison Chambers, 32 Nassau Street,
Dublin D02 YH68, Ireland, https://eu-contact.penguin.ie.

*For my mother, Ginny Constantine, whose words of wisdom
I still quote in life and on the page. You are dearly missed.*

DON'T OPEN YOUR EYES

Annabelle

"You're a monster!" I scream, my chest heaving as my heart pounds wildly. His eyes bulge, his face flushes red, and he looks like he wants to kill me. I back away as he closes the space between us. I'm wedged between his body and the kitchen counter. I hate him right now with every fiber of my being. I shove at him with all my strength, but he doesn't budge. I watch, helpless, as his hands reach up and circle my neck. He begins to squeeze. I can't get a breath. I claw at his arms to no avail. My vision blurs. Blindly, I reach my arm behind, my fingers fumbling until they close around the handle of a butcher knife. With every ounce of strength I have left I pull it from the block. I swing my arm around and aim the knife at his chest. He releases his grip and drops his arms, backing away. I cough and rub my sore neck. He nonchalantly walks toward the door to the garage, his hand lingering on the handle a moment, then opens it. "Oh, I forgot to tell you, I just got news I won best doc. It'll be in next month's Connecticut Magazine. *Thanks for voting." He winks and walks out the door.*

Annabelle Reynolds's eyes flew open, and she sprang to a sitting position. Her face was wet with perspiration, and a feeling of utter terror flooded her senses. She drew a deep breath, and her eyes darted to the figure sleeping next to her. She slipped from under-

neath the covers and grabbed her robe from the bench at the end of
the bed, covering her naked body. Shaking her head, she went into
the bathroom and turned on the shower, glancing at herself in the
mirror. She splashed cold water on her face. *You're being silly. It was
just a dream.* Yet the image of the two of them fighting, her husband's
face red and contorted with rage, had seemed so real. It was especially jarring because they hardly ever argued.

Today was their wedding anniversary. Two children, one dog, two
guinea pigs, and too many goldfish to count later, and she was happy.
As happy as she could be, despite everything that had happened
before—when she had still believed in happy endings. After she'd
married James, she'd promised herself that she'd put it all behind
her. Over the years, Annabelle had tried to forget about the loss—to
appreciate all she had gained. And even though there would always
be a part of her that missed him, a part of her that couldn't let him
go, she had to keep reminding herself that there was no point in
missing something that was never meant to be. So, she did her best
to think of him less often, every year trying harder to force herself to
forget, to be happy. But maybe being happy was asking too much.
Enough, she thought. *Shake it off.*

She brushed her teeth, mentally reviewing everything on today's
agenda. After she dropped the girls at school, she had to swing by the
drugstore to pick up an anniversary card for James. Then she had a
full day at work. As she stepped into the shower, she spoke her daily
gratitude affirmations aloud. "I'm thankful for my husband, my children, our good health, our beautiful home. I'm thankful for a job I
love, and good friends." She felt a little foolish doing this, but her last
client, a successful author of self-help books, had told her how benefi-
cial a gratitude practice was, not only to mental health, but physical as
well. Annabelle tried to be open-minded, so she'd committed to trying
it for sixty days to see if it made any difference. She was on day ten now.

"Mind if I join you?" James's voice cut through her thoughts as
he entered the bathroom.

"Please do."

He opened the door to the large shower and stepped inside.

"Happy anniversary," he said as he wrapped his arms around her and nuzzled her neck.

"Happy anniversary." Annabelle turned and kissed him, trying to dismiss the earlier feelings of terror from her dream. "Why don't we do this more often?"

A banging on the door made her pull back.

"Mooom, Parker's throwing up! I think he ate another sock."

She adored their golden retriever, but at times like this, not so much. Annabelle looked at James and rolled her eyes. "And that's why . . ."

"I'll go. Finish your shower." He stepped out. "Olivia, I'll be right there," he called through the door.

Half an hour later, Annabelle was dressed and downstairs. She walked into the kitchen, the smell of bacon filling the air. It was her favorite room of the house, featuring a built-in fireplace with a cozy sitting area, a custom-made farm table, and double French doors opening to their deck overlooking their swimming pool. Her mother had always said that the kitchen was the heart of the home, and some of Annabelle's best memories were of the two of them sitting and talking in their tiny kitchen around their worn wooden table. How she wished her mother was here now. She felt a pang of regret that her mother would never see her settled and content in such a beautiful place. Annabelle had never imagined that one day she'd be living in a gorgeous house, walking distance to the beach, and close to downtown Bayport, one of Connecticut's most charming towns. Parker ran up to her and nudged her with his nose as if sensing her sudden melancholy. She reached out to pet his head. "I hear you ate another sock, buddy."

"He's fine now. Someone must have left their socks out." James gave Olivia a meaningful look.

"Wasn't me!" their eleven-year-old protested.

"Well, I'm glad he's okay," Annabelle said, hoping to ward off a lecture from James.

He had made a full breakfast for Olivia and Scarlett: omelets, turkey bacon, toast, and an array of fruit. Annabelle gazed at her girls. Scarlett was a carbon copy of Annabelle—light brown hair and green eyes. James often commented that they were both the typical wholesome and natural, girl-next-door types. Annabelle thought it was cute when people commented on how alike they looked, but lately Scarlett seemed annoyed by it. Olivia was all James: blond and blue-eyed, with his bow-shaped mouth. But her sunny personality came from Annabelle.

James handed Annabelle a portable mug. "I made your coffee with oat milk and no sweetener. Consuming all those artificial sugars is bad for you."

"Yes, Doc," she said, resisting the urge to roll her eyes. She'd add some sweetener after he left. A couple of Splendas were not going to kill her, but it was pointless to argue with him. "I'm looking forward to our anniversary dinner tonight." They had reservations at her favorite restaurant in New York City, a little more than an hour's drive from their house.

"Me too. Mom's coming over at six to stay with the girls."

Scarlett made a face. "We don't need a babysitter. I'm fifteen. Gram doesn't need to come over."

"It's nice for there to be an adult around with us being an hour away," James said.

Scarlett rolled her eyes. "Come on, Dad. It's not like you're leaving the country. You'll just be in the city."

Annabelle and James looked at each other. "Well," she began, "she does have a point. What do you think?"

James scratched his beard and shifted his gaze to Scarlett. "I don't know. You and your sister tend to fight. Not sure you're the best person to be in charge."

"Give me a chance. Aren't you the one so big on us learning responsibility?" Scarlett asked.

Annabelle suppressed a grin and said nothing, waiting to see his response.

He moved his head back and forth as he considered it. "Okay, we'll give it a try." He glanced at his watch, then gave Annabelle a peck on the lips. "You'd better hit the road if you don't want to be late." He looked over at the girls. "Take your plates to the sink and grab your backpacks."

"I got it. You should get going, or *you're* going to be late," Annabelle said.

"Right. Have a good day, everyone."

A few minutes after he left, Annabelle cleared the table while the girls gathered their things. They filed out and got into Annabelle's Volvo XC90. Once they were on the road, she gave Scarlett a quick look.

"Make sure you're not on your phone all night. I don't want you to ignore your sister."

"I won't. We'll watch a movie or something."

"And no one coming over," Annabelle said.

"Okay, Mom. Got it. Geez."

"I'll tell you if she does anything wrong," Olivia piped up from the back seat.

"I'm not going to do anything wrong. Ugh!"

"And you call me right away if there's a problem," Annabelle said.

"There won't be a problem! What did you get Dad for your anniversary?"

"Remember the photo of the four of us on the beach last summer at the Cape?"

"Yeah, you made us all dress alike like a bunch of dweebs," Scarlett said.

Annabelle laughed. "It's a great photo of everyone! I had it done in oil paints for Dad."

Scarlett didn't seem impressed. "Hmm. That sounds nice, I guess. Um, so, I was wondering—"

"What?"

"Did you have any other serious boyfriends before Dad?"

Annabelle's hand tightened on the wheel as an image formed in her mind. For the second time that day, the old pain returned. All these years later, she still felt like a part of her was missing. "Why do you ask?" Annabelle made her voice light, buying time.

"Just wondering, you know, if there was anyone really special before Dad. Like, did you know right away that Dad was the one?"

"Do you mean, was it love at first sight?"

"I guess."

Annabelle was careful to measure her response. "I don't believe in love at first sight. Your dad and I were friends first, and I fell in love with him gradually. But it's better, I think, because he's not only my husband, he's my best friend." What she didn't tell her daughter was that once upon a time, she had very much believed in love at first sight. Back when she was young and naive and hadn't had her heart broken. She'd experienced that all-consuming, head-over-heels, mad love that poets and philosophers wrote about, and it had nearly destroyed her. Maybe her knees didn't buckle when James kissed her, but that kind of feeling didn't last anyway. What they had was better, more real. The kind of love that would sustain her, not obliterate her.

Scarlett made a face. "Doesn't sound very romantic. Who were you dating before him?"

Annabelle decided to sidestep the question. "Listen, the romantic love you see in the movies isn't real. Real love is—" She glanced over to see if Scarlett was listening and saw that she had put her AirPods in and tuned her out. She sighed. The teenage years were certainly living up to the stereotype. Annabelle was close to both girls, making sure to do special things one-on-one with each of them. Olivia and Annabelle went to the bookstore together every week, ordered hot chocolates, and chose a new book to read together. Scarlett and Annabelle's thing was scary movies. They'd make a large bowl of popcorn, turn the lights way down, and snuggle under a blanket. But lately, Scarlett wasn't even interested in doing that. Annabelle supposed it was normal—this pulling away—but it didn't make it any easier. Thank goodness Olivia was still her same sweet self.

Annabelle pulled into the parking lot of their school.

"Bye, Mommy," Olivia said as she jumped out of the car. Scarlett got out without a word.

"Have a good day," she called after them, but they ran ahead without looking back.

"You too, Mom," she said to herself, shaking her head.

JAMES HELD UP HIS GLASS of wine. "Here's to us, and to many more years together."

He looks so handsome tonight, Annabelle thought. He seemed to get better looking each year. When they first met, she thought he was a bit geeky. Back then he wore thick black frames, and his hair was too short for her taste. But now, with a touch of gray at his temples, contacts, and a more fashionable haircut, he reminded her a bit of Jude Law. Annabelle touched her glass to his and drank. "I love it here," she said, looking around. "All the stress of the day melts away as soon as I walk in the door."

He smiled at her. "You look gorgeous. I love that dress on you. How do you manage to get sexier every year?"

Annabelle had on her silver Irina halter dress—a little shorter than she liked, but if there was anywhere to wear it, it was New York. And she wanted to make tonight a special night. She'd even had her hair blown out so that it was extra shiny and straight for the evening. Annabelle wasn't into labels, but her mother-in-law had given her a gift card to a boutique where the least expensive item was nine hundred dollars. So she'd splurged and bought it for a New Year's party last year. "Thank you. Maybe later we can try to make up for what we missed in the shower this morning."

"That's a deal," James said. "We should come here more often. We don't get into the city enough anymore."

"Then it wouldn't be as special." The first time they'd come to Per Se was after they'd had Scarlett. Annabelle had been sleep-deprived and exhausted, and James had surprised her with a week-end away. Her in-laws had come to stay with the baby, and he had booked them a suite at the Waldorf. The first night they'd ordered room service; she fell asleep soon after and slept for fourteen hours. When she woke up around noon, he'd booked her a facial and a mas-sage and had made dinner plans at Per Se. His thoughtfulness was one of his most endearing qualities.

James reached into his pocket and pulled out a small box, wrapped in forest-green paper with a gold ribbon. "For you."

"I thought we were going to wait until we got home to exchange our presents."

"I couldn't wait. Go on. Open it."

Annabelle tore the paper and pulled out a small velvet box. When she flipped the top to reveal what was inside, she gasped. "Oh my gosh, James. This means so much." Tears sprang to her eyes. "How did you do this?"

"I got the name of a jewelry restorer and had it fixed."

She gently lifted the diamond and sapphire ring and held it in the palm of her hand. It had belonged to her mother, and to her grandmother before her. But it had been damaged when her mother had fallen on a sidewalk years ago, when she was in the end stage of Alzheimer's. The gold had been badly scratched, and some of the stones had fallen out. Her mother's aides had been so concerned with getting her to the hospital that no one thought to look for the stones, and they were never recovered. But now it looked like noth-ing had ever happened to it. She slipped the ring on her finger and held her hand out, admiring it. It felt like she had a part of her mother back.

"How is it that you always know the perfect thing to do?"

"I'm glad it makes you happy."

She reached out and took his hand. "*You* make me happy. Thank you so much for this." She blew out a breath. "I can't believe it's been nine years since Mom's been gone. But at least when I think of her now, it's when she was well. It's almost like those awful years never happened."

"I wish I had known her before she got sick. But I'm glad I was able to see glimpses of the real her. And she loved you, Annabelle. That much was obvious, even at the end."

Annabelle smiled. "She loved you too. From the moment she met you, she thought we were a couple, back when we were just friends. It's like she knew right away that we were meant to be together." She took a sip of her wine, a feeling of contentment washing over her. "This is so nice. As much as I love our family time, it's great to have time with just us, especially with your crazy work schedule."

"Couldn't agree more. Speaking of work. I forgot to tell you. Good news. I won best doc again this year. It'll be in next month's *Connecticut Magazine.*"

Annabelle gasped.

James gave her an amused look. "Well, you don't have to look so shocked."

She forced a laugh. "I'm just happy for you. Congrats! Why didn't you mention that you were in the running?

"Didn't want to jinx it."

She raised the glass to her lips with a shaking hand and took a long sip, her dream coming back to her full force.

2

Scarlett

Zoe Barnes was such a bitch! Scarlett could still feel the steam coming out of her ears when she got home from school. She'd barely said a word on the drive home, not that Dylan noticed. Scarlett's mom had hired her a year ago to pick up Scarlett and Olivia from school when they had after-school activities, and to stay at the house until their parents were home from work. Even though Scarlett didn't need a babysitter anymore, Dylan was pretty cool and didn't bug her too much. Besides, Olivia still needed to be taken care of, and Scarlett didn't have time for that. Now Dylan was too busy talking to Olivia about her stupid science project to notice that Scarlett was upset. It would be nice if she could at least ask Scarlett if everything was all right.

She went straight to her room and slammed the door, kicking off her shoes and blaring music from her phone as she opened Instagram. As she scrolled through, her stomach dropped at the story Zoe had just posted. A selfie of her and Ethan at the mall, their faces smushed together. Why had she ever told Zoe about her crush on Ethan? I mean, she'd only liked him forever. It was like a scene straight out of *Mean Girls*. Zoe had promised to find out if Ethan liked Scarlett, only to snag him for herself. And then when Scarlett got upset, Zoe turned everyone in their friend group against her. But what made it so much worse was that Zoe and she had been friends since first grade. They'd gone on each other's family vacations, spent every summer at the same camp, and had sleepovers almost every weekend. Zoe had been the one Scarlett called when she got her first period, the one who held Scarlett's hand in the ER when she had sprained her ankle ice-skating and had to wait for x-rays at the hospital. Zoe was always Scarlett's go-to person. But when they started high school this year, everything changed. Zoe went out for cheerleading, turned into this ultra fashionista, started giving more weight to clothes than the people wearing them, and began treating Scarlett differently. She was critical of Scarlett's appearance and complained that she was a Goody Two-shoes because she refused to vape like all the cool girls. Scarlett wasn't interested in spending hours on makeup and clothes, was too much of an athlete to risk her lungs for an e-cigarette, but Zoe was all about being cool. Still, Scarlett had never expected her betrayal, especially not in such a hurtful fashion. Zoe was a different person now.

Scarlett took a deep breath and exhaled, blinking back tears. She missed her friend—the old Zoe. The one who had cared about her for who she really was. But maybe that Zoe was gone for good.

She sighed. She couldn't keep holding on to what used to be. She would find new friends—ones who wouldn't stab her in the back. She wasn't going to let Zoe's betrayal ruin her school year.

Her door burst open, and Olivia walked in. "Hey, Dylan and I are making chocolate chip cookies. Wanna help?"

"Knock much?" Scarlett snapped. "No. I don't want to consume a thousand calories in sugar."

"Okay, geez. Don't bite my head off."

"Shut the door!" Scarlett yelled after her, but Olivia was already halfway down the stairs. Huffing in irritation, Scarlett got up and slammed the door again. Little sisters were so annoying. Her phone pinged and she grabbed it, her heart racing when she saw the name on the screen. Ben. Who needed stupid Ethan Manchester anyway?

She hadn't told anyone about Ben yet. She'd been given all the lectures on meeting people online, stranger danger, blah, blah, blah. But Ben was all right, and he lived far away—in Chicago. Besides, all they were doing was texting. It's not like she was telling him where she lived or anything. He'd messaged her on Discord. She was part of a Taylor Swift fan server, and they chatted off and on there until he suggested they move offline and text. After that he didn't participate much in the Discord server. He said he was getting a little tired of Taylor Swift. She knew what he looked like from his Instagram profile—he was sixteen and they had a lot of the same hobbies. They both loved sailing and tennis, and both weirdly hated pizza. She didn't know anyone else who didn't like pizza, but they both agreed that it was totally overrated. She had told him that she lived in Connecticut, close to New York, and that they often went there. He was impressed and said he'd always wanted to go to New York. She didn't give him her actual address, her father's words ringing in her head. She wasn't allowed to put where she lived or where she went to school in any of her social media posts. But she felt bad keeping things from Ben. She didn't want him to think she didn't trust him. Plus, he gave really good advice. She opened the message.

Ben: Your "friends" still being jerks?

Scarlett: Yah

Ben: They are 🔪 F em

Scarlett: Yeah BTW Thx for the
advice about no more sitters—so
much bttr then having grndprnts here

Ben: NP. U r not a baby. What's the mascot
of your HS? Hopefully, something cool.
Ours is so lame. A muskrat.

Scarlett: The Falcons

Ben: Very cool!

A knock at the door made her look up from her phone. "Scarlett, time to come down and do homework," Dylan said.

"Okay, coming." She texted Ben that she had to go, swung her legs over her bed, and opened her door.

When she got downstairs, the smell of fresh baked cookies wafted over her. She eyed the plate of chocolate chip cookies and couldn't resist grabbing one. It didn't escape Olivia's notice.

"I thought you didn't want to eat a ton of sugar."

"Shut up."

"Hey, you're not allowed to say that."

"Whatever."

Dylan looked over. "I don't see any homework."

Scarlett rolled her eyes and retrieved her backpack from the hallway, bringing it to the kitchen table. She pulled out her math book and got to work. It was hard to concentrate though. She kept thinking about Ben. Maybe she should be more open with him. He wasn't hiding anything from her; he had even told her where he lived and what school he went to. She knew his birthday too. She debated whether or not to talk to Dylan about it, but she was afraid Dylan would tell her parents, and she knew what they would say. At least she knew what her dad would say—he'd have a cow.

But then again, he worried about everything. They had to text him the minute they arrived anywhere, and when they were on their way home. He rarely let them go to sleepovers—only if he knew the parents well. Even then, he didn't like it. He would have a conniption if he came home and the door was unlocked. Nothing bad ever happened in their neighborhood, but he was always like, "you never know" and "be careful." And he was a total freak about privacy. Constantly checking her socials to make sure her pictures had no personal information. So over the top. Her mom wasn't quite as bad, but she always wanted to keep the peace, so she'd go along with her dad. Scarlett had considered talking to her about Ben but decided to keep it a secret. After all, her mother had secrets of her own.

3

Annabelle

I'm having dinner at Marco's but for some reason the menu says Blue Fig. The tablecloths are different too. They have a French Country look—yellow and blue. I take a sip of my iced tea and hand the menu back to the waiter. I smile at my client. "Thank you so much for trusting us with your business. I'm excited to develop a social media plan for you. Can you tell me a little more about your dreams for your business, your reach-for-the-stars vision?"

She begins to speak, and my phone vibrates with a text. I apologize as I glance at the screen. James. Again. He knows I'm at a business dinner. Why does he keep texting me? She resumes talking, and not five minutes later my phone buzzes. But instead of a text tone it plays a weird song I've never heard, with the line "Just because you're crazy doesn't make you crazy." I grab the phone and silence it, looking at my client in embarrassment. "Sorry— my kids must have changed my text tone." I glance at the screen. The message simply says PICK UP! "I'm so sorry. This is my husband."

She murmurs her understanding, even though she looks annoyed, and I go to the restroom and place the call.

He answers right away. "You need to come home."

"What's the big emergency?" I ask, not bothering to keep the hostility from my voice. I surprise myself with my tone.

"I'm sick of looking at your empty chair every night. This is getting out of hand. I'm a doctor, and I don't work as much as you."

"I'll be home when my client dinner is over. And don't text me anymore." I disconnect before he can say anything else and turn off my phone. We don't normally talk to each other like this. Why is he being such an asshole?

"Babe, wake up." James gently nudged her shoulder. "You slept through your alarm. I'll take the girls to school. My first appointment canceled on me."

Annabelle's eyes flew open and she startled at the sight of him, still feeling the residual anger as she came fully awake. What was it with these damn dreams? At least this one was banal. No homicidal husband in it. "Thanks," she said as she jumped out of bed, trying to shake it off. She had a meeting first thing this morning and would have to be fast or she'd be late.

"Maybe we should turn in earlier. This isn't like you. Is it too much screen time at night?" James said.

She didn't have time to discuss her sleeping habits. "Sorry, honey. I'm late. Gotta get going."

"Okay, have a good day." He leaned down and kissed her.

She skipped her morning affirmations and thought about her dream. James had never behaved in the way she was dreaming. Sure, he could be a little overprotective, but it was only because he cared so much. It made him happy to look out for all of them. Sometimes it was annoying. But he was always good-natured about it and backed off when she told him to. He was the one who made sure everyone took their vitamins, got their flu shots, and were never a day late for annual checkups. It was freeing in some ways since she didn't have to worry about those things. She supposed it came with the territory of being married to a doctor. She did wish that he'd let his hair down a little bit more. And she could do without the disapproving looks she got when her second glass of wine at a party turned into a third. James rarely drank, only on special occasions, and then never more than one drink. As a neurologist, he said he knew too much about the brain to subject his own to the effects of alcohol. But all his fussing was because he loved her so much. And he never tried to prevent her from working or placed traditional gender roles on their relationship. He respected her career and knew it meant as much to her as his did to him. And despite the fact that he earned a lot more than she did, and had a nice trust fund from his parents, he never once suggested that she stay home since they didn't need the money.

Before going downstairs, Annabelle stepped out onto the balcony that overlooked their front yard and inhaled the crisp air. The maple trees were magnificent, their leaves turning gorgeous shades of red and green. Fall was her favorite time of year; she made a mental note to remind James that they were going apple picking that Saturday. She reluctantly returned to the bedroom, grabbed her phone, and went downstairs.

AT THE OFFICE, ANNABELLE'S MORNING passed quickly in meetings. Her boss, Madeline, popped her head in around noon.

"Do you have time for lunch? Something I'd like to discuss with you."

Annabelle picked up her phone and scrolled to the calendar. "I'm free till two. Where should we go?"

"Marco's was sold and it's under new management. A friend of mine knows the new chef. It's called Blue Fig now. Today's the first day it's open."

Annabelle's head snapped up. "What did you say?"

"Marco's is now called Blue Fig. Just reopened."

"Did you mention that to me yesterday?"

Madeline gave her a strange look. "Uh, no. I was off, remember? I just heard about it yesterday myself."

"Oh, someone else must have told me. Okay, I'll meet you at the elevator in five."

Annabelle leaned back in her chair, momentarily stunned. She'd dreamed about this. So strange. She must have read about the name change somewhere.

She grabbed her purse and walked to the elevator where Madeline was waiting. They'd been working together at the public relations firm for almost ten years and even though Madeline was Annabelle's boss, they'd become close friends. She was in her early sixties, an attractive, vibrant woman who was well-respected by the entire team. The two of them had closed down a company happy hour on more than one occasion.

When they were seated at their table, Annabelle was disquieted to see that the tablecloths were the same as the ones in her dream. She ran her hand over the linen fabric. She realized with a start that she'd also dreamt about the blue vase that held sunflowers. She tried to think about where she may have seen them before. It was one thing to know the name—it had most likely been advertised and her subconscious picked it up. But there would be no way for her to know what the new decor was like, unless she'd seen a picture somewhere.

"Madame, would you like a drink?" the waiter asked.

"Club soda, please."

"Same for me," Madeline said.

"Am I in trouble or what?" Annabelle joked.

Madeline smiled. "Not at all. I'll just come out and say it, Derrick and I are moving."

Annabelle's eyes widened. "You're kidding. When? Where?"

"We've been talking about Charleston for a while. Kirby and her husband are expecting in the spring, and we want to be close to our grandchild. I've accepted an offer with a firm down there."

The news left Annabelle momentarily speechless. She'd had no idea Madeline was even considering moving. She assumed she would stay at the company until she retired. But if Annabelle's children lived out of state, she'd be tempted to move too. "I get it. But I'm going to miss you. Are you going soon?"

"I've given a month's notice."

"Do you know who's going to take your place?"

"Well, that's what I wanted to talk to you about. I was thinking that you might want to."

"Really? Wow, I don't know. Have you discussed this with Michael?"

Madeline nodded. "Yeah. We both think you'd be terrific. And I can tell you, he's great to work for. I think you'd do well with him. You love innovating, and he's very open to trying new things."

Annabelle was excited at the prospect, but her elation was tempered with trepidation. "I'm flattered. My heart wants to say yes right now, but I need to talk it over with James. It's a lot more travel, which I wouldn't normally mind, but the girls are still young and his schedule is crazy." Her dream came back to her again: James complaining that she was never home.

"I understand. You should take some time and think about it. Discuss it with James. I'm not gonna lie, it's a trade-off. Kirby was only a little older than Scarlett when I took the position, and I missed a lot. But I love what I do, and now she's all grown up with her own life. For me, it's about balancing who I am as an individual with who I am as a mom. It's different for everyone. But I wanted to offer it to you first before we start looking at external candidates."

"When do you need my answer?" she asked, her mind racing.

"Within a week?"

Annabelle nodded. "I can do that. So, have you guys found a house yet?"

Their talk moved to the personal as they finished their lunch. Annabelle's thoughts were buzzing in the background with this new opportunity. Their arrangement was perfect right now. She had time with her kids in the mornings, taking them to school. And then Dylan filled in for a few hours until she was home from work. If she took this job, she'd need to be in earlier, which meant she'd lose that time in the mornings with them. And there would be more wining and dining of clients, which meant more nights out, as well as travel every month. It was a lot.

On the other hand, if she turned the promotion down, she was pretty much sealing her fate at this company. She wouldn't get the opportunity again. She knew how the corporate world worked. She wished her mother was here; she'd know what to advise. She thought of all the sacrifices her mother had made to ensure that she was there for Annabelle as much as possible. Annabelle was proud to be a working mom, and believed it was a good example for her daughters, but she'd always struggled with the major life choices.

Somewhat of a fatalist, she believed it was the things we gave little thought to that shaped our destinies. Her whole life could be different right now, based on her selection of an elective back in college. And then her world shifted again, simply because a class was canceled at the last minute. What gave her comfort about those instances was that she hadn't been in control. Yes, you could agonize over leaving five minutes later or going to CVS versus Walgreens, but living life that way was paralyzing. Everyone went about their daily activities without thinking how those small decisions could have monumental consequences. But who you married, where you moved, what job you took—those you could control. And if you screwed those up, then you would have no one to blame but yourself.

On the drive home, Annabelle pulled into a quick market and walked up to the counter. "Pack of Marlboro Lights, please." The minute she was out the door, she tore the pack open and lit one up. Taking a deep drag, she felt her whole body unclench. She smoked it down to the filter, then started to throw the pack away, but thought better of it. She was spending a fortune buying a new pack every time she had the urge. She stashed it in a pocket in her purse and pulled out lemon-scented hand sanitizer, rubbing it all over her hands. She got back in the car, rolled down the windows, and popped a mint in her mouth. James would have a fit if he knew. But what he didn't know wouldn't hurt him.

4

Before

Annabelle sat in the armchair, watching her mother sleep. Her mother had gotten so much worse in the past six months. It was terrifying how quickly her mind had been ravaged, leaving her a shell of the woman Annabelle knew. Moving her here was the most difficult decision of her young life. But when she'd come home from class a month ago, just in time to put out the kitchen fire her mother had started, she knew it was time to listen to her aunt and stop trying to take care of her mother on her own. It didn't make it any easier though. And when her mother had those brief moments of lucidity, it pierced Annabelle to her core as she tried to explain why she couldn't bring her mother home.

It had always been just the two of them, or at least as far back as most of Annabelle's memories went. Her father had been there for the first six years of her life, but she could barely summon a memory of him, and the way he'd abandoned them left her with no desire to ever see him again. Her mother had worked tirelessly as a nurse, taking the midnight shift so that she could be there to see Annabelle off to school, and be home to make her dinner and help with homework. Only now that she was an adult herself did she realize what a toll that must have taken on her mother. Her life had revolved entirely around Annabelle—getting home at seven-thirty in the morning, then sleeping until Annabelle came home, only to have a precious few hours to herself before leaving again at eleven-thirty. When Annabelle was younger, their upstairs neighbor would come and stay, but once Annabelle was a teenager, she stayed alone. Her mother never complained, always had a smile on her face, her mood even and sunny.

What advice would her mother offer her now? Annabelle had read that often Alzheimer's changed someone's personality. People became angry and combative. Fortunately, that wasn't the case with her mom. She could hold on to that, be grateful for that. That's what her mother would do. But Annabelle didn't feel grateful. Rage and grief were the emotions that took turns consuming her. Her mother was only fifty-six. Now that Annabelle was in her senior year of college, it should be her mother's turn to have time for herself. It wasn't fair to either of them, but no one ever said that life was fair. She grabbed a tissue from the table next to her and dabbed her eyes, now wet with tears.

"How you doin', hon?" Sonya, one of the nurses, walked in, her voice quiet, her eyes kind.

Annabelle looked up and shrugged, not trusting herself to speak.

Sonya walked over and put a hand on Annabelle's shoulder, giving it a gentle squeeze. "I know it's hard, sweetie. But we're taking good care of Miriam. You've been here all morning. Go get yourself something to eat." She glanced at the bed. "She'll be asleep for a while. I'll bet you have some studying to do."

"Okay, yeah, thanks." Annabelle gathered her backpack and walked out to her Honda Civic. She had a ton of reading to do, as well as some movies to catch up on. As a communications major, Journalism in the Movies wasn't something she would likely need for a marketing career. But she had room for two electives, and it fit with her schedule on Tuesdays and Thursdays, giving her the other three weekdays free to visit her mother. She couldn't deny that it was interesting, but whether her fascination was the subject matter or the

professor was up for debate. Professor Bennet, "call me Randy," was
a dead ringer for Jake Gyllenhaal. No stuffy man in a tweed jacket,
but jeans and a black T-shirt that showed off his perfect pecs and
washboard abs. All the girls in the class were mesmerized, but Annabelle was the one he'd noticed.

She thought back to that first day in class. She'd been rushing,
stuck in traffic, and ran into the room ten minutes late. Professor
Bennet was speaking and when Annabelle opened the door he
stopped, and all eyes turned to look at her. She could feel her face
turn red. Scanning the room for an empty seat, she spied one near
the back but tripped in her haste, dropping her purse. All its contents spilled onto the floor. The pounding in her ears increased when
she heard the buzz of laughter in the classroom, but she couldn't tear
her gaze away from him. Crystal-clear blue eyes, a mischievous
smirk, and tousled sandy hair that looked as though he'd just gotten
out of bed. He stopped teaching, leaned down to help her retrieve
the items from her purse, and she thought she'd die when he handed
her a tampon. When his fingers met hers, there was an electric current. As cliché as that sounded, she felt it. She could see in his eyes
that he felt something too.

From then on, there were surreptitious looks, lingering eye contact, and knowing smiles. But it wasn't until a month later that he'd
invited her to meet for coffee. Coffee turned into dinner, dinner into
drinks, and drinks into breakfast. They had been seeing each other
for a month now. It was against the rules, but for once she didn't care
about the rules.

Annabelle fired off a quick text letting Randy know she was
heading back to her apartment, promising to call him later. She put
the car in drive, turned on the radio, and sang along to Coldplay as
she drove.

Twenty minutes later, she arrived at the property she rented in
Norwalk—an apartment over the garage of a small Cape Cod. The
owner was sweet, a woman in her eighties who baked cookies and
pumpkin bread, always putting some aside for Annabelle. Annabelle

had had to sell their house to afford her mom's facility and pay her college tuition. There had been enough left to cover her rent here, a steal at $900 a month. If she was careful about her spending, she'd be okay until she graduated and got a full-time job.

She grabbed the newspaper from the driveway and put it on Mrs. Miller's doorstep, then carried the now-empty garbage can to the back of the house. Unlocking her door, she climbed the stairs to her studio apartment and turned on some lights.

Her stomach was rumbling; she realized she hadn't eaten since breakfast. Rummaging through the cabinets, she settled on a can of lentil soup and poured it into a pan to heat. She was exhausted. How was she going to get through all that reading without falling asleep? Her phone pinged, and she smiled when she saw the name on the screen. Randy.

I miss you. Sleepover?

Her face flushed as images of their lovemaking the night before came unbidden. She hesitated only a moment before answering.

Be over in an hour

His reply came immediately.

Don't forget to forget your p.j.s

What the hell? It was only an elective. She could ace the next quiz.

5

Scarlett

Scarlett usually slept as late as possible before getting up for school, but she and Ben had started texting in the mornings, so she found herself eagerly awakening at six-thirty. She loved starting her day with him, especially knowing that she was facing social obliteration once she reached school.

Ben: GM

Scarlett: Hey how was ur wknd. What'd you do?

Ben: NMU

Scarlett: Some tennis. Then I wanted to watch the new Halloween but Olivia said it was too scary. Had to watch some baby movie instead.

Ben: That sucks.

Scarlett: IKR

Ben: Didn't she get to pick where you
went to lunch too? Does she always get her way?

Scarlett: IDK Now that you say that . . .

Ben: Must be hard. I'm an only so . . . IMO
sounds like ur Mom favors ur sis

Scarlett: SRSLY u may b right. What's ur mom like?

Ben: Pretty cool works a lot urs work?

Scarlett: Yeah—she does social
media stuff for a company so she's
all over me monitoring mine. Eye roll

Ben: Pretty cool job tho what company?

Scarlett inserted a link to her mom's website.

Ben: Cool! GTG. Wish I could go with you
to school and put those witches in their place

Scarlett smiled. It felt so good to have someone like Ben wanting to defend her, to protect her. It made what she was going through at school a little bit easier.

Scarlett: Thx! TTYL

She put her phone down and stretched. She needed to get up, but she could hear the shower going, so Olivia must have beaten her to it. She felt kind of bad keeping Ben a secret from her sister. But Olivia would tell their parents, and Scarlett couldn't let that happen. When the time was right, she'd let Olivia in on everything. As much as she teased her younger sister, she really loved her. Olivia was like this little ball of sunshine, seeing the good in everything. Scarlett looked forward to the day when they were both older, and their age difference would be insignificant. Her mother was always telling her how much she wished she'd had a sister, and how lucky Scarlett was that she had Olivia. But for now, it seemed Olivia was still the innocent child, while Scarlett felt as though she were teetering on the edge of adulthood.

Lately, she found herself thinking about the future. Even though she still had four years of high school, she was worried about college. Everyone kept drilling into her head how important it was to prepare now. Get good grades. Volunteer. Do extracurriculars. It was exhausting trying to juggle schoolwork with practice and games, then sailing on the weekends. Sometimes she wondered if her parents kept their schedules so packed to ensure there would be no time to get in trouble. This feeling of being hemmed in, of her world being too controlled by her parents, was relatively new. It was like there was a fire inside her now, and one wrong look or word from her parents could make it erupt. One minute she wanted to run to them for comfort, and the next she wanted to scream at them to stay out of her life. She'd tried to talk to Olivia about it, but she didn't understand. Sometimes Scarlett felt as though she was going crazy.

SCARLETT GRABBED HER LUNCH FROM her locker and headed to the cafeteria. She took a seat at her usual table, but she was the first one there. Zoe had texted her to meet them in the cafeteria—said she was ready to make up. But where were they? She looked around the crowded room alive with chatter, scanning the table to see if her friends were sitting somewhere else. She froze when her eyes met Zoe's. Zoe was sitting at a table with Ethan and his lacrosse buddies. She raised her eyebrows and pursed her lips, then turned her gaze back to Ethan, moving closer to him. Scarlett wanted to scream. Her face grew warm when she saw Zoe's new clique of three sitting down across from her.

Zoe had sent that text to mess with her. They were still freezing her out. She bit the inside of her lip, willing herself not to cry. Screw them. She wasn't about to let them see how humiliated she felt. Scarlett took a deep breath, gathered her things, and stood. She would find new friends. Friends who weren't so petty as to ignore her like they were back in elementary school or something.

She walked three tables over to where Avery, a girl from her English class, was sitting with two girls Scarlett didn't know. "Okay to sit here?"

Avery shrugged. "It's a free country."

Scarlett sat down and unwrapped her lunch. Her mom had packed her a turkey and cheese sandwich, along with an apple and some almonds. Her father was always pressuring her to send them to school with a balanced lunch. There had been cookies left over, and she'd snagged a small bagful this morning. She put them in front of her. "Help yourself."

Avery hesitated, then reached out and took one. "Thanks." She took a bite. "Pretty good."

Scarlett pushed the bag toward the other two girls. "Want one?"

"I'm good," they both said.

"So, what happened to your clique? How come they ditched you?" Avery asked.

Scarlett shook her head. "Doesn't matter. I thought they were my friends, but—"

Avery looked across the room to where Zoe was sitting and then back at Scarlett. "Let me guess. It was over a guy?"

"Maybe."

"Well, if you ask me, you're better off without all of them, including Ethan. That guy may know how to spin a lacrosse stick, but he can hardly string two sentences together."

Scarlett nodded. "I guess I got distracted by how cute he is."

"Cute only goes so far. Don't you want to be with someone who has brains too?"

"I don't care about Ethan anymore. He's a jerk. Zoe can have him. I'm more interested in getting to know someone else right now anyway."

6

The Wife

He's hiding something. I found a key for a post office box in his brief-case. When I asked him about it, he pretended he had no idea where it had come from. But he's hidden things before, and I can always tell when he's lying. He's definitely lying now. So I kept the key. Told him I'd throw it out, and to his credit, he didn't argue. Probably be-cause he figured then I would drop it. But that's where he was wrong. While he slept, I pulled his corporate Visa card from his wallet and took pictures of it. The next day I called the bank and told them I needed the past couple of statements. The charge for the post office box was right there. The post office was understanding about my forgetting my box number. The key fit, and I found out his secret.

Annabelle

Annabelle had to give Madeline her answer tomorrow. She'd been mulling it over for the past several days and was planning to discuss it with James tonight. He'd been on call for the last three nights since two of his partners had come down with the flu. They'd finished dinner, and the girls had gone upstairs to their rooms to do their homework. Annabelle was checking her emails on her laptop while James loaded the dishwasher.

"Tea?" asked James, after he finished.

"I'm okay."

"Come on. Some nice chamomile will relax you." He made two cups and brought them over to the large island, sitting next to her.

"What's going on? You've been preoccupied."

She took a sip of her tea. She reached out and squeezed his hand. He could read her so well. "I've been wanting to talk to you about something. Madeline's leaving, and she offered me her job. But I'm not sure what to do."

His face lit up. "That's great, babe. Congratulations! What's the problem?"

"Well, it's a lot more hours. Late nights. More travel. I don't know."

"Is it something you want?"

"I mean, yeah, I love what I do. I'd have a lot more creative control. I'd be overseeing the whole team. In some ways, there'd be less daily work, but I'd have more meetings, at least in the client acquisition phase." She exhaled. "The girls are both still young. I worry that I won't be there when they need me. What do you think?"

"I think it's your decision. There are bound to be regrets either way. If you don't take it, you may always wonder if you should have. And if you do, you'll wonder if you shouldn't have."

Annabelle rolled her eyes. "Now I understand why you went into medicine instead of philosophy." She laughed. "I get that there's an upside and a downside to both. But which is the right decision?"

"And I get that you like to know how things are going to turn out; I understand there's been a lot of uncertainty in your past. But you know as well as I do that there are no guarantees. We can always get more help if you decide you want to go for it."

"I know. But I don't want to miss the important things."

James gave her a tender look. "I understand that. But you're a wonderful mother, and the girls are happy and well-adjusted. You don't have to give up your dream job for our children. But on the other hand, I don't think you should feel pressured to take it just because it's a promotion." He stood and gave her a peck on the lips. "I know you'll make the right decision."

She stayed there after he left, thinking through her options, then looked up when she heard footsteps. Olivia walked over to her, clad in her pajamas.

"Can you come up and read to me?"

"You got it, sweetie." Even though Olivia was a good reader, this was a bedtime routine that she'd established years ago, and both girls still enjoyed it. She followed her up the stairs, and they stopped at Scarlett's door. Annabelle knocked.

"You ready for story time?"

"I don't feel like it tonight. Go on without me." Scarlett didn't look up from her phone.

"Everything okay?" Annabelle asked.

She gave Annabelle an annoyed look and sighed loudly. "Fine! I'm not a baby. I don't need you to read to me."

Olivia looked up at her mother. "What's her problem?"

Annabelle didn't answer but called in to Scarlett. "Okay, honey. I'll come by and say good night afterward."

Olivia jumped into her bed and pulled the covers up to her chin.

"Scarlett's been really grumpy lately."

"Maybe she's tired." But Annabelle was concerned. She'd noticed it, too, and had chalked it up to her being a teenager. But now she wondered if something else was going on. The one time Annabelle could always count on Scarlett's guard being down was at night. Annabelle enjoyed the bedtime routine, when the girls would tell her about their days or confide things they were worrying about. If she took the new job, she might not be around to notice these kinds of things.

"Mooom!"

"What, honey?"

Olivia raised her eyebrows. "Are you gonna read? You're staring into space."

"Yes, of course." She picked up *The Lion, the Witch, and the Wardrobe.* "Let's see, where were we? Oh yes, chapter three." She began to read, and blessedly for a little while, her thoughts were only on the story and taking delight in Olivia's reactions. After half an hour, she closed the book and stood, leaning over to kiss her daughter on the cheek.

"Good night, love. Sweet dreams."

"You too, Mommy," Olivia said, her eyes already closing.

Annabelle passed Scarlett's room, then went back. She hesitated for a moment and then knocked.

"Come in," Scarlett called.

"Is everything okay, sweetie?"

Scarlett shook her head. Annabelle moved closer to the bed and saw that her eyes were filling. She sat on the edge of the bed and took her daughter's hand.

"Honey, what's the matter?"

Scarlett groaned. "I hate social media!" She picked up her phone, swiped a few times, then handed it to her mother. "I posted this pic yesterday, and I only have ten likes. Luna posted practically the same picture, and she got like fifty."

It was a selfie of Scarlett holding a Starbucks cup. Her lips were puckered in that teen selfie way, and her cheekbones looked more defined than usual. She must have used a filter.

Annabelle put the phone down. "Honey, social media is all about facades. It's not a true barometer of anything."

Scarlett raised her eyebrows. "That's rich, coming from you. Aren't you, like, the queen of social media at your job?"

"That's why I'm telling you, it's all curated images that often have no resemblance to reality. It's a tool to sell things, yes, but it's dangerous to tie your self-esteem to it. Maybe you should take a break from it for a while."

Scarlett rolled her eyes. "You don't get it, Mom. That's how it is now. It's all about how many followers and likes you get. I usually get a lot more."

"I'm sorry. I guess I forgot how tough high school can be. We didn't have to contend with social media, but I know what it's like to want to be more popular."

Scarlett's brow creased. "Weren't you the homecoming queen or something?"

"Yes, but when I was a freshman, I had braces and frizzy hair. All I wanted was to look like Maggie Brown, the most popular girl in school."

Scarlett smiled. "I didn't know that. I thought you were always this beautiful and confident."

Annabelle brushed a hair from Scarlett's forehead, touched by her words. "You're sweet. But no, I was kind of shy. *You* are beautiful inside and out."

Scarlett leaned forward and surprised her with a hug. "Thanks, Mom." She leaned back in her bed. "Gotta get back to my homework."

Annabelle rose. "Good night, sweetie. I love you."

"Love you too," Scarlett said, already looking down at her book.

Annabelle was troubled as she left. There was no shortage of articles on the damaging effects of social media, especially on teenage girls. She thought of her daughter's comment about her job. Was she part of the problem? But what choice did she have? Her expertise was marketing, which these days was mostly online. She hadn't connected her work with what many experts were citing as an unhealthy fixation on image. The clients she represented were professionals with products or services aimed at adults. As with anything, there were two sides to social media. It was a great tool for gaining exposure and connecting with others, but it could also be a gateway to misery. Especially for vulnerable teens who decided that their value was determined by how well-liked their posts were. She'd keep a closer eye on Scarlett. She was glad that at least she'd restricted Olivia's access to it until she was older.

Annabelle went downstairs to let James know she was turning in. She'd read in bed for a while and try to get a good night's sleep. Maybe the morning would bring wisdom. She'd only read a few pages when her eyes became heavy. Putting the book on her nightstand, she turned off the lamp, sank into bed, and closed her eyes.

I'm in a hotel room. It's beautiful with a large balcony overlooking the ocean. The door's open and the salt air wafts through, beckoning me. The sun is beginning to set as I walk out to the balcony. The sky is painted in brilliant pinks and purples, and the sound of the waves crashing on the shore makes the scene complete. I stand next to the railing, soaking in these last magical moments of daylight. When I glance at the table, there are two wineglasses filled halfway with a crimson liquid. Who am I here with?

Turning around, I look into the room, but it's empty. Suddenly I realize I'm hugging someone. A man. He's tall, and I feel completely at ease in his arms. We don't speak, we hold each other, and it feels right. I can see his reflection in the glass balcony door—the back of his head. I try to make out his features but they're blurry.

My phone rings. It's on the table next to the wine, and James's name flashes on the screen. I extricate myself from the man I'm hugging, whose long brown hair I can see now. It's not James.

A pang of regret fills me when he releases me from his arms. I pick up the phone and enter the room again.

"Hello?"

"I need you to cut your trip short."

"What's going on?"

"It's Scarlett. She was vaping in school. They suspended her. Do you know how bad vaping is for you? This is really serious!"

"I can't believe she'd do that. She knows better. Are you sure she was vaping?"

An impatient sigh. "She denies doing it but come on. She was caught in the bathroom with a bunch of other girls. She's been hanging out with new people since the rift with Zoe."

"I'll talk to her when I get back. One more day."

"You need to come home now. She needs you. You're gone all the time, and I think this is her way of rebelling."

"I can't miss my meeting tomorrow. You know that. You'll have to handle things until I get home. I'm not her only parent, you know! And it's not like I haven't had to do plenty on my own. I never asked you to come home when you were on call all night. How many nights have I spent with sick kids by myself?"

His voice softens. "I know. I'm not trying to make you feel guilty for working. I'm worried about her, Annabelle. I wish I could get through to her on my own, but she needs you."

"I'll try to book a red-eye for tomorrow night instead of waiting until the next day. But that's the best I can do."

"If you say so."

I end the call and throw the phone on the bed. It's then that I notice the television is on and an emergency announcement interrupts the program. A plane crash over Atlanta. Flight 108. I grab the remote and turn the volume up. Everyone is feared dead. A chill runs through me. There's a loud blaring, and I look around to try to find where it's coming from. Is the smoke alarm going off in the hotel? The man is still standing on the balcony, his back to me.

"Hey, do you hear that?" I shout.

"Annabelle, wake up," James says, gently shaking her. "You must have been dreaming. You were yelling."

She sat up with a start. "Um, yeah. I thought there was a fire. Only a dream," she mumbled, still half-asleep. He held her phone in his hand. "Your alarm was going off. You should change it to music. I've told you these harsh noises are not good to wake up to."

She fell back against the pillow, still tired. "Yeah. I'll do that. I need a few more minutes."

"Okay. I'll get the girls' breakfast going."

She closed her eyes, reliving the dream, trying to make sense of it. Who was the man on the balcony? She would never cheat on James, especially given what had happened to her in the past, but the dream seemed to indicate that she was. She could still feel the sense of completeness she'd felt in his arms.

Annabelle had never met her grandmother, but her mother had told her that she used to have elaborate dreams. Dreams that sometimes came true, and that scared her mother. Annabelle hadn't thought much of it at the time, but now she wished she could ask her mother more about it. Lately, it was as though she was living in another dimension. She wasn't doing anything different. No new medications or diet changes. Although she was doing that gratitude thing. Maybe she was tapping into her subconscious more. She didn't like it. She'd have to google it and see if that was even a thing. One thing was for sure, her subconscious was screaming at her not to take the job. Her reservations about not being available if her children needed her weighed heavily on her. She would tell Madeline no.

When she got downstairs, James handed her a cup of coffee.

"Morning, everyone," she said.

"Morning, Mommy," Olivia replied, giving her a big smile. Scarlett mumbled a hello without looking up from her phone.

Annabelle arched an eyebrow, turning to James. "I'm not going to take it."

His eyes widened. "Oh, okay. What made you decide?"

She gave a slight nod of her head in the direction of Scarlett and Olivia. "I don't want to be traveling so much right now."

He smiled. "Can't say I'm not glad. I kinda like having you around."

"That's nice to hear," she said. She clapped her hands. "All right, kiddos. Time to get going."

"You didn't eat anything," James said.

"I'll grab something at the office later. Not hungry."

He handed her a banana. "At least have this. You know your blood pressure gets low if you wait too long to eat."

"Yes, Doctor. Go see your actual patients."

He didn't move, still looking at her.

"Oh, for heaven's sake!" Annabelle peeled it and took a bite. "Happy?"

"Good girl." He kissed her on the top of her head and left.

She gave the rest of the banana to Parker. *Good girl.* What, was she a dog?

On the way to school, Scarlett took her AirPods off and turned to her mom. "Oh, by the way, I'm going to the mall after school with my friends."

"Okay. How are you getting there? Is Zoe's mom picking you up?"

"Zoe and I aren't friends anymore."

This was news to Annabelle, but she flashed back to her dream. Had Scarlett told her, and she'd forgotten? "Since when?"

"Since she stole my crush and turned our friends against me."

"Who's your crush?" Olivia piped up from the back seat.

"None of your business," Scarlett said.

"Who cares anyway," her sister shot back.

Annabelle pulled up to a stoplight and turned to look at her.

"Honey, I'm so sorry. You two were always so close. Why didn't you tell me?" She put a hand on Scarlett's arm, but she pulled away.

"It's no big deal. I'm hanging out with some other girls now."

Zoe's mom and Annabelle had always been friendly, if not close. They all belonged to the same yacht club, and the girls had taken sailing lessons together every summer for the past eight years.

"If you want to talk—"

"I'm good."

Annabelle pulled up to the school, her stomach now in knots.

"Love you girls. Have a good day."

She thought about her dream again. Who were these new friends? Was Scarlett getting in with the wrong crowd? She would talk to her about it tonight. One of the reasons she had decided to send the girls to the public school was so that they'd form friendships with others close by. The schools were terrific, and most of their friends sent their kids there as well. But James's parents, Charlotte and Art, had been disappointed when they'd learned that she and James weren't sending them to St. Luke's, the school James had attended. But the public schools in Bayport were some of the highest rated in the country. It was the one thing Annabelle had been firm about. There was no way they were going to spend in excess of a hundred thousand a year for middle and high school, when their schools were so good. But it wasn't only about the money. Annabelle wanted them to have friends in their own community. It was one of the few times she'd argued with James's mother. His parents had offered to pay for the girls. The four of them had been out to dinner, and Annabelle could see that James was wavering.

"Thank you for the generous offer, but it's not only about the tuition. We believe it's better for the girls to be closer. St. Luke's is a forty-minute drive with traffic; it's much more convenient for them to go here. And the public schools are excellent."

Charlotte had frowned. "They're adequate, but I wouldn't say they're excellent—"

"They're ranked very highly. I don't wish to debate this, Charlotte. We want our girls to be down-to-earth, not entitled."

Charlotte raised an eyebrow. "You don't seem to think living in a million-dollar-plus home is entitled, so why are you against private school? St. Luke's is a quality education and will better prepare them for their futures," Charlotte said. "It certainly helped James get into medical school."

It had taken every bit of Annabelle's self-control not to lose her temper. "And that's what's so great about having your own children: You get to make your own choices."

James finally spoke up. "Mom, the matter's settled. Please respect our decision."

To her credit, Charlotte never brought it up again, and she was right there cheering at all the girls' plays, sporting events, and school activities.

Annabelle turned the radio on and tried to quiet her thoughts. A few minutes later, her phone rang. James. She pushed answer on her steering wheel.

"Miss me already?" she teased.

"Did you hear about the plane crash?"

Her heart stopped. "No, what crash?"

"Over Atlanta. Early this morning. Over two hundred people dead."

Annabelle

James's words shocked her so much that Annabelle almost ran a red light. She slammed on the brakes just in time.

"Annabelle, are you okay?"

"Yeah, I got distracted and almost didn't stop at the light. I'll call you from the office."

"I'm so sorry. I shouldn't have called you while you're driving. Be careful."

She pulled into a gas station after the light changed and put the car in park, her heart hammering in her chest. Hands shaking, she rummaged through her bag and found the pack of cigarettes. She put down the window and lit one. Pulling out her phone, she navigated to a search engine to look up the crash. Her eyes scanned the page, the pit in her stomach growing. She held her breath when she got to the flight number: 108. *My God . . .* It was the same as in her dream. What was happening to her?

She took a deep breath and called her best friend, Kiera. They'd grown up together and had been inseparable until college, when Kiera went to the University of Maryland. She'd met someone there and gotten married after college. Now Annabelle only saw her in person on the few weekends a year they managed to clear their schedules and get away together, but they texted often. The phone rang twice before Kiera picked up.

"Hey, aren't you supposed to be at work?" Kiera asked. She was a freelance editor who worked from home.

"I'm on my way, but I need to talk to you."

"What's wrong?"

Annabelle could hear the concern in her voice.

"Something really weird's going on. I'm having these bizarre dreams, and I think they're starting to come true."

"What do you mean? What kind of dreams?"

She told Kiera about the last two but for some reason withheld the one where James was choking her. "I mean, the restaurant thing could have been a coincidence. But how could I dream about a plane crash before it happened?"

"I don't know. Are you sure you did? The crash happened early this morning, I think around six A.M. What time was your dream?"

"Not sure. I woke up at seven."

"Could you have heard about it on TV or something and incorporated it into your dream?"

Annabelle considered this. She'd thought her phone alarm was a fire alarm in the hotel she was dreaming about. But they didn't have a television in their bedroom. And if James had been listening to the news, he would have mentioned the crash before they left this morning. "I don't think so. Do you really think I could have dreamt about it after it happened?"

"Maybe. I mean, there has to be a logical explanation. I've known you your entire life; I think I'd know if you were psychic." Her tone was teasing, but Annabelle didn't laugh.

"I guess you're right. Maybe there was some kind of freak Siri thing where the report played on my phone. That must be it. This is why you need to move back to Connecticut. You're the only one who can talk me down from the ledge."

"I'm only a phone call away. Get to work, but call me later. We can FaceTime tonight and have a glass of wine. Sounds like you could use some girl time," Kiera said.

"You're on. I'll text you later. Love you."

"Love you too."

She put the cigarette out in her coffee. Feeling better, she got back on the road and headed to the office. She was now even more certain that turning down the job was the right thing to do. Regardless of whether or not her dreams were foreshadowing actual events, she wasn't prepared to put in the kind of hours that the position required. But she wondered if the man in her dream was part of the reason she was turning down the job. Was she worried that she'd be unable to resist temptation?

When Annabelle got to her office, she shut the door, sat down at her desk, and typed "psychic dreams" into her search bar. As she read article after article, she began to feel validated. Apparently, these types of dreams were more common than she thought. Some sources said that up to a third of people reported having some type of precognitive dream. Precognitive dreams predict the future and, to be classified as such, must be recorded prior to the event happening, either by telling someone or writing it down. These dreams were known to cause a lot of stress. *No kidding,* she thought. She typed in "how to stop psychic dreams." Some advice was to reduce stress. *Seriously?* She kept clicking. There were lots of articles on protecting yourself from psychic attacks; some of them were way out there. She leaned back in her chair, thinking. There had to be a reason this was happening to her. Instead of trying to stop them, she needed to understand the dreams, to figure out the reason she was having them. She couldn't explain it, but she had a strong feeling that ignoring them would have catastrophic consequences.

9

Before

"Don't you think it's a little creepy that he's your professor? I mean, does he do this all the time?" Kiera asked.

Annabelle dipped her fork into her salad and tilted her head. "He's only been teaching for a year. He's, like, twenty-nine. So it's not like he's some old professor. And we clicked from the beginning. It's a stupid rule. The grading is objective, no essays, so I'm not getting special treatment."

"If you say so. When do I get to meet him?"

She wasn't ready for Randy to be put under Kiera's scrutiny yet. There were no secrets between her and Kiera, and Annabelle thought of her as a sister. They'd become friends in kindergarten and stayed that way through high school. Kiera was now in her last year at the University of Maryland, and they saw each other only on holidays and the occasional weekend. She had secretly hoped her friend would choose to stay in Connecticut and go to UConn like she had, but Kiera had been ready to spread her wings. Annabelle missed her desperately but understood. She would have studied farther from home herself if her mother hadn't gotten sick.

"When you're back for Christmas break. Promise. He won't be

my professor anymore, and we'll be able to go public. He's nervous about anyone finding out right now."

Kiera arched a brow. "I hope he's not a player. I've never seen you this head over heels."

"I like him a lot, but I'm keeping my head. Right now, Randy's about the only good thing in my life. Mom is getting worse every day. It's so hard."

Kiera reached out and put her hand on Annabelle's. "I'm so sorry. I've always loved your mom. You know I used to wish she was *my* mom. I hate that you're both going through this."

Kiera was the only person other than her aunt that Annabelle would let visit her mother. Her mother had been well-liked, and friends and colleagues tried to stay in touch. But as she grew worse, Annabelle knew that her mom wouldn't want them to see her in the state she was in. After a while, they stopped trying, and Annabelle was grateful. Her aunt Celia lived in North Carolina and was seldom around. At times Annabelle wished she lived closer, but due to the distance, she hardly knew her aunt, so she wasn't sure she'd be much comfort anyway.

"Your mom loves you. I know you guys don't always see eye to eye, but take it from me, you'd miss her if she was gone," Annabelle told Kiera.

Her friend looked down at the table, then back at her. "You're right. I'm sorry. That must have sounded so ungrateful."

Annabelle shook her head. "No, no. I'm just saying. Anyhow. You're getting pretty serious with Marshall. What are your plans after graduation?"

"I wasn't going to say anything, but we're getting a place together. I think I'm gonna end up staying in Maryland."

Annabelle forced a smile. She liked Marshall, and she was happy for her friend, but she couldn't help but feel bereft at the thought of Kiera living two hundred miles away. "I had a feeling. Ugh. I'm going to miss you. Does this mean you're going to be a Ravens fan now?"

Kiera chuckled. "You know I'd never abandon my Patriots."

They finished their lunch, and Annabelle checked her watch. "We'd better get moving. Your train leaves in an hour."

The ride to the train station was filled with general conversation, and Annabelle felt a deep pang of sadness when it was time to say goodbye. She held back her tears as they hugged, and she watched as Kiera disappeared into the station. Their lives had turned out so differently. Kiera was enjoying the traditional college experience, making new friends, going to parties, and doing the whole sorority thing. Annabelle had wanted that, too, and her mother had taken her on the full college tour her junior year of high school. She'd narrowed down her choices; her top three had been Boston College, Cornell, and University of Chicago. She'd been accepted at all three. She'd decided on Boston College but had felt guilty about leaving her mother.

"Nonsense," her mother had said. "It's time for you to fly the coop. I'm happy for you. You worked so hard, got a full ride; there's nothing holding you back. I can't wait to see all the great things you're going to do."

They'd gone out to dinner to celebrate, and it was one of the happiest nights of her life. But then a few weeks later her mother started forgetting things, getting lost, and everything changed. Her mother was a nurse; she knew the signs. She got tested quickly, and the devastating diagnosis soon followed.

Her mother had insisted that Annabelle get her degree, even if that meant staying local. And she was getting a good education at UConn. It was just that sometimes it felt like she was in a more adult version of high school. If she had lived at the Storrs campus, it would have been a different story. But the Stamford campus was small, mostly commuters, so she hadn't made any close friends. Maybe if she'd had the time to join one of the clubs, it would have made a difference, but her free time was split between studying and visiting her mother—and now some stolen nights with Randy. It was her last year, so she supposed it didn't matter anymore.

Besides, if she'd gone away to school, she'd never have met

Randy. Annabelle hadn't been honest when she'd told Kiera that she was keeping her head. She was crazy in love with him, but she hadn't told him that yet. It was old-fashioned, but she wanted him to say it first. And so far, he hadn't. The hiding wasn't helping either. The only time she could go to his apartment was when his roommate was on call for the night. Randy was überparanoid about someone finding out about the two of them. One more month, and they wouldn't have to hide anymore. But a part of her worried that when the semester ended, the relationship would too.

Scarlett

Scarlett had been hanging out with Avery ever since she'd eaten lunch with her two weeks ago. Now they sat together every day. Avery wanted to learn how to play tennis, and Scarlett was teaching her. They practiced every day after school now. The other two girls who'd been at the table that first day were only around occasionally. Avery said she'd rather be alone than hang out with anyone who wasn't real. She was big on that, and Scarlett thought she was pretty cool. Not at all like Zoe, who judged everyone by what they wore or what their bodies looked like. Avery didn't diss other people. She said small-minded people talked about others, while great minds discussed ideas. Something like that anyway. It was a quote from Eleanor Roosevelt, who Avery said should be an example to every woman.

Scarlett wondered if one of the reasons it was easier for Avery to be independent was because she'd moved around so much. Avery's father was a navy pilot, and this was the sixth school she'd gone to. Scarlett thought that sounded kind of cool. You could reinvent yourself whenever you felt like it. Scarlett had been friends with the same people since she was five. It was hard not to get stuck in everyone's idea of who you were.

They had just sat down to have lunch when Zoe, Brittany, and

Chloe walked by their table and made a point of turning their heads in the opposite direction. It was obvious they were ignoring Scarlett.

"Real mature," Scarlett called after them.

"Don't let 'em see they're getting to you," Avery said. "You only need, like, one really good friend," she told Scarlett. "Trying to fit in with the popular group makes you a drone." She put the word *popular* in air quotes. Avery wanted to be an investigative journalist and was always observing people.

The truth was, Avery could have fit in with any group she wanted. She was really pretty and smart, and funny too. She was what Scarlett had heard her mother refer to as "effortlessly beautiful." Avery didn't wear much makeup, and she dressed casually. She had shiny black hair, blue eyes, and one of those perfect turned-up noses that Scarlett would have killed for. She wished she could be more like her new friend, and not care about what others thought. But she did care. She couldn't help sneaking a look over at Zoe's table and wondering if they were laughing at her. She forced herself to look straight ahead and ignore them.

"Ben said they're a bunch of losers, and I should ignore them."

"Totally. He sounds like a cool guy. Where does he live again?" Avery took a bite of her sandwich.

"Chicago. I wish he wasn't so far away. We both want to meet up. Do you think I should ask my parents? Maybe they could help me arrange something."

Avery gave her a look. "You're joking. No, don't tell them. From what you've said about your dad, he'd totally freak out. Especially since you've done this behind their backs. They're not going to help you go meet some random guy. Give it time. You don't want to blow it, and then never get to meet him. Maybe later on, you can figure out how to talk to your parents about him. For now, I'd keep it quiet. But like I said before, you need to FaceTime him and make sure he's who he says he is."

Scarlett nodded, even though she had no intention of doing that.

She liked texting. It gave her more time to think about how to respond. If they talked on FaceTime and Ben asked personal questions, she'd be put on the spot, maybe say something really dumb.

"Let me see his picture again," Avery said.

Scarlett navigated to Ben's Instagram. "Here." She handed Avery her phone.

"He's really cute!" She slid the phone back across the table. "Time to head to class. By the way, steer clear of the bathroom by the library before last period."

"Why?"

She leaned in. "Don't tell anyone, but I heard some teachers talking in the hall this morning, when I came in early to use the writing lab. They've been trying to catch a group of girls who've been vaping in the bathroom. Every time they try to catch them, the girls flush the vapes."

"If they know when they're doing it, why doesn't a teacher go in the bathroom at that time?" Scarlett asked.

"They've tried, but then the girls don't do it, and they can't put someone in there all day."

"So what are they gonna do?"

"Right before last bell, they're going to seal up the toilets so the vapes can't be flushed. Then they'll go in a couple minutes before and catch 'em."

"Are you going to tell them?" Scarlett asked.

"No, if they're dumb enough to pollute their lungs, that's their problem. I'm going to record it so I can write about it."

As Scarlett walked to her class, an idea came to her. She'd go and be Avery's backup. Why should she miss out on the excitement? It was time she stopped leading such a boring life. She wished she knew what her life's ambition was. Avery was lucky to know what she wanted to do. Scarlett loved sailing, and she was good at tennis and most sports, but that wasn't a job. She did love to read, but she didn't want to be a librarian or English teacher. Her mom was a marketing whiz who knew everything there was to know about social media and getting clicks, but Scarlett only liked doing that for fun. And she didn't think she had the stomach to go into medicine, like her dad. Olivia said she wanted to be a doctor, but maybe that was because she was only eleven and thought it would be neat to do what their dad did. Maybe Scarlett could be a detective. She liked trying to figure things out, to find out what secrets others were hiding. She'd already started snooping around her own house, because both her parents were definitely hiding something.

She fidgeted as her science teacher droned on and on about amoebas. Finally, the bell rang. Grabbing her backpack, Scarlett ran down the two flights of stairs and tried to push open the door to the bathroom.

"It's full!" a girl's voice called out.

"I just need a minute," Scarlett said. A moment later the door opened a crack, and she slid in. The girl who'd opened the door slid the trash can back against it. Avery was right; six girls were vaping. She walked past them to the last sink and pulled out a lip gloss from her backpack, trying to look nonchalant. One of the stall doors was closed, and she could see Avery's green Nikes reflected in the mirror. Her heart began beating furiously as she anticipated the teachers barging in. Just when she thought it was a false alarm, the trash can started to move, and a teacher called out.

"Open this door immediately!"

The girls ran to one of the stalls and tried to throw the vapes in the toilet, but they landed on the ground. There was cellophane adhered to the toilets. The door burst open and Ms. Barlow, the assistant principal, came in.

"All of you, head to my office. You're suspended."

"What? We didn't do anything," one of the girls said.

Ms. Barlow walked over to the stall and pointed to the vapes on the floor. "Let's go."

They began to file out. She looked at Scarlett. "Come on."

"But I wasn't vaping. I was only using the mirror."

"Nice try. Let's go."

Scarlett glanced at the last stall and saw that Avery's shoes weren't visible. She must be standing on the toilet seat. In her fury, Ms. Barlow hadn't even looked in that direction. Scarlett left the bathroom, trying to figure out how she was going to explain this to her parents.

Annabelle

There was a plumbing leak in our office building and we've all been sent home. I head to the grocery store and call James at his office to see if he wants me to pick anything up for him. He doesn't answer his cellphone, so I dial the office.

"Neurological Specialists."

"Hi, Daisy. It's Annabelle. Is James with a patient?"

"Hi, Annabelle. Um, no, he canceled his morning appointments. Said something came up and he'd be in later this afternoon."

"Oh, that's right. I forgot. Thanks." The last thing I need is to add fuel to the rumor mill. There has been plenty of drama over the years at his practice with some of his partners.

I hang up, perplexed. James didn't mention anything to me. Curious, I open my "find me" app and look for his car. I frown. It looks like he's parked at the Phoenix Motel, a seedy place in the next town over. I put the address in my GPS and drive there. When I arrive, I see his black Range Rover is parked in front of one of the rooms. I park my car on the other side of the stairway so it's out of sight, but where I can see the room. What the hell is he doing here? He comes out of the room, stops, and turns back around, the door still open. He's talking to someone in the room, his face animated, and his words punctuated by his *finger stabbing the air. I can only hear bits and pieces until his voice rises and a female voice from inside the room shouts.*

"You need to stop this. Annabelle can't find out."

A woman comes out and grabs him by the shoulders. I can only see the back of her. A towel is wrapped around her head, like she's come straight out of the shower.

"What the hell. I need to go!" he shouts.

"Quiet! Don't make a scene!" she says, pulling him back into the room. The door slams shut.

I'm stunned. James is cheating on me? It can't be. The one thing I've always been certain of was his devotion. But what else would he be doing in the middle of the day with a woman in a motel?

"Mommy, Mommy!"

What is Olivia doing here?

A strong push on her arm woke her up. "Mommy, wake up! Parker ate another sock!" Olivia was pulling on her arm. It was James's day to get the kids ready. Her alarm hadn't even gone off yet.

"Okay, okay. Coming. Where's Daddy?"

"He had to leave. His phone rang, and he said to come get you."

Annabelle grabbed her robe and followed Olivia from the room and downstairs where a disgusting-looking sock lay in the middle of the rug in a pile of vomit. Of course, Parker wouldn't throw up on the wood floor instead. Annabelle fetched some paper towels and got to work. When she was finished, she called out to Olivia.

"Okay, all cleaned up. Go get dressed. We need to leave in half an hour. Where's your sister?"

"In her room. Texting, of course."

Annabelle tried James's cell, but he didn't answer. He must have gotten called into work on an emergency. She thought about her dream again. This one didn't worry her. James would never in a million years cheat on her. His fidelity was one of the main reasons she'd married him. Maybe these weird premonition-like dreams were over, and she was back to good old-fashioned regular dreams.

*   *   *

MADELINE UNDERSTOOD ANNABELLE'S DECISION. "I get it. This is the right choice for you, and I'm proud of you for making it. I know it wasn't easy." Annabelle sat across from the woman who would no longer be her boss in a few weeks.

"Thanks, I appreciate it. Just make sure you hire somebody great for me to report to. I've been spoiled."

Madeline laughed. "I can't promise that he or she will be as great as me . . . but Michael had someone in mind, in case you didn't accept."

"Oh? Who?"

"He's from the California office. Looking to relocate to the East Coast, to be closer to family. You probably met him at our corporate retreat last year. Riggs Larson."

Annabelle made a face. "Really? He'll be my new boss?" She had taken an instant dislike to Riggs when they'd been paired for one of the ridiculous bonding exercises that were de rigueur at these corporate team-building conferences. She loved the company, but, come on, they were adults there to do a job, not live together. He'd been one of those seemingly nice, polite people who were actually self-serving and pushy. Plus, that name: Riggs. So pretentious. And now she'd be working for him. It almost made her want to rethink her decision.

Madeline's brows went up. "Not a fan?"

"I didn't spend much time with him. He sort of rubbed me the wrong way, but I really don't know him."

"I don't know him well, either, but Michael thinks highly of him. He's run the Client Services division for three years, and their client base has gone up each year. Clients seem to like him too."

Annabelle wondered what his subordinates thought of him, but she didn't ask. She'd turned down the job, so she had no right to criticize their choice. But it would be fine; she knew how to get along with others. Besides, at her level, there wasn't much oversight necessary. She spent all her time either with her clients or doing work for them.

She stood up. "Guess I'll head back to my office." She was halfway through the door when she stopped and turned around. "When is he starting?"

"Next week. He'll shadow me for two weeks, and then take over."

Annabelle nodded. "Got it."

When she got back to her office, she noticed that she had two missed calls from Scarlett's school. Her heart began to race as she listened to the voicemail.

"Mrs. Reynolds. This is Audrey Barlowe. Scarlett's fine, but there was an incident, and I need you to come to the school. Please call me as soon as you get this message." She dialed the school's number from her office phone.

"Front Office."

"Yes, this is Annabelle Reynolds. May I speak with Vice Principal Barlowe?"

She was put on hold, and a moment later, a woman's voice spoke.

"Mrs. Reynolds?"

"Yes. What's going on?"

"Scarlett was caught in the bathroom vaping. We've been trying to identify the girls who have been doing this for a month now. She's been suspended for two days."

Annabelle gasped. "Scarlett doesn't vape! This has to be a mistake." She flashed to her dream, and a chill ran through her.

"It's no mistake. I saw her myself."

"I'm on my way."

"No need. When we didn't get in touch with you, I called your husband. He's on his way now."

"Okay, I'll talk to Scarlett, and make sure this doesn't happen again."

"I'd like to schedule a meeting with you, your husband, and Scarlett, to discuss this. It's quite serious. She's only fifteen, and vaping is illegal at that age. Not to mention the health risks."

Annabelle was getting irritated. "I'm aware of both the law and the health risks, as is my husband, who's a doctor. We will be addressing this with her. You said a two-day suspension. Am I to assume that she may return to school on Friday?"

"Yes, you may. But I still think—"

"We'll call the office and schedule an appointment."

"Good. Until then."

What a sanctimonious prig! You would think Scarlett had been caught doing cocaine. Yes, vaping was bad, and she was way too young to be doing it. But was it really necessary for the four of them to meet and talk about it? She and James were capable of parenting their child. Annabelle was sure that this was something new; something Scarlett had gone along with, trying to fit in with her new friends. Scarlett was an athlete, concerned about being healthy. This was an aberration—she'd just been going through a rough time.

James was going to have a fit, though. She could just hear his lecture. Guilt sliced through her. She should have taken the time to talk to Scarlett about her estrangement from Zoe. She'd been so distracted trying to decide whether or not to take the promotion that she'd neglected her daughter. She grabbed her purse and briefcase, then swung by Madeline's office.

"Scarlett's not feeling well. I'm going to head out and work from home the rest of the day."

"Okay. Hope she feels better."

"Thanks."

As she drove home, she thought about her dreams again. She could still see it all in vivid detail, as if it were a movie. The plane crash that had actually happened—and now this. In her dream, James had blamed Annabelle for Scarlett's vaping. But unlike the dream, she wasn't out of town on a trip, embracing a strange man on the balcony.

There had to be a logical explanation. She'd noticed how out of sorts Scarlett had been lately, snapping at everyone, and shutting them out. Had there been a subtle sign about the vaping that Annabelle's subconscious had picked up on? Or maybe it was her guilty conscience for hiding her smoking from James. It had to be something like that because the alternative was terrifying. If she couldn't find a reasonable basis for knowing about that plane crash and Scarlett's vaping, it meant that her dreams were not dreams at all, but rather *were* actually glimpses of the future.

12

Before

"Can we go home now?" Annabelle's mother asked, as soon as Annabelle walked into the room. Miriam was sitting in a chair at the small table in her room, an open photo album in front of her.

"Hi, Mom." Annabelle took a seat next to her. "That was a fun day," she said, pointing to the picture of the two of them in front of the Christmas tree in Rockefeller Center. It had been taken when Annabelle was still in high school.

Miriam pointed to the picture at the bottom of the album, of their old house in Fairfield. "I want to go home."

Annabelle swallowed and took her mother's hand in hers. "We had to sell the house, Mom. It was a lot to take care of. That's why you're here. So you can have some help."

Miriam didn't answer right away, then looked over at her daughter. "Did you pass your driver's test?"

Annabelle nodded. "Yep. Do you want to go for a drive?"

Her mother shook her head. "I'm tired. I think I'll take a nap. Sorry, honey, you'll have to make your own dinner tonight."

"It's fine, Mom. Let me help you."

She got her mom settled into bed, even though it was only three o'clock. Miriam barely ate these days and was always exhausted.

Within minutes, the soft sound of her snoring filled the room. Annabelle leaned back into the armchair next to the bed and closed her eyes, summoning memories of better days. She hated seeing her mother disappear before her eyes, becoming a stranger. Her deepest fear was that over time, the memories made with this new version of her mother would eclipse the cherished ones of her as she used to be.

When it became apparent that her mother would be sleeping for a long while, Annabelle decided to go home and get some studying done before going to Randy's place. His roommate was on call again, so the coast was clear. She hated being here after five, when her mother would become even more confused, to the point where she sometimes didn't even recognize Annabelle.

She was surprised to see Randy's car when she pulled up to her apartment at Mrs. Miller's house.

"Hi, wasn't I supposed to come to you?"

He leaned in and kissed her. "James is home, so I came here."

Disappointment filled her. This meant they'd have only a few hours together, since Mrs. Miller was not a fan of overnight guests. Annabelle liked and respected her too much to give her any flak about her rule regarding "gentlemen callers," even though it was outdated. But she had a good thing here, and she didn't want to rock the boat.

"I guess we can order takeout. My fridge is pretty bare."

"I'm not really hungry. For food anyway," Randy said, raising his eyebrows and giving her a meaningful look.

When they entered her apartment, he pulled her to him and kissed her. Her knees almost buckled; their chemistry was off the charts. She ran her hands through his hair as they fell onto the sofa, peeling off clothing and throwing it to the floor. Desire flooded her as he kissed her neck and continued down her body. Randy wasn't her first, but she'd never felt this intensity with anyone else. "Do you have a condom?" she whispered, her breath coming in short bursts.

"Shit, no. I'll pull out."

A little voice warned her to stop him, but this felt too good, so she silenced it and gave in to the sweet surrender of her body and Randy's becoming one. When it was over, they lay together, wrapped in each other's arms.

"I love you," Randy said, his lips against her head.

Those words made elation and relief flow through her. "I love you too," she replied. A sense of contentment and joy filled her. For the first time in a long time, she didn't feel regret for what might have been. This was proof that she was exactly where she was supposed to be.

Annabelle

When Annabelle pulled into the garage, James's Range Rover was already parked in its space. Her stomach tightened in anticipation. As she opened the door to the kitchen, she heard angry voices.

"I didn't do it! I already told you. I was only there because Avery was doing a story on it. I wanted to see them get in trouble."

"I'm sorry, Scarlett, but that doesn't make any sense. If what you say is true, then why didn't Avery get in trouble too?"

"Because she was hiding in the stall, and Ms. Barlowe didn't see her. If she had counted the vapes on the floor, she would have seen there were six of them, and seven of us. I can't believe this shit!"

James's face turned red. "Watch your language, young lady!"

Parker ran over to Scarlett, sat at her feet, and started pawing at her leg. She reached down absentmindedly to stroke him.

"Calm down, everyone. This isn't solving anything. Even the dog is upset!" Annabelle said, moving into the kitchen.

Scarlett's face was wet with tears. "I don't vape! And now this is going to go on my permanent record. It's not fair!"

Annabelle wanted to believe her. "Let's all sit down. Start from the beginning. Tell us exactly what happened."

"I already told Dad! Call Avery if you don't believe me."

"Who's Avery?" Annabelle asked.

"My friend. Pretty much my only friend now. She wants to be a reporter. I only went in there because I thought it would be like an adventure, watching something happen as it went down. I didn't think I'd get blamed for something I didn't do."

"So, you're saying the vice principal didn't see you with the vape?" Annabelle asked.

"No! Because I didn't have one. The girls barricaded the door with a trash can so they'd have time to throw the vapes out if a teacher came. But earlier that day, the teacher blocked off the toilets. When she came in, the girls went to throw them in, but they landed on the floor. She assumed I did it, too, because I was there. Then she told us we were all suspended. But no one had a vape in their hand."

Annabelle looked at James. "Well, that doesn't sound right, does it?"

James scoffed. "The girls blocked the door, then they tried to throw the vapes in the toilet but the administration had cleverly put plastic wrap under the seat. I can see how that's a pretty good case for the administration."

"Well, that may be so, but I think we need to fight this. As Scarlett said, it will go on her record, which up until now has been exemplary." She turned to Scarlett. "Will Avery back up your story?"

"Definitely."

"Okay. I'm going to talk to your vice principal tomorrow. We believe you, and we're going to stand up for you. Right, honey?" She gave James a pointed look. She could tell he wasn't convinced, but he nodded.

"Right, but—"

Annabelle groaned internally, waiting.

"We're giving you the benefit of the doubt. If we find out that you've betrayed our trust, you'll be in a lot more trouble than a two-day suspension," he said.

Scarlett's lips drew together in a tight line. "Way to have faith in me, Dad." She bolted from the room, but not before Annabelle saw more tears rolling down her face. They heard the slamming of her door. Annabelle spun around and glared at James.

"Really? What was that?"

He threw his hands up. "What do you mean?"

"You acted like she was on trial or something. She's never been in trouble before—"

"That's not true," he interrupted. "Are you forgetting she got detention last month for walking out of class without permission?" Annabelle's eyes were drawn to his clenched fists and the image from that horrible dream flashed in her mind. *Get a grip,* she scolded herself. She looked James in the eye, enunciating every word for emphasis.

"And are *you* forgetting that she had her period, and the idiotic substitute wouldn't let her go to the bathroom? That doesn't count!"

He threw his hands up. "You always defend her. That's part of the problem. Scarlett can do no wrong in your eyes. Neither of our kids can."

She was stunned into silence. Yes, she could be permissive at times, but she wasn't blind to her children's faults. She just didn't nitpick every little thing the way James did. When they were first together, she had found his ways steadying and comforting. Her life had been in chaos for so long that it felt good to give up control to someone else. And he was a good father—but why did he have to expect so much? They were still children, after all. Maybe she did give them a pass a little more often than she should, but if so, it was only to mitigate the stringent code of conduct he expected of everyone. Her mother-in-law was fond of saying that they balanced each other out perfectly. Annabelle prided herself on being a good mother, and it felt like James was telling her that she was failing. "Are you criticizing my parenting?"

He waved his hands. "No, no, I'm not. I'm merely saying I think they take advantage of your good nature sometimes."

"And I feel like I'm on a tightrope. Always balancing how to keep everyone happy without offending someone. I just want peace!"

"What's going on? Is something bothering you?"

Annabelle started to tell him about her dreams, but then she hesitated. James was a man of science, his worldview based on facts. For the most part, she'd always been the same way, scoffing at psychics who claimed to know the future. But if she couldn't discuss this with her husband, what did that say about their marriage? And they had a good marriage. Didn't they? A good life. She reached out and took his hands in hers.

"Something *is* bothering me. I've had some strange dreams lately, and some of them have come to pass."

Confusion played over his face. "What do you mean, 'come to pass'?"

"That plane crash? I saw it in my dream. I was in a hotel, and it was on the news. And I also dreamt that you called me and told me that Scarlett had gotten suspended for vaping. I dreamt all this *before* either thing happened."

His mouth was partly open, and he looked dumbfounded. "I don't know what to say, other than . . . that's impossible. You must have heard about the crash."

"I thought the same thing. But what about Scarlett? That just happened today. I dreamt about it a couple nights ago."

He kept shaking his head, looking off into the distance. "I think you're mixing things up somehow. Maybe these dreams are disturbing your sleep. Sleep deprivation can play tricks with your mind."

Now she was getting frustrated. "I'm not sleep-deprived. And dreams happen in the REM state, the deepest part of sleep."

"Well, actually REM isn't the only stage in which you dream."

She stood up. "Whatever. You're probably right. It's nothing."

"Annabelle—"

"I'm going to go check on Scarlett. You should probably get back to your office."

Why did James always have to be the expert on everything. Just because he'd gone to medical school, he thought he knew it all. "Sleep deprivation can play tricks with your mind," she mimicked in a singsong voice as she headed up the stairs to Scarlett's room. She wasn't crazy. She would keep a dream journal and write down everything from now on. But she wouldn't discuss it with James. She would have to add it to the list of secrets she was keeping from him.

Scarlett

Scarlett's eyes opened when she heard her text tone. She rolled over and grabbed her phone, swiping. She smiled.

Ben: GM r u still in trouble?

Scarlett: My lame dad doesn't believe me

Ben: So ur suspended?

Scarlett: No mom gave them shit—I go back today

Ben: Sorry about ur Dad

Scarlett: Cuz he's a liar—so he thinks everyone else is too

Ben: Sucks

Scarlett: Maybe I shld tell my mom about u and our plan

Ben: Not yet

Scarlett: Why not? I think she'll be cool
with it. I don't like lying to her

Ben: What if she shuts it down. U said she
monitors all your socials. Can u really
trust her? U know she'll tell ur dad
and he sounds overly strict

Scarlett: I guess ur right. Ok

Ben: Have a good day at school 😊

She put the phone down and got out of bed. Her feelings for Ben
grew stronger every day. It was crazy; she felt like she'd known him
forever. She still couldn't believe how lucky she was to have found
him. Every time she thought about the future, she was so excited she
thought she would burst. It took all she had to keep quiet when her
mom kept asking her what was making her so cheerful. She wanted
to tell her, but then her dad would find out, and that would ruin everything.

Avery was waiting for Scarlett by her locker when she got to
school.

"You're lucky you got out of your suspension," Avery told her. "I
heard the principal changed it to an expulsion, since two of the vapes
had pot in them."

"Seriously?" Scarlett would have been mortified if that had happened to her.

"Yup. I don't know what your mom said, but you should thank
her."

"My mom can be very persuasive. She should have been a lawyer. And thanks for sticking up for me with Ms. Barfo," Scarlett said.

"No prob. I wish you would've told me you were planning on
coming. I would have warned you to hide."

"No big deal. All good now."

"Are you still chatting with Ben?"

"Yeah. The more I get to know him, the cooler I think he is. You wouldn't believe how much we have in common. It's freaky. We like the same shows, the same music. He's seen every single episode of *Lost* too!"

Avery pursed her lips. "I've been thinking. All that stuff is on your Insta, right? Do you think maybe he's just saying he likes the same things?"

"Why are you being so harsh about him?"

"Naturally cynical, I guess. You *have* seen *Nightline*, right?"

"Oh, come on! He's not a pedophile."

"Seriously, have you guys FaceTimed yet? You know, to make sure he's not catfishing you. I saw a movie about some old guy pretending to be a hot young guy, and then when they met up, he tried to kidnap the girl."

Scarlett rolled her eyes. "He's not catfishing. I can see other friends' comments and stuff on his Insta. I don't want to FaceTime him. I want the first time we see each other to be in real life."

Avery gave her a skeptical look. "I think you should at least Face-Time once. You need to do your due diligence."

"You're such a journalist! I know you're trying to help, but I know who he is. Look, I can't tell you everything yet. I promised him I'd keep it secret for now. You have to trust me. I know for sure he's who he says he is. I have proof. Okay? Just leave it at that."

Avery raised her eyebrows. "It's your funeral."

The bell rang, and they parted ways. Scarlett appreciated Avery's concern. She was turning out to be a true friend; so different from Zoe, who was still being a total bitch. But Avery didn't have to worry. Ben was someone she could trust. In fact, she was starting to think he was the only one she could trust and who wasn't lying to her. Ben had pointed out the holes in the stories her parents had told her. A few months ago, she'd been given a school project about heritage. Her father had refused to sign the permission slip to allow her to have her DNA tested, claiming it was a violation of privacy and could be used for other things down the road. He was such a freak about stuff like that. But now she understood the real reason he was insistent that she not do the DNA test. He didn't want her to find out the truth.

15

Before

The semester was finally over. Randy had invited her over and had promised to cook her a special dinner. Annabelle used the last of her weekly budget to pick up an eight-dollar bottle of wine. She hoped it wouldn't give them headaches. As she walked up the sidewalk to his house, she noticed two silhouettes standing in the living room. *Must be his roommate,* she thought. It boded well that Randy was ready to introduce her.

She rang the bell, and the door swung open. Randy greeted her with a smile and a peck on the lips. She looked over his shoulder to see a nice-looking guy with blond hair and glasses watching them.

"This is James, my roommate," Randy said, taking her coat and moving out of the way so James could shake her hand.

"Nice to meet you, Annabelle," James said.

He held her gaze, and for a moment she felt strangely uncomfortable. "You as well," she replied, dismissing the feeling.

They moved into the kitchen, where an open bottle of wine and two glasses were waiting on the island. Randy filled them and held his glass out for a toast.

"To not being your professor anymore," he said with a laugh.

They clinked glasses and drank. The wine was delicious, and although she didn't know much about wine, she could tell it was defi-nitely a higher quality than what she'd brought. She looked at James. "Randy says you're a doctor."

"Resident. Finishing up my first year."

"Is it as much of a slog as they make it look on *Grey's Anatomy*?" she asked.

He smiled. "Kinda. But the attendings aren't as mean. And noth-ing is happening in the on-call rooms, sadly."

They all laughed.

"Enough about me; Randy tells me you've got one more semester to graduate. Have you thought about what you want to do?"

"Something in marketing, digital strategy."

"Any specific industry?"

"I like to change things up. I'll try to get a job with an agency that represents a variety of clients."

"She's brilliant. Any company would be lucky to have her," Randy said.

She shook her head. "Thanks, but you don't know anything about my marketing acumen—only that I can ace my film exams."

"I can tell these things," he insisted.

"I think I'll take off and give you guys some privacy," James said. "Have fun. Hope to see you again, Annabelle."

"Bye." James's last remark made her wonder if Randy had a pa-rade of women coming in and out. Why would he have to hope he'd see her again? After he left, she decided to be up-front.

"Did you tell James that we've been seeing each other, or does he think this is our first date or something?"

He gave her a puzzled look. "Why?"

"I'm curious why he'd say he hoped to see me again. Wouldn't he kind of figure I'd be around?"

Randy got up and walked over to her, putting his hands on her shoulders. "Of course. He knows I'm nuts about you. I'm sure he didn't mean anything by it. And besides, you're the first girl I've had over here since I moved in."

She suddenly felt foolish. She'd never behaved so insecurely with anyone before. She thought the university rule archaic and stupid, but she had to admit that there *was* a power dynamic inherent in it that favored the professor. For the past two months, she'd allowed Randy to set the pace and call the shots. Despite knowing there was a reason he'd kept her a secret, it made her feel tawdry.

"Yeah, okay, you're right. I'm just glad we don't have to hide it anymore."

"Me too. Dinner's gonna be ready in about forty-five minutes. How about an appetizer?" He kissed Annabelle deeply, moving his hand to her breast and lightly caressing her. Her stomach fluttered with butterflies, and she leaned into him. He took her hand and they walked to the staircase. But before they could ascend, the doorbell rang. She straightened up, trying to regain her composure.

"Expecting someone?"

"Nope. Hold the thought."

She waited by the staircase as he went to open the door. Her stomach dropped when she saw that it was another girl from her class, Darla, or Darlene, she couldn't remember. But she'd noticed her—with her jet-black hair, short skirts, and killer body. What the hell was she doing here?

Randy seemed surprised to see her. "Darlene, what are you doing here?"

Darlene looked past him to Annabelle, and her smile was replaced by a frown. "Class is over, so I thought you might be able to come out and play. You said there are no rules against it now, but I can see you've already found someone else to play with."

"I'm sorry if I gave you the wrong impression, but . . ." Randy's words trailed off and he blew out a breath.

Darlene narrowed her eyes, staring at Annabelle for a long moment. "No worries. My bad. Have fun. Guess you're the teacher's pet." She turned and stomped down the sidewalk. Randy shut the door and walked back to Annabelle.

"I'm sorry. I don't know what that was about."

"What did she mean about your telling her there were no rules now? Did something happen between the two of you?"

His face turned red, and he looked at the floor. "Look, I'm an idiot, okay? She hit on me at the beginning of the semester. I was in my office grading papers, and she came in. She asked me out, and I told her it wasn't allowed."

Annabelle could see there was more he wasn't telling her. "And?" she pressed.

"And she kissed me."

Annabelle went cold. Kiera's words about Randy being a player resounded in her mind.

"Did something else happen?"

"I kissed her back, but then I told her it wasn't going to happen. It was before you and I had coffee, I swear. Nothing else happened, and I didn't want it to. I told you, I love you."

Annabelle wanted to believe him, did believe him, but the mood was spoiled. Her appetite was gone, too, but she wasn't going to let this blow up into a big fight. She looked him in the eye. "Whatever happened before we were together is cool. Just don't lie to me. I'm only going to ask one more time. Was that really all there was to it, or did something more happen?"

He looked down at the floor. "A few kisses, and she initiated it. But then I made her leave."

"Why would she think she could show up at your house? And how did she know where you live?"

"I don't know. Honestly. She must have looked it up. I mean, I'm listed. I guess she figured she'd take her chances."

"Let's just eat and forget about it," Annabelle said.

They returned to the kitchen and continued drinking wine and chatting as though everything was fine. But a little doubt had nestled in Annabelle's mind, and she knew it wouldn't leave as easily as Darlene had.

16

The Wife

He thinks he's so smart, so tricky. I pretend that I don't know about her. That I'm oblivious to everything. He leaves the house earlier every day. Even when he's here, his mind is elsewhere. He stays in his office until late and comes to bed after I'm asleep. The last time I never proved anything, but this time I will. I'm not going to turn a blind eye.

I turn the knob on his home office and enter. He's careful, so I'm not optimistic that I'll find any clues, but I have to try. I sit down at his desk and pull on the center drawer. Locked. I rummage around for a key, looking under the blotter, in the pencil cup, moving papers on the surface—but there's no key. I glance at the built-in bookshelf lining the wall. I don't have time to search there. I'm already running late; I have a client meeting at nine with a woman who recently discovered her husband has been living a secret life for years. She wants me to take him to the cleaners, and that's what I intend to do. They don't call me a "ball-buster" for nothing. I've made a good living, helping women make their husbands pay dearly in a divorce. My reputation is well known. Unfortunately, my husband is aware of it, too, which makes him very hard to catch.

17

Annabelle

Annabelle left work early with a raging migraine. *It must be stress,* she thought. She hadn't had a headache this bad in years. It was three o'clock, and the house was quiet. Scarlett had a soccer game, so Dylan and the girls wouldn't be home until close to five. If it didn't feel like a nail was boring through her skull, she would have loved to have surprised Scarlett by going, but all she wanted to do was lie down in a dark room with an ice pack on her forehead. After downing three ibuprofens, she went upstairs. She tried to quiet her thoughts, but she kept replaying the discussion between her and James about her dreams. When she'd tried to talk to him about it again, he'd cut her off midsentence. She wasn't crazy, and she wasn't imagining things. The plane crash, the restaurant, Scarlett's vaping. It was all too much to be a coincidence.

She remembered her mother telling her about the time her grandmother had dreamed about her husband clutching his chest and falling over. She'd begged him to go to the doctor and get checked out. He didn't listen. A week later, he had a heart attack and died. Annabelle's mother said it was a curse that her mother had to bear, seeing these horrible things and no one believing her. And now it was happening to Annabelle.

She finally drifted off into a fitful sleep.

It's pizza night and Parker sits at my side, his head on my leg, waiting and hoping I'll share some crust with him. I know I should scold him, but he's so adorable with that sweet face and limpid brown eyes that I don't. When James isn't looking, I break a piece of crust and hand it to him under the table.

"Nice try," James says, "I saw it. That dog has turned into a pest because you all spoil him."

"It's not fair. We get to eat whenever we want. Parker has to wait for us to feed him," Olivia says.

James shakes his head.

Scarlett's phone pings, and she stands up to retrieve it from the counter.

"Not during dinner!" James admonishes.

She rolls her eyes. "It's about a homework assignment. I'll just be a sec." She gets up and reads the text. "Oh, shoot!"

"What?"

"I forgot! I need a poster board for my presentation. I thought it was due Friday, but it's tomorrow."

I groan. "Scarlett! How many times have we asked you to plan ahead?"

"It's okay, I'll run you over to the store. We can swing by the grocery store too. I'm running low on my protein shake," James says.

I clear the table after they leave, then open my laptop to jump on a Zoom call with the West Coast office. After a while, I look up and see it's almost eight-thirty. They've been gone for over an hour and a half, and the shopping center is only a few miles away. A feeling of unease comes over me. I pick up my phone, go to the "find me" app, and look up James's phone. It shows him on the road but not moving. I try to navigate to his contact info to call him but the phone freezes. My fingers poke the screen and nothing happens. Why can't I call him? I turn to go in search of the house phone but it's like I'm stuck in quicksand. I can barely move. The doorbell rings. A sense of dread overcomes me. I don't want to answer it. Something inside is telling me that once I do, my life will never be the same. My legs feel leaden. The doorbell rings again. I make my way to the hallway, again, in slow motion as my legs don't seem to get the message that I need them to move. When I finally reach the door and open it, a police officer is standing there. "No," I whisper before he says anything.

"Mrs. Reynolds?"

I nod.

"May I come in?"

I open the door without a word.

"Can we take a seat?"

"My husband was in an accident. Wasn't he?"

He sighs deeply. "A pickup truck going the wrong way collided head-on with his car at 7:05."

"And?"

"Your husband and your daughter are dead."

Annabelle woke up with a cry, her eyes open, her pulse racing. "Thank God it was only a dream." And then she heard the words and doubled over in terror. A dream or another premonition?

18

Before

Christmas arrived, and the only thing making it bearable was Randy. Annabelle and her mother had always celebrated the holidays with joy, accumulating traditions over the years. She bought her mother a small tree and had hoped to decorate it with her, but Miriam just stared at it as if she had no idea what it was. Even putting some of their cherished ornaments on it hadn't jogged her memory.

Today Annabelle would meet Randy's whole family. They arrived at his parents' house, and she felt her stomach flutter with nerves.

"I hope they like me," she said, smoothing down her dress as they got out of the car, holding the gift basket she'd brought for them.

"They're going to love you. My sisters can't wait to meet you. If they try to give you the third degree, feel free to ignore them." He laughed. "They can be a little much sometimes."

As soon as they walked into the house, everyone descended upon them, shouting their hellos, hugging, and kissing. As an only child, it wasn't a scene Annabelle was used to, but it made her wish they were *her* family. How wonderful it must be to have so many people to love.

"Hi, Annabelle," his mother gushed as she pulled her into a hug. "We've been dying to meet you."

"Thank you for including me in your Christmas," Annabelle said.

"You're more than welcome," Randy's father boomed, also giving her a warm hug. "Come on in and meet everyone."

Randy's three sisters were lovely, not at all the way he made them sound. They whisked Annabelle off and got her some eggnog. The four of them sat together for over an hour, laughing and getting to know one another. By the end of the day, Annabelle was smitten with all of them. As they were driving away after dinner, she turned to Randy.

"I had such a good time. Your family is great."

He grabbed her hand. "Thank you for coming today. Everyone loved you, like I knew they would."

"They were wonderful. This isn't an easy day for me. I'd like to stop and see my mom."

He looked at his watch. "Didn't you say nights aren't the best time for her? Maybe it's better if you go in the morning."

She hesitated. He was right about that, but still, she felt guilty letting the day go by without seeing her mother.

"Yeah, but still. You don't have to come with me. Let's go to your house, and I'll get my car."

"Okay."

She was disappointed that he didn't offer to go with her but said nothing. It was hard enough for her, so maybe she was expecting too much from him. But after she'd spent the whole day with his family, it would have been nice if he could spare a little time for hers.

ANNABELLE WAS NOW SPENDING HALF her nights at Randy's house. James didn't seem to mind, and the three of them had fallen into a companionable routine on the nights James wasn't working at the hospital. They'd have dinner together and play a game or two afterward, before she and Randy would retire to his room.

It was her turn to cook tonight. She'd looked up a recipe for lasagna since that was Randy's favorite dish. She wished she'd realized how complicated it was before undertaking it, but as she watched him take a bite, she was pleased to see him nod approvingly.

"Best I've ever tasted," he said.

Annabelle put a forkful in her mouth. The sauce was bitter, and the noodles not fully cooked. She grimaced. "Liar," she replied, laughing. "I'm not sure it's supposed to be crunchy."

James took a heaping helping, ate a forkful, and then arched an eyebrow. "It's the most *interesting* lasagna I've ever had. The raisins are a nice touch."

She pushed the plate away from her. "Pizza on me. This is inedible."

James pulled out his phone and ordered a pizza. Then he smiled at Annabelle. "I've got it. You're still a student." He put his phone back in his pocket. "On its way."

"Thanks," she said, grateful that she wouldn't have to dip into her dwindling cash. She appreciated James's thoughtfulness. She knew he couldn't make that much as a resident, but he always did small things to make it easier on her.

"How was your mom yesterday?" James asked.

"In a happy mood. Didn't ask to go home, so I'm hoping she's getting used to it there."

"Did you play some of the old songs she liked?"

Annabelle nodded. "Thanks so much for suggesting it. She actually remembered some of the lyrics and was singing along. It was the first time in I don't know how long that I saw a genuine smile on her face."

"It's amazing what music can do. I suggest doing that each time you see her," James said.

"Yeah, I was thinking of getting her a CD player and some CDs, so the nurses can play music when I'm not there."

"Great idea," Randy said.

"I have one I don't need. You can take it if you like," James said.

"That would be great, thank you." She yawned. "I'm wiped. I'm going to take off. I've got a full day of classes tomorrow. I want to stop and see Mom in the morning."

"Are you sure? The pizza's not even here yet," Randy said.

"Yeah, you guys enjoy." She'd been staying over a lot lately, and she was getting too used to it. She didn't like the way she was start- ing to depend on Randy, and the last thing she needed was for Mrs. Miller to get upset that she was gone so much and ask her to move out. She said goodbye and drove home.

When she got to her apartment, she microwaved some ramen and ate it in front of the television, but her mind wandered. Her period was three weeks late. She hadn't yet said anything to Randy, but she was worried. She was never late. She glanced over at the box sitting on the coffee table. She hadn't been able to work up the nerve to take the test yet. She was graduating in a few months, and she needed to find a job soon after. What the hell was she going to do if she was pregnant? She cursed her stupidity in not stopping Randy that night they'd had no condom. If she was pregnant, it had to have happened then. That was almost two months ago. When would she be due? Was it exactly nine months from conception?

Sighing, Annabelle opened her laptop and googled it. A preg- nancy calculator came up. She input the date of her last period and her possible conception date, then hit enter. Confetti filled the screen and the message: *Congratulations! Your due date is Septem- ber 13. You are 5 Weeks Pregnant.* She gasped out loud.

Calm down, she told herself. Maybe she was late because she was under so much stress. That happened sometimes. "Just take the damn test already," she said out loud. Taking a deep breath, she picked up the box and went to the bathroom, following the instructions. She left the stick on the counter and set her phone timer for ten minutes. She went back to her computer and navigated to the Facebook pro- file she'd been monitoring ever since her mother had gotten sick.

There he was, looking happy and relaxed on the slopes with his current wife and their twin daughters. The girls looked to be around nine or ten; adorable, blond-haired, and blue-eyed, like their mother. His wife was younger than he was—by at least twenty years. But time had been kind to him. In his late fifties, he could easily pass for fortysomething. His hair was still thick and only sprinkled with gray, which on a man always looked distinguished. She clicked through the photos, her gut tightening with anger. They were in Switzerland— Davos. They all had on fancy-looking jackets, ski glasses, and skis. His wife, Olga, was leaning into him with an arm around the two girls who stood in front of her. She was model pretty, and Annabelle wondered how he had snagged her, and if she knew he had ditched his first family. She didn't know if he was the one who'd made the money or if he'd married into it, but she would bet it was the latter. His wife didn't have any social profiles, so Annabelle wasn't able to find out too much about her, other than a few articles about her parents and their large endowments to Princeton, their alma mater. Annabelle felt confident that his good fortune was not of his own making. Gerard Morgan (previously George Morgan), the name he was now using, listed his occupation as an entrepreneur with some vague language about investments and digital currency. He was certainly not discriminating with his Facebook friend requests, as it had taken her no time at all to put up a fake profile, with a photo of a stunning blonde, and send him a friend request, which was speedily accepted.

Annabelle hadn't seen him in person in over seventeen years. He'd left when she was six. Her last memory of him was when she'd fallen off her bike and gashed her leg. He'd taken her to the Emergency Room for stitches, holding her and assuring her that she would be fine. She could still remember the smell of his aftershave, and the way the stubble of his beard felt against her cheek. He'd held her hand while they stitched her up, making up a fairy tale in which she was the princess whom the evil witch had made fall. Afterward, he took her for ice cream, a triple-dip chocolate cone. A few days later, he was gone. Her mother told her that he'd had to go far away for work, and that she hoped he'd come back soon. As she got older, and her mother couldn't protect her any longer, she found out the truth: that he'd left them with no intention of ever returning. Even though in the divorce agreement he was responsible for alimony and child support, he left the state and never sent a dime to her mother. Annabelle never heard from her father again. To this day, she hated chocolate ice cream.

When Annabelle was older, she wondered if perhaps her mother had prevented him from getting in touch or intercepted his communication. But what she discovered broke her heart and made her love her mother even more. Despite his abandoning her, her mother had tried to get in touch with him over the years, beseeching him to stay connected to Annabelle for her sake. She'd even offered to legally absolve him of any financial obligation if he would only make time for his daughter. All her letters were returned to her with *Return to Sender* in bold letters. When she'd asked her mother why she hadn't sued him for the alimony and child support, her mother had shaken her head sadly.

"I never wanted you to be in the middle of a legal battle, and I didn't want to spend my time and energy fighting in court. I made enough to take care of us. Your father is not a good man. For your sake, I tried to convince myself that having him in your life was better than not. But he wanted to move on. I never wanted you to feel like raising you was a burden. You didn't belong to him anymore, so I didn't want to pull him back into our lives."

Now her mother was incapable of changing her mind and going after him for what she was owed. The money from the sale of the house wouldn't last forever, and Annabelle would be damned if she'd put her mother in an inferior facility. When it became clear to her that she wasn't going to be able to afford it on her own for much longer, she decided she would find him and make him pay. Now that her mother was incapacitated, Annabelle had the right to represent her legally. From her internet searches, she was pretty sure that he was still legally responsible for all those years he paid nothing. Serendipitously, her landlady's son was an attorney. He had promised to ask around at his law firm for a family attorney willing to take her case pro bono. For her mother's sake, Annabelle was going to do whatever she had to do to make him pay restitution. He owed her that at least.

The timer on her phone went off and she stood. Time to face the music. She went into the bathroom and picked up the stick.

19

The Wife

I've always known he was a little bit kinky. I mean, the kinds of things he talks about are not normal. He's always been drawn to the dark side, but as long as he's only talking about it and not actually doing it, I always figured, what's the harm? Some of the chat rooms he's in are disturbing. I don't understand the attraction. But again, talk is cheap. Maybe I should have taken more of an interest in the things that interest him, because I feel him drifting away more and more. I found the research he's done on her. He's learning everything he can, so that he can ingratiate himself with her. I won't let him get away with it.

Annabelle

The next day, Annabelle was still haunted by her dream. It had rattled her so much that instead of ordering pizza, as they always did on Wednesdays, she'd texted James and told him she was making tacos. They had finished eating when everything began to play out just as in her dream. The text. The forgotten poster board. And James's needing more protein powder.

"I'll take her," Annabelle said. She would go a different way, and they would avoid the horrible accident.

"Don't you have that Zoom with the California office in half an hour?"

Shit, how could she have forgotten? "I'll go afterward."

"No, it's fine. Besides, you don't know how long you'll be. It's no big deal. I'll take her."

She looked at the clock. Six-thirty. The accident in her dream was at 7:05. Should she just tell James? No, he would dismiss her again. She needed to stall, keep them here at least until seven. Then they would be in the store when the accident happened, not on the road coming home.

"Okay, okay. But can I see you upstairs for a minute before you go?"

He gave her a puzzled look. "Okay."

"Hurry up," Scarlett called after them. "I still have to do the assignment once I get the poster board."

When they reached their bedroom, James looked at Annabelle expectantly. "I didn't want to have this conversation in front of the girls," she began.

"What is it?"

"I was wondering if you could prescribe me some migraine medicine. I don't want the girls thinking that, you know, I'm trying to get drugs or something." She wasn't really worried about that, but it was the only thing she could think of to stall him. And she knew it would spark him asking lots of questions.

He cocked an eyebrow. "It's not like you're asking me for oxy or something. But back up. When did the migraines start? I didn't know you were getting them again."

She sat on the bed, hoping he'd follow suit and more time would pass. "Well, um, I think it's stress. Since Madeline left, and I have a new boss. I had to come home early yesterday because it was so bad."

"Babe, I'm sorry! You should have told me. What can I do to help? Of course I can prescribe something, but it's more important to cut out the underlying cause. And if it's stress, you need to reduce it."

"What do you recommend?"

He tilted his head. "Meditation. I've been trying to get you to do that for a while. I can show you some apps to download. And don't get mad, but alcohol can also be a trigger."

She glanced at her watch. Six forty-five. She needed a few more minutes. If they left here at ten till, they'd get to the store right at seven and be at least fifteen minutes. But what if they weren't for some reason? She should make them wait until 7:06. That was the only safe thing to do. "Alcohol, really? So, you think even having some wine on the weekends could cause a headache later?"

He warmed to the topic. "Yes, studies have shown—" Annabelle tuned out while he spoke for the next several minutes about the evils of alcohol.

"Okay, I'm gonna head out."

"Wait. Can you show me those apps? I don't want to get the wrong ones."

"Now?"

"Yeah, it'll only take a few minutes, please?" She pulled her phone from her pocket and handed it to him.

When he was finished, he gave the phone back to her.

"So how do I know which ones to use?" she asked.

James spent another few minutes explaining. She looked at her watch again. Six minutes past seven. She abruptly stood. "Great, thanks. I better get to my Zoom." She was now seven minutes late, but she didn't care. Before he could leave, she pulled him to her and kissed him deeply, closing her eyes and holding him tight to her. When she released him, he looked at her in surprise.

"Well, that was nice. What brought that on?"

"I love you."

He leaned in and gave her another kiss. "Love you more. Let's pick this up again later tonight." He winked and headed downstairs.

After James and Scarlett left, and she had Olivia settled watching a movie, Annabelle joined the Zoom, apologizing for her tardiness. It was eight o'clock when she finished and they still weren't home. She began to sweat. Had something happened anyway? She saw headlights through the curtains and ran to the window, her heart in her throat. She breathed a sigh of relief when she saw that it was James's Range Rover.

She met them in the hallway.

"I was getting worried," she said.

James rolled his eyes. "It was crazy. Traffic backed up all the way on Route One. Terrible accident. Pickup truck driving in the wrong lane caused a head-on collision. Ambulance and police everywhere. Looked pretty bad."

Annabelle

I'm in my office, working on a new file. It's someone Riggs brought in, a crime podcaster who wants to build up his social platform. Riggs is asking me to hand off another client to Mitch, so I can take him on. I glance at my watch and sigh. Two o'clock. Riggs's inaugural staff meeting took over an hour, and now I've got to scramble to finish everything before I leave. I've got two hours before I need to pick up Olivia from gymnastics practice. I spend the next hour assembling a transfer package for the Morgan account. I walk over to Mitch's office, but his lights are out.

Sherry, our admin, walks by. "Are you looking for Mitch?"

"Yes, is he gone?"

"Yeah, you just missed him. He wasn't feeling well."

"Okay, thanks."

I go back to my office and am about to navigate to the podcaster's website when my phone rings. I glance at the screen. Now what? I think as I snatch it up.

"Mrs. Reynolds?"

"Yes?"

"This is Coach Calhoun. Olivia fell off the balance beam. She's in a lot of pain; we think she may have broken her arm."

"Oh my God. I'll be right there."

*I run from the office and press the button for the elevator repeatedly.
Come on! What's taking so long? Frustrated, I run to the stairwell. It's
eight floors but I'm pumped so full of adrenaline that I don't care. I pull
the handle on the door, but it won't open. I yell, "Open, dammit! Let's
go!"*

"Annabelle, wake up."

James is standing over her. "You were yelling. Another nightmare?"

She sprang up and jumped out of bed. "Yeah." She hadn't told
him that she'd dreamt of the pickup truck. She had no way to prove
to him that she'd seen it before it happened. She had written it down
in her journal, but she could hear him saying she could have written
it after the fact. But it was irrefutable proof to her that she was seeing events before they occurred. Did that mean, though, that every
dream was a premonition? She'd always had an active imagination
and remembered her dreams—but they were the typical forgotten
homework assignment, being naked in public, all those types of anxiety dreams. These dreams were different. Could Olivia truly be in
danger or had Annabelle manufactured this dream out of anxiety
because of the ones before that had come true? She would have to
see how the day played out.

"Yeah, I guess," she answered, not making eye contact. As she
dressed, a pervasive sense of doom filled her. Annabelle was normally an optimistic person. She'd been through a lot in her life, but
she always did her best not to let her circumstances get her down.
She supposed she'd inherited that trait from her mother. After her
father had abandoned them, her mother could have become bitter
and angry. But Annabelle never heard her say a bad word about him.
She thought back to her mother's response when Annabelle had
asked her why she didn't hate him or speak ill of him.

"Hate is like drinking poison and hoping the other person dies,"
she'd said. "Besides, life's too short to live that way. I prefer to count
my blessings. And you are my number one blessing."

She always made Annabelle feel like the most important person in the world. So, when it was Annabelle's turn to take care of her mother, she'd done her best to treat her with the same love and devotion her mother had showered on her. She felt so alone right now. She wished James was more open-minded and that he would help her to figure this out. But he kept invalidating her fears about her dreams. She used to like how confident he was, that he always knew what was right. Now she found him overbearing. Was what had always felt to her like a blanket of protection actually him being controlling? But maybe that wasn't fair. James was fiercely loyal to his family, always one step ahead, doing his best to make sure nothing on the outside penetrated his protective shield. What Annabelle wanted right now, though, was a partner, someone to take her seriously. She didn't need protection—she needed understanding. She'd been so young when they'd married, right out of college, before she'd had time to live as an adult. She'd become a wife and a mother so much sooner than she'd ever planned. Her dream had been to travel the world before settling down, but an unplanned pregnancy had put an end to that. Annabelle inhaled deeply. She needed to look ahead, not back. No good would come of thinking about the past.

She pulled out the notebook from her nightstand and scribbled down her latest dream. Then she went through the motions for the rest of the morning and got the girls off to school. By the time she arrived at her office, she'd forced the dream from her mind.

MADELINE WAS GONE NOW; ANNABELLE needed to give Riggs a chance. Today was their first staff meeting, and she was surprised to see an assortment of pastries and fruit on the conference table. Riggs greeted her with a toothy smile as he welcomed her. She'd done a little online investigating on his Facebook page and was surprised to discover that he was only thirty-one. She would have pegged him closer to forty. He reminded her of an overgrown frat boy in his preppy polo and chinos, his vocabulary peppered with pretentious phrases and buzzwords. She noticed that he kept the Armani case to his tortoiseshell glasses on display at the table. His dark hair was parted on the side and kept in place with some sort of pomade.

"Good morning! Nice to see you again, Annabelle. Hope you're hungry."

She wasn't, but the coffee looked good, and she poured herself a large cup. Her colleagues began to trickle in, and by nine everyone was there and seated.

"I know Madeline typically assigned clients based on your individual areas of expertise, which is great. But I'd like to ensure that everyone continues to develop and has the opportunity to learn new skills."

Annabelle groaned inwardly. If he was going to tell her she was the new TikTok expert, she would throw a cinnamon bun at him.

"With that in mind, I'd like to try something new. I want to pair each of you with someone who has a specialty you don't yet have. This way the client still gets an expert, but you all get to learn something new."

Annabelle looked around the room. Everyone was doing their best to keep their expressions impassive. Riggs droned on for another fifteen minutes, extolling the virtues of developing a "deep bench" along with a few more sports metaphors before he finally opened it up to questions.

Mitch, a newer hire in his early twenties, spoke first. "How is this going to impact our stats? Who takes the lead and gets the credit?"

"Great question, Mitch. The person with the expertise takes the lead, but that same person will be second in a team where someone else is the expert."

It sounded like a nightmare in the making. Annabelle took a deep breath and modulated her voice. "The clients like one point of contact. I'm assuming that won't change. That this, um, training, will be behind the scenes?"

Riggs gave her a condescending smile. "I'm so glad you brought that up, Annabelle."

He must be a Dale Carnegie fan. Annabelle didn't think folks loved hearing their names used as much as Riggs clearly believed they did.

"Yes, the client's needs will come first, as always. My method may require everyone to put in longer hours for a while, but I'm confident that it will be worth it to each of you to acquire new skills. A winning team takes practice."

She tuned out the rest of what he was saying and finally, after another half an hour, the meeting ended. She gathered her things and stood, but Riggs stopped her before she could leave.

"Annabelle, could I have a minute?"

"Sure."

Everyone else filed out, a few casting curious looks at her before leaving. Riggs shut the door.

"I didn't want to say this in front of the group, but you don't need to partner up with anyone. You're already well-versed in everything we do here, Annabelle. They wouldn't have offered you the job otherwise."

"Oh, I didn't realize—"

"That I knew I was the second choice?"

She laughed uneasily. "I'm sure you weren't second. It's just I was already here." She didn't know why she was trying to placate him. A man would probably have taken the compliment.

"Is that all?" she asked.

"No. I wanted to let you know we have a new client that I want you to handle. It's the first client I'm bringing in, and I want to make sure he's well taken care of. Annabelle, I'd like you to offload the Morgan account to Mitch."

She thought of her dream. Her stomach tightened. This was freaking her out. "Okay, Riggs. Who is it?" *Please don't say a podcaster,* she thought.

"Name's Chase Sommers. He's an investigative journalist and has a podcast. He wants to grow his audience. I told him you're the perfect one to help him." He handed her a file.

She gulped, breaking out in a cold sweat. What the hell was happening? "Okay, great. I'll, um, put together a package for Mitch on Morgan." She swallowed several times, hoping he didn't notice her discomfort.

"Great. We'll do a face-to-face with Chase next week. In the meantime, do an assessment of his current socials, website, et cetera, and then you and I can meet beforehand to discuss a plan of action."

"Sounds good."

Annabelle returned to her office, put down the folder, and glanced at her watch. Two o'clock. She thought about her dream again. It was all unfolding in real time. After finalizing the Morgan file, she emailed it to Mitch, then walked over to let him know she'd transferred everything. His office was dark. It was all coming true. Her heart raced as she waited for what she knew would happen next. Sherry walked over.

"Looking for Mitch?"

Annabelle couldn't catch her breath for a moment. "Did he go home sick?"

Sherry gave her a strange look. "Yes. How did you know? You just missed him."

Annabelle ran back to her office and picked up her phone, her heart racing. Olivia would be going to gymnastics practice any minute now.

"Bayport Middle School."

"This is Annabelle Reynolds. I need to pick up my daughter Olivia. Please make sure she doesn't go to gymnastics practice. I repeat, make sure she does not go to practice. Have her wait for me in the office."

"Is everything okay, Mrs. Reynolds?"

"Family emergency. But please don't alarm her. Tell her every-thing's okay, but I need her to come home early today."

"All right."

She grabbed her bag and raced out of the office, hoping she wasn't too late. What if something even worse than a broken arm happened to Olivia? She couldn't lose another child.

Annabelle

Annabelle rang the bell at the school entrance, tapping her foot nervously as she waited for the guard to buzz her in. It seemed like it took forever for him to scan her license and print out a visitor's badge; she was practically jumping out of her skin by the time she reached the office. She threw the door open and ran in, looking around frantically for Olivia. She was nowhere in sight. Where was she? Had they let her go to practice?

"Where's my daughter?" she blurted out, her breath coming in short gasps.

"Excuse me?"

"Olivia Reynolds. I called saying I'd pick her up—"

The woman looked up from her desk. "Oh, yes. She'll be right back. She went to the bathroom."

As Annabelle waited, she thought about her dream again and wondered briefly if she was overreacting. Was she going to spend her life worrying about everything and trying to dodge accidents? But what choice did she have? She'd already seen some of her dreams come true. What if she hadn't stopped James and Scarlett the other night? The door swung open, and Olivia walked in. Annabelle heaved a sigh of relief. She was doing the right thing.

"Sweetheart, there you are!"

Olivia walked over and gave her a hug. "Why did you pick me up early? I'm missing practice."

Annabelle put her arm around her daughter and ushered her out of the office. "Let's go. I'll explain outside."

Once they were in the car, she turned to look at Olivia in the back seat. "I wanted to surprise you. Have one-on-one time. I've been working so much lately, and I miss you. I thought we'd go get ice cream sundaes."

"I miss you, too, Mommy, but I feel bad missing practice."

Annabelle felt bad as well, but she was too nervous about her dream to ignore it. Not after everything else that had come true already. "Don't worry, sweetie, your coach understands. It's only one practice."

She pulled up to the ice cream shop, and they went inside. "Why don't you grab us a table, and I'll go order our sundaes?" She knew how her daughter liked hers—two scoops of chocolate with chocolate fudge and chocolate jimmies. Annabelle almost gagged ordering it every time. She ordered a vanilla sundae with nuts and caramel for herself. She glanced over at Olivia as she waited at the counter while they made their sundaes. Her heart swelled. Olivia was such a sweet and sunny child. She'd practically been born with a smile on her face. Even as a baby, she'd rarely cried. So different from Scarlett, who had screamed her head off the first three months of her life. Olivia was that rare child who made everything easy, and Annabelle loved her to pieces.

"Watch where you're going," a male voice shouted at the entrance. Annabelle turned to see what was happening. A young man in a jean jacket with a buzz cut was pointing his finger into the chest of a man facing him. The other man was older, dressed nicely in a suit, his face red and eyes narrowed.

"You bumped into me, asshole," the older man said. "Learn some manners."

Annabelle watched as if in slow motion as the young man pushed the older one and he began to fall in Olivia's direction. She lunged toward Olivia and grabbed her just in time to get her out of the way. The table and chair were knocked to the floor. Olivia's eyes widened and she held on to Annabelle, who was shielding her with her body.

"What is wrong with you?" she yelled at the two men. "Look what you've done!"

They both stared, open-mouthed, as Annabelle crouched down and gently touched Olivia's cheek.

"Olivia, sweetheart, are you okay?"

"I'm fine, Mommy."

Annabelle's heart was pounding in her chest. She held out her hand to her daughter. "Come on, let's get the ice cream to go."

23

Before

Two lines. Shit, shit, shit. What was she going to do now? Annabelle stared at the stick, almost hypnotized, as her life flashed before her eyes. If there was ever a time she needed her mother, it was now. She stood up and threw the test into the trash. She and Randy had only been together a few months. They were nowhere near the point in their relationship where plans for the future had been made. She loved him, and he'd said he loved her, but they were still in the infatuation stage where everything the other did was charming. She had no job, and how would she find one when she was visibly pregnant? No one would want to hire someone who would be out on maternity leave a few months later. And Randy wasn't financially stable yet. A professor's job didn't pay that much, and he was just getting started doing freelance writing for some of the local papers. This was a disaster.

She contemplated calling her aunt Celia, but quickly dismissed the idea. They weren't close, and it wasn't fair to burden her. Celia had enough to worry about with her sister's illness. Annabelle had no idea how Randy was going to react, but if she had to hazard a guess, it wouldn't be good.

She picked up her phone and sent a text to James.

Can you meet me for coffee tomorrow?
I can come to the hospital. Need to talk
to you. Pls keep it between us for now.

James would be a good sounding board. He knew Randy well, as they'd been roommates for a couple of years now. She stared at her phone, willing it to light up with a response, but nothing. He was probably doing rounds. She put the phone down and her hand moved to her stomach and rested there. It was hard to believe that there was a living being inside of her. She wondered if it was a boy or a girl. Annabelle knew that she wanted children one day, but between taking care of her mother, finishing school, and needing to make a living, this was the worst possible time. Her mother had always told her that everything happened for a reason. Could there be any good reason for this? Her thoughts and feelings were so conflicted; she desperately wished she could get her mother's advice. Maybe she could. Her mother still had moments of clarity, albeit brief and sporadic. She'd talk to her in the morning.

She checked her phone again and saw that she had two messages. The first was from James, confirming tomorrow at eleven. The next message was from Randy.

Sorry you had to leave. My bed is
lonely without you. Love you. xo

She started to type a response, then deleted it and typed an x and an o. Suddenly she was bone-tired. She fell into bed and turned off the light. Maybe morning would bring clarity.

ANNABELLE WAS RELIEVED THAT SHE didn't have any classes today. She would be too distracted to pay attention anyway. Her mother was awake and finishing her breakfast when Annabelle arrived.

"Hi, Mom," she said, giving her a peck on the cheek and sitting across from her at the small table.

"Hi, darling, no school today?"

Annabelle shook her head. "I don't have classes on Monday."

Miriam's brow wrinkled. "What do you mean? High school is every day."

"I'm in college, remember?"

"Oh," Miriam said, but Annabelle could tell she was still confused.

"Listen, Mom, I have something I need your advice on."

"What is it?"

She took a deep breath. "I'm pregnant."

Her mother's smile transformed her face. "That's wonderful! Who's your husband, again?"

"I'm not married, Mom. It was an accident, and I don't know what to do."

Miriam leaned back in her chair and studied her for a long moment. "You take your vitamins and wait for the baby to grow. A baby is a blessing." She stopped and looked up at the ceiling. "I had a baby. I was so happy when I found out I was pregnant. Best thing that ever happened to me." She turned her attention back to Annabelle. "What's your name again, honey?"

"It's Annabelle, Mom. I was your baby."

Miriam grew quiet. Annabelle could tell she had gone to that other place again, somewhere unreachable by those around her, but somewhere good, Annabelle hoped. Maybe Miriam was back in time at some happier place. At least that's what she told herself. She let the subject drop and spent the next hour following Miriam's lead in conversation until her mother was tired again and ready to rest. It was almost time for Annabelle to meet James, so she kissed her mother and slipped from the room.

On the drive to the hospital, she debated the wisdom of telling James about the baby before she told Randy. What if James told him that she'd done so? Randy would be so hurt. But she was terrified of what Randy might say. She hoped that James would at least give her enough insight to prepare herself.

When she reached the cafeteria, he was already there, seated at a table with two cups of coffee waiting. He stood as she approached and kissed her cheek.

"Thanks so much for taking the time to see me," she said.

"Of course. Your message had me worried. Is everything okay?" The kindness in his eyes broke her, and she burst into tears.

"Hey, hey. What's going on?" He slid his chair next to hers and put an arm around her.

It took her a moment to compose herself enough to speak. "I'm pregnant."

James moved his chair back to its original position. "Oh, wow. Does Randy know?"

"Not yet. I just found out last night. I wanted to talk to you first. You know him so well. How do you think he's going to handle this?"

"Um, I—I don't know. How are *you* handling it?"

"I'm freaking out, naturally. This is the worst timing. How am I supposed to get a job if I'm showing? My head is spinning."

"Well, you have options."

"I know I do. But I'm not ready to think about those yet. I need it to sink in a little more. The timing sucks, but I'm sure there are a lot of people who thought the timing sucked, and they can't imagine their lives without their child. It seems like the worst thing now, but who knows? Maybe it's okay. Oh, who am I kidding? It's terrible." She put her head in her hands.

"It's okay. You have time. Nothing has to be decided right now. But Randy's a good guy. I'm sure he'll support you in whatever you want to do. And I'm here for you, too."

She reached out and squeezed his hand. "I know. Thank you. You've been such a good friend. Between my mom and now this, I feel like I'm always running to you with my problems."

He didn't say anything. And she felt something pass between

them—or at least something coming from him—that made her think he thought of her as more than a friend. She hoped she wasn't taking advantage of him. She was in love with Randy and didn't want to give James the wrong idea. "I probably should have talked to Randy first. Please don't tell him I came to you. I love him so much, but we've only been together a few months. I would never want him to feel like I was trying to trap him, as old-fashioned as that sounds."

"You have my word. I won't say anything to him. But you should talk to him as soon as possible. You shouldn't have to shoulder this alone."

"I know. I'll talk to him tonight."

"I'll make myself scarce, try to grab an extra shift, so you two can be alone."

"Are you sure? I hate to keep you out of your own house."

"It's no problem. I can always use the extra dough."

"You're a doll. Thank you."

Annabelle hugged James and left feeling marginally better. He was right. Randy was a good guy, and he was the one who'd encouraged her to throw caution to the wind that night. Just because she was the woman didn't make this her fault. But then again, regardless of the fault, she was the one who had to deal with the consequences. She thought of her mother's words. Could this child be the best thing that had ever happened to her?

24

Annabelle

They were finishing dinner when Olivia let it slip that Annabelle had picked her up from school early.

"Mommy took me for ice cream instead of gymnastics. And these two men got in a big fight. I almost got knocked from my chair!"

James turned to look at Annabelle, his eyes narrowed.

"What? Why wasn't she at gymnastics?"

"Hey, that's no fair!" Scarlett piped in.

"I wanted to do something special with Olivia today. No big deal. Scarlett, I'll do the same for you."

James gave her a puzzled look. "So you left work early? I don't understand."

She sighed. "Can we change the subject?" She gave him a look. "We'll discuss it later."

After both girls had left the table, she put a hand on his arm before he could get up. "I didn't want to say this in front of Scarlett and Olivia. I picked her up early because I was afraid she was going to get hurt at practice."

"Why?"

She bit her lip. "I know you think this is all in my head, but I'm telling you that I'm dreaming things before they happen."

"Annabelle, not this again. I think—"

"Hear me out. I dreamt about the pickup truck accident. It's the reason I made sure you and Scarlett didn't leave until after 7:05 that night."

His mouth dropped open. "Annabelle, this is too much. Why wouldn't you have just told me that? Are you sure you didn't dream it afterward? I can't believe you wouldn't have said something if you had."

Frustration made her want to scream. "I didn't tell you because you wouldn't have believed me! You would have ignored me and left, and it would have been *you* in that accident." She closed her eyes for a moment, trying to compose herself. "Look, there's more." She relayed everything that had happened at her office today, and how the events had mirrored her dream. "I thought if I could make sure Olivia didn't go to practice, I could prevent her from breaking her arm, like I prevented you and Scarlett being in an accident."

"What did Olivia mean about men fighting?"

She told him about the incident.

"If you hadn't gotten to her in time, she could have been hurt then. Don't you see, you could have made it worse. You can't go around behaving this way. A knee-jerk reaction to these dreams."

She felt the heat rise to her face. "What about the accident you could have been in the other night?"

"I don't know, Annabelle. I still think you must have dreamt about it afterward, but even so, I mean maybe it was a fluke. What I do know is that this is not the way to live. It's not possible to predict the future, and you can't live in fear of these dreams coming true. Olivia would have been fine if you'd left her at school. And the last thing I want is for our children to develop an anxiety disorder because you're allowing your subconscious to torment you."

"Well, that's just—"

Her cellphone rang and she stood up, grateful for the interruption. She glanced at the screen. Olivia's friend Sophie's mother.

"Hi, Laura."

"Hi. Did you hear what happened at gymnastics today?"

Annabelle's hold on the phone tightened. "No, what?"

"The balance beam tipped over. Loose bolts on the legs or something. Anyhow. Poor Margaurite fell and broke her arm. Had to have surgery."

25

Annabelle

I'm standing on the same balcony again. I'm mesmerized watching the setting sun over the ocean. Arms entangle me in an embrace, and I'm whispering words of comfort to the man who holds me. "That must have been so hard. Thank you for telling me." After a long moment, he releases me, and I see his face. He's handsome, with wavy hair and deep blue eyes. "Boyish good looks" is the phrase I'd use to describe him. My eyes are drawn to the dimple above his smile. I feel an overwhelming sense of camaraderie and affection.

"Shall we have another glass of wine before we go down to dinner?" he asks.

I nod. He goes into the hotel room and retrieves a bottle of red, topping off the glasses sitting on the table. We both sit down and pick up our glasses. He lifts his to toast.

"Here's to being seen," he says. We clink our glasses, then drink.

"I'm so grateful to be able to talk to you about this. My wife wants to leave it in the past, but I can't. I need to talk about them. It feels wrong not to, as though they didn't matter."

I nod. "Exactly. My husband is the same way. I have to keep it all bottled up inside. It feels so good to be able to share it with someone who can relate." I should feel disloyal, sitting here with a man who isn't my husband, talking about intimacies that should be shared only with James, but I don't. Instead, I feel grateful. Justified even. We're both quiet suddenly, the only sound the crashing of the waves. An impulse comes over me and I stand, holding out a hand.

"Let's go swimming! I've been dying to jump in the ocean since we got here."

"Only someone from the East Coast would want to swim in the Pacific in October." He grins. "What about dinner?"

"We can stop by the restaurant on the way down, and see if they can push back the reservation."

"Okay, why not."

"I'll meet you downstairs. I'll go change."

I head to my room, which is next door. It's the first time I've stayed at Shutters, the first time I've been to Santa Monica, and I love it. As soon as we arrived, I felt as though it was somewhere I could live. I grab my one-piece from my suitcase and change. If James were here, he'd have laughed off my suggestion as silly and insisted we keep our dinner reservation. But the man I'm with is so different. It hits me that I don't know his name. In fact, I don't know what we're doing here at all. Am I having an affair? No, that can't be right. We'd be sharing a room. This must be a business trip. All I know is that for the first time in forever, I feel validated and free. I push James to the back of my mind. I don't want anything to ruin this, whatever this is.

When I get downstairs, he's waiting for me, and he's remembered to bring towels. He takes my hand, and together we run down the beach toward the water, like two kids. He lifts his arms and pulls off his T-shirt. I stare at his flat stomach and well-muscled chest. It's obvious that he works out. He catches me looking, and I feel the heat spread to my face as I quickly look away. I suddenly feel shy about taking off my cover-up.

"Come on, Reynolds, lose the dress."

I take a deep breath and pull it over my head, sucking in my stomach.

"Ready?" he asks.

"Yep," I say as we both run to the water.

"Come on, gotta do it fast," he says, splashing me. I squeal, then dive under the surface. It's freezing! I pop back up at the same time he does, staring at the water dripping from his curls. We're both shivering.

"That was great, but—" I say.

"Time to get out," he finishes. He grabs my hand as we hastily make our way out of the water, running to beat the wave inches from crashing over us. We both collapse on the sand, laughing so much that we can hardly speak. Finally, we stand up, rubbing our arms to warm them. There's sand stuck to his cheek and I have the urge to brush it off, but I hold back.

"I guess we should get out of these wet suits and change for dinner," I say as I get to my feet.

"Yeah. We should definitely get out of these suits."

Our eyes meet, and he holds my gaze a beat longer than necessary. Conflicting emotions run through me. He picks up one of the towels and drapes it over my shoulders. It feels intimate and caring. I start to walk back toward the hotel before the moment turns into something that I'll regret. But as I walk away from him, the only thing that I feel is regret.

"Annabelle, wait. I have something—"

Annabelle's alarm roused her from her dream, and her eyes flew open. She still had butterflies in her stomach as she pictured the man again, his twinkling eyes, the curly hair, and his fit physique. She couldn't remember ever fabricating an entire person in her dreams before. She'd had the occasional dream about a celebrity crush or an old boyfriend, but the man in this dream was so vivid, so real. She'd never seen him before, of that she was sure. She would have remembered.

She suddenly felt guilty. She was happily married to a wonderful man. So what if they didn't agree on everything? Even after finding out about Margaurite breaking her arm at gymnastics, James wouldn't change his position on Annabelle's dreams, insisting that it was a crazy coincidence. She attributed it to the fact that as a medical doctor, he had a hard time believing in anything that couldn't be scientifically proven. In every other way, though, he was supportive and thoughtful. Husbands didn't have to be in sync with every facet of their wives, after all, that was what girlfriends were for.

Annabelle spoke aloud. "I'm grateful for my family. I'm grateful that Olivia wasn't hurt. I'm grateful for my job. I'm grateful for my husband." But even as she spoke her affirmations out loud, her mind drifted back to the man with the arresting blue eyes.

26

Before

Annabelle twirled the stem of her wineglass in her hand, hoping that Randy wouldn't notice she'd yet to take a sip. She'd arrived at his house a little while ago and was trying to work up the nerve to tell him her news.

"What do you think about going to the Bahamas over spring recess?" Randy asked, taking a long swallow of his wine.

"Um, yeah, maybe. But there's something I need to talk to you about first."

He put his glass down. "What is it?"

She blew out a pent-up breath. "Okay so, remember a while back, when we didn't use a condom?"

His eyes grew wide. "Yeah?"

"Well, turns out we should have. I'm five weeks pregnant." Annabelle looked straight ahead as the words left her lips, afraid to meet Randy's eyes.

"Oh. I was not expecting that. What, I mean, how are you . . . what are you thinking you want to do?"

"I'm not sure. I guess I was wondering what your thoughts were."

He stood up and began to pace, not speaking for a few minutes, then came back over and sat down, taking her hands in his. "Look, I love you. This is a shock for sure, but I'm here whatever you decide. I've always wanted kids, and if you want . . . I mean, it happened quickly, but we know how we feel about each other."

She looked deep into his eyes, trying to discern if he was merely trying to make her feel better, or if he was sincere. "I was really freaked out at first, but, yeah, there's a part of me that thinks maybe it's meant to be. I think I'd like to keep it. I've always been a believer in fate. But what about money? You're still trying to make a name as a journalist, and no offense, I can't believe the university pays its professors that much."

"None taken. And you're right. I'm not rolling in it, but we can figure it out. If you move in here, that saves your rent."

"What about James? It's not fair to him for me to move in. And then when the baby comes, what then?"

"Slow down. You're due when?"

"September."

"It's February. James won't care if you move in now. You're here a lot anyhow, and he adores you. Our lease renews in August, so at that point he can find a new roommate, and you and I will get a place together."

"I don't need to move in yet. Everything's happening too fast. I haven't even decided for sure what I'm going to do. I'm still worried about finding a job. I mean, who's going to want to hire me when I'm out to here?" She held her hands out in front of her stomach.

"You'll find a job." Randy bit his lip. "You know what, let me check with a friend of mine. He's got a marketing company that does social media for a bunch of brands."

"That would be great," she said, her spirits soaring. This was going so much better than she'd dared hope. She put a hand on his arm. "Are you sure about this? I need to know that you really want this. I couldn't take it if you started to resent me."

He gave her a tender kiss on the lips. "Annabelle, I love you. I'm not going anywhere."

Scarlett

Scarlett was alone in the house. Dylan had taken Olivia to her dental appointment for braces. Olivia wasn't even upset about having to get them. If it had been Scarlett, she would have been super pissed about having wires in her mouth and having to give up gum, but Olivia took it in stride like she did everything. Sometimes Scarlett wished she was more like her sister. But she agreed with Ben; you were born with your personality, so no sense in wishing you were someone else.

Her science teacher had done a unit on nature versus nurture, which Scarlett found fascinating. Her teacher said the debate was still going on, with some people believing that your behavior and choices were hardwired into you, while others believed that your environment had more to do with who you became. Scarlett decided she was in the nature camp. She and her sister were raised in the same environment, but they were as different as night and day. Her teacher pointed out that due to their age difference, they didn't have the same parents. That time would have changed them, and when Olivia came along, they may have acted differently toward her than Scarlett at the same age. But Scarlett thought about her friends at the yacht club, Dana and Ruby, who were identical twins, yet their personalities were super different.

If genes made you who you were, then she wondered who she took after. Definitely not her father, who was all about order and structure. And even though she looked like her mom, her personality was nothing like hers. Her mom was so easygoing, more like Olivia. Scarlett didn't think she was like Gram and Granddad, either. She didn't remember her grandmother on her mom's side because she had died when Scarlett was only four. She had a grandfather, too, but her mom wouldn't say much about him, only that he wasn't in her life. So, who was she like? It bugged her and made her feel like she didn't belong anywhere.

She walked upstairs, went into her parents' bedroom, and opened her mother's closet. *She sure has a lot of shoes,* Scarlett thought, looking at them all lined up on shelves on one of the walls. Everything was organized so neatly, with all Annabelle's purses on their own shelves, and her clothes sorted by style—suits in one section, dresses in another, and blouses in their own space. But it was nothing compared to Gram's closet, which was twice the size of this one, and where all her handbags had their own silk bags with the designer's name on them. Her mom called Gram a "clotheshorse," which Scarlett thought was a weird expression.

But she wasn't here to look at her mom's clothes. She was trying to find something. She was looking for anything her mother might have held on to from the time before she was married. Scarlett was sure there had been someone her mother loved before her father. Because she was convinced that her mother had gotten pregnant before they were married, and she also believed that it wasn't by the man she called "Dad." That was why he'd been so adamantly opposed to Scarlett taking the DNA test. But what he didn't know was that she had forged her parents' signatures and had taken it anyway. And now she had the proof that they were a pair of liars.

Annabelle

James spritzed cologne on his jacket and glanced over at Annabelle, who was finishing her makeup.

"We're going to be late," he said, shaking his head.

"You know I hate to arrive right on the dot. It's three houses away. We'll be fifteen minutes late, tops. Fashionably late."

"You say fifteen, but that means a half an hour." He walked over and kissed the top of her head. "Try to move it along, please."

Every first Friday of the month, five couples in the neighborhood, including James and Annabelle, alternated hosting a "First Friday Fiesta." All their neighborhood activities had cute names like that. It was a little cringeworthy, she'd admit, but James loved the sense of camaraderie and belonging their neighborhood provided. Her friend Kiera joked that Annabelle was becoming a Stepford wife, but the women were anything but subservient robots. They were smart with varied careers and backgrounds. The neighborhood she'd grown up in was friendly but not social, and while she enjoyed a party as much as the next person, it sometimes got a little old, hanging out with the same group so often, hearing the same complaints and jokes.

Tonight's party was at the home of Phil and Anita, a couple she and James often played tennis with. Phil was a dentist, and Anita was an editor for a large publishing company.

Annabelle finished with her makeup and got dressed. It was a beautiful October evening, but it would be cool, even with outdoor firepits. Most of these gatherings took place outside until it turned too cold. She slipped on a pair of black silk pants and a champagne camisole. A red silk jacket completed the look. When she went downstairs, the girls were watching a movie, Parker on the couch in between them.

"What did I say about letting the dog on the sofa?" she asked, only half serious. All he had to do was look at her with those big brown eyes, and her resolve melted.

"He likes to sit with us," Olivia said, beginning to pet him.

"All right. Scarlett, keep your sister company. We shouldn't be too late."

James looked at his watch. "I stand corrected. You made it in fifteen."

She gave him a stiff smile in return. Did he have to make a point out of everything, even if it *was* to concede that he'd been wrong? It was tiresome. They stepped outside, and he put an arm around her as they walked down the sidewalk.

"Listen, babe. I don't want to be a party pooper but take it easy on the wine tonight. Remember we promised Scarlett we'd go sailing to Port Jeff in the morning, and I don't want you to have a hangover."

"You act like I'm an alcoholic or something. Just because you hardly ever drink, don't try to make me feel bad for having a few glasses of wine on the weekend."

James sighed in exasperation. "I'm not saying you're an alcoholic. Why do you have to be so dramatic? I'm simply asking you to take it easy, so we can get an early start tomorrow."

"Fine." Her mood spoiled, she didn't even feel like going now.

"Thank you," he said, completely missing the note of annoyance in her tone.

They walked through the gate and around to the large backyard, where music was playing and white twinkling lights gave the patio a festive feel. The bar was set up in the pool house, and four firepits were surrounded by cozy seating areas, but most of their friends were standing around the patio. Anita approached them as they came in.

"Welcome! Phil's been waiting for you, James. Wanted to ask you something— Oh, here he comes."

Her husband joined them, and Annabelle thought once again how much better he would look if he shaved that ridiculous mustache. Every time she saw him, an image of a villain tying someone to the railroad tracks came to mind.

"Hey, I picked up that 5-Star Baller's Choice from Honma Beres. Watch out next Saturday!"

James whistled. "You must have done a lot of root canals this month."

Phil laughed. "I do okay."

James arched an eyebrow. "I decided to pull the trigger on the Damascus Grand putter."

"Nice. Let's hope you don't snap that one in half when you miss your putt." Phil turned to Annabelle. "Your husband is quite the hothead on the course. But then again, I guess I'd be pissed, too, if he was the one who'd gotten the hole in one that day."

Annabelle needed a drink. She couldn't stand here another minute listening to these two one-upping each other. She turned to Anita. "Shall we leave the golf talk to the boys?"

Anita looped her arm through Annabelle's as they walked away. "So, I invited the new neighbors from fourteen. He's a builder, and she's a therapist. Rumor has it that he left his first wife for her."

"What kind of therapist?" Annabelle asked, not taking the bait. Anita was nice enough, but her fondness for gossip left a bad taste in Annabelle's mouth. It was one of the reasons that she never confided anything to her. She remembered her mother often repeating the adage: *If a person talks to you about others, they will also talk about you to others.*

"Some sort of holistic practice doing Reiki, acupuncture, that kind of thing. She has weekend retreats to help people realize their goals in life and self-actualize, or something." Anita waved her hands. "I'm not sure about all of it, but it's in Westport, and from what I gather, she does very well. Anyhow, I thought they'd make an interesting addition to our group."

"Are they here?"

"Right over there." She pointed.

Annabelle looked across the yard to see an attractive couple walking toward them. They both looked to be in their early forties. He was tall with blond hair and she was a redhead, who, as she got closer, Annabelle saw was stunning.

Anita introduced them. "Juliana, Kenton, this is my dear friend Annabelle. She's three houses down, at seven."

"Nice to meet you, and welcome to the neighborhood," Annabelle said.

They made small talk for a while, then moved in to join everyone else. Annabelle headed to the pool house and poured herself a glass of pinot noir. Still annoyed, she held it up in a silent salute to James, who was watching her from across the pool. She was about to go sit with some friends by one of the firepits when Juliana appeared in front of her.

"Anita tells me that you're a social media genius."

Annabelle laughed. "I wouldn't say genius, but I know a thing or two about it."

"I'm looking for help growing my business. I'd love your card."

Annabelle pulled out her phone and navigated to her dot card. "Have your phone?"

"Um, yeah." Juliana dug in her purse and brought it out.

Annabelle brought up her digital card and held the phone next to Juliana's. "Voilà."

Juliana looked at her in surprise. "Very cool. Love this. I just save and it goes to my contacts?"

"That's it."

Juliana put her phone away then poured herself a glass of white wine. "I already see that I can learn a lot from you."

"Tell me about your center. Anita said it recently opened?"

Juliana held her gaze for a long moment. "You should come by. I'll give you the tour. We're traveling for the next few weeks but will be back by the first of next month. We have all sorts of healing modalities: meditation, energy healing, craniosacral therapy." She took a sip of her wine. "But I think you're interested in something else."

Suddenly Annabelle felt uncomfortable. Juliana's gaze was searing. She felt as though the woman could see into her very soul.

"You've had great loss in your life. You're still mourning someone very deeply," Juliana added.

Annabelle felt her eyes tear up. She blinked, trying to keep them from spilling over. "Everyone's had loss."

Juliana nodded. "Yes. But there's unfinished business waiting for you."

Annabelle took a step back. She didn't want to hear any more. "I'm going to go find my husband." She began to walk away.

"Annabelle?"

She turned back around. "Yes?"

"They're real."

"Pardon me?"

"Your dreams. They're real."

Scarlett

"Come on, you promised you'd play cards with me," Olivia whined. She nudged Scarlett, who was in the middle of texting Ben. Scarlett was beginning to regret her proclamation that they no longer needed a sitter. At least Olivia wouldn't be bugging her every five minutes if Gram was here. She swatted her sister's hand.

"Okay, okay. Give me five." Her fingers flew over the phone.

Ben: Did you go sailing today?

Scarlett: Tomorrow morning

Ben: Wish I could go with you

Scarlett: Me too. Gtg. Pesty sis needs attention

Ben: K. BTW Did u find anything else?

Scarlett: Not yet. I think I should just ask her about it

Ben: She'll just lie—you need to do more
digging. Hold off for now—I mite b coming
to ur town

                    Scarlett: Seriously? That would be awesome

Ben: Yeah. I'll keep you posted. We'll meet any day now

                                      Scarlett: GR8

Scarlett put the phone down and picked up the deck of cards, dealing out the hands for Go Fish, Olivia's favorite game.

"Who are you texting all the time? Your boyfriend?" Olivia asked, trying to grab Scarlett's phone.

"Cut it out! None of your business."

Olivia rolled her eyes. "I thought Zoe stole your boyfriend."

"It's not stupid Ethan, okay? Why do you have to be so nosy? It's my life. Stay out of it."

Olivia teared up, and Scarlett was filled with guilt. "I'm sorry, Liv. Look, it's just a friend, okay? I don't really want to talk about it yet, but I will. Let's play cards."

"You used to tell me everything. I don't get why you have secrets all of a sudden."

It was true. They had always been close, but in the past couple of years or so, after Scarlett had turned fourteen, then fifteen, the gap between them became wider. Olivia was still interested in kid things, and Scarlett just wasn't. Olivia thought their parents were perfect; she'd always gotten along so easily with them. She didn't think their dad was too strict, or that their mom gave in to him too much. When Scarlett tried to talk to her about them, to complain, Olivia had gotten upset and defensive of them. She was still in that phase where she saw them as some kind of saints or something, not real people.

But Scarlett looked deeper. She didn't like the way her mother's personality changed when their dad was around. One minute she'd be all funny and loose, and the next she was like a soldier at attention, making sure the kitchen was perfect, or that Scarlett and Olivia weren't eating too much junk food. It wasn't like she was afraid of him exactly, but it was like she didn't want him to disapprove or to be disappointed. But it seemed to Scarlett that he was *always* disappointed one way or another. At least as far as she was concerned. She could tell that he still didn't believe she hadn't been vaping. It had surprised her that day, the way her mother had stood up for her and made her dad go along with it. It made Scarlett feel good, like maybe she could confide in her mom, after all. That was when she decided it was time to tell her all about Ben. She had planned to talk to her tomorrow, but she'd respect Ben's wishes and wait until he let her know if he was able to come to Connecticut. It would be much better if her mom could meet him and see that he was a great person.

She looked at her sister. "I'm not keeping secrets from you. I'm just texting a friend. No big deal." She'd have to tell Olivia the truth soon, but she intended to protect her from it for as long as possible. Because when it came out, Olivia's image of their perfect parents would be shattered beyond repair.

Annabelle

Annabelle spun around and looked at Juliana. "What did you say?"

Juliana gave her a benign smile. "That your dreams are important. Whatever it is that you aspire to."

"No. You said they're real. My dreams are real."

"Yes, that's what I said. Your dreams or aspirations are real. You should strive for them."

Annabelle felt foolish suddenly. She needed to get a grip. Of course, Juliana wasn't talking about her actual dreams. She ran a center dedicated to helping people achieve their best selves. She smiled at Juliana. "I'll keep that in mind."

"There you are," James said, walking over to them. "Anita sent me to get you both. It's time for charades."

"We'd better scoot then," Juliana said as she walked away.

"You coming?" James asked.

"Yeah. Be right there. I'm going to refill my wineglass," Annabelle said.

He arched an eyebrow. "Okay, but remember, we're—"

"I know. Sailing tomorrow," she snapped.

He looked taken aback and put up his hand. "Sorry."

He headed back toward the pool. She filled her glass and took a long sip, watching everything from a distance. Suddenly it all struck her as so superficial and meaningless. As her gaze drifted from person to person, Annabelle realized that she knew them no better now than when they'd all first met. Sure, there had been shared confidences among the women—mostly marital woes—but if she was honest with herself, those discussions had occurred from the beginning. How much of their so-called intimacy was real friendship and how much a by-product of too much wine? With everything she'd been dealing with lately, it hadn't even occurred to her to call any of these women for advice. Instead, she'd reached out to her friend Kiera, two hundred miles away.

Annabelle was beginning to wonder if her whole life was window dressing. Not her children, of course. She loved them with a ferocity unlike anything she'd ever known. And she loved James, but did he really know her? Or maybe the better question was, had she let him see the real her? What would it be like to have a husband she didn't have to hide her occasional smoking from? One with whom she could share the broken pieces of her heart, not just the whole ones? Would he love her if he knew everything about her? Was that what the man in her dreams represented? Someone with whom she could shed her inhibitions, who could embrace her wild, childlike self?

"Annabelle, come on, we need you on our team," Sybil, her next-door neighbor, called out.

"Coming." She navigated her way down from the pool house. They all made their way inside and went to the large living room where two oversize sofas sat opposite each other. The group split into teams, and as per usual, the husbands and wives were on opposite ones. She was with Sybil, Anita, Mary, Belinda, and Juliana.

Before they all sat, Belinda looked down at the coffee table and gasped. She pointed to a blue sculpture that looked like a balloon animal. "Anita, you didn't tell me you bought a new Koons! It's fabulous!"

"Phil surprised me with it. It's the *Balloon Monkey (Blue)*. I simply adore it. Be right back, girls, I need to grab some scorecards."

When she walked away, Belinda whispered to Annabelle. "That cost over twenty-five grand. Can you believe it?"

Annabelle was stunned. "How do you know?" she asked.

"She showed it to me online last month. So pretentious, don't you think?"

Before she could answer, Anita returned.

"Ready? We're up—Belinda's going first."

Annabelle sat next to Anita and waited for Belinda to start.

She made a circular motion with her hands.

"Movie," Juliana called out.

Belinda nodded.

She held up four fingers.

"Four words," Annabelle said.

She nodded again.

She put her hands together, and then rested her cheek on them and closed her eyes.

"*Sleeping with the Enemy*!" Sybil yelled.

Belinda shook her head and held up four fingers.

"Fourth word," Mary said.

Belinda made a motion with her hands toward herself.

"Come," Annabelle guessed.

Belinda nodded.

"Okay, fourth word is *come*," Anita confirmed.

Belinda held up two fingers.

"Second word," Sybil said.

Belinda nodded and again put her cheek on her hands with her eyes closed.

"Not sleeping, um, asleep?"

Belinda shook her head again.

Annabelle knew and her stomach tightened. "Dreams," she said, her voice wooden.

Belinda nodded.

"Blank, dreams, blank, come. Oh, *What Dreams May Come!*" Anita yelled, a huge smile on her face.

Annabelle's blood ran cold.

Before

Annabelle had made her decision. She was going to keep the baby—and not just because Randy had responded favorably. In fact, she'd done her best to take him out of the equation entirely. If she was going to do this, it had to be for the right reasons, and she had to be prepared to do it alone, if it came to that. She knew all too well that men made promises, only to break them. Not that she thought all men were like her father, but if she'd learned anything from what he'd done to her mother and her, it was to always know how to take care of yourself.

Instead of waiting for Randy to find her a job, she'd already begun applying for marketing jobs that she could start now. If she was able to secure a few freelance projects, it would go a long way in helping her stay afloat. So far, nothing had gelled, but she would stay on top of it.

She grabbed her backpack and walked down the stairs. When she opened the door, Mrs. Miller was standing there ready to knock.

"Oh heavens, you gave me a start," she said, laughing. "I was going to see if you were free for dinner tonight. I'm making a nice roast, and I thought you could use a home-cooked meal."

Annabelle was touched. She was supposed to have dinner with

Randy and James, but they would understand. "That's so sweet. I'd love to. I'm going to stop by and see Mom after my three o'clock class, so I should be back around six. Is that good?"

"Perfect." She turned to leave, then stopped. "Oh, I almost forgot, Mitchell said he found someone to help you. With your mom's back child support."

"Oh my gosh, that's great!"

"Mitchell gave him the paperwork you left with him. Here's his name and number." She handed Annabelle a handwritten note.

"Thank you so much. I can't tell you how much I appreciate it."

"Of course."

"See you tonight."

Annabelle was relieved as she drove to campus. Her father definitely had the wherewithal to pay for everything he owed. Between the back alimony and back child support, it should be well into the six-figure range and would be more than enough to take care of her mother for a long time. She only hoped he wouldn't put up a fight and delay things. She supposed she could get in touch with him, appeal to his conscience, but she couldn't bear the thought of groveling to him. No, she'd rather put him in jail first. What would his wife think if she knew that her husband was capable of turning off his emotions so easily? Did he care at all about his new children, or were they, like her, disposable?

The ringtone that came through her Bluetooth ended her musings. It was her mother's assisted living facility. She pressed answer on the screen.

"Hello?"

"Ms. Morgan?"

"Yes, is my mother okay?"

"She's going to be okay, but I'm sorry to tell you that she fell, and we think she broke her arm."

Annabelle's heart began to race. "What happened?"

"There was a fire drill and she got up from the bench when the nurse turned around for a minute and tripped on the sidewalk. The ambulance just left and is taking her to Norwalk Hospital."

"I'm on my way."

She ended the call and pressed the voice command button in her car. "Call James," she said. After three rings, he answered.

"Hey, what's up?"

"My mom fell! She's on her way to Norwalk Hospital. Can you meet us in the Emergency Room?"

"Of course. I'll meet the ambo and stay with her until you come."

"Thank you."

She suppressed the urge to lay on the horn when the idiot in front of her slowed down at the green and made them miss the light. She tapped the wheel nervously, willing the light to change faster. *Don't panic,* she told herself. It wouldn't do any good for her to get into an accident. Thank God James was there. He'd been to visit her mother with her a few times, so hopefully, her mom would recognize him. She was going to be so confused. And what if she needed surgery? Anesthesia was the last thing her mother's brain needed. It could hasten her decline even more.

She pulled into the parking lot and ran in through the double doors.

"I'm looking for my mother. Miriam Morgan. She was brought in by ambulance."

The woman typed something in her computer, then nodded. "Yes, they took her back. I'll have someone come and get you to be with her."

"Thank you."

Moments later, James walked out. She ran up to him. "How is she?"

"Confused and upset. Come on, I'll take you to her."

She followed him back. She could hear her mother before she even saw her.

"Where am I? Who are you? I want to go home."

"Mom, you hurt your arm. The doctors are going to fix it," Annabelle said.

Miriam looked down at her arm and tried to move it, then winced in pain. James was at her side instantly, taking her hand in his and speaking to her in a quiet tone. "Try not to move your arm. We're going to get you all fixed up. Nothing to worry about. Annabelle's here, and I'm here. We won't leave you."

Miriam smiled at him. "Oh, I'm so glad you're here." She looked over at Annabelle. "I like your young man. You've made a good choice."

Annabelle felt her face grow warm, and she looked at James sheepishly. "No, Mom . . ." She let her words trail off. What was the point in making a big deal out of it? Chances were that James would be forgotten by tomorrow. But Miriam didn't stop there.

"How long have you been together?" she asked James.

James didn't miss a beat. "I've known your daughter for a few months now. She's a lovely person. You did a wonderful job raising her."

Miriam beamed. "Thank you, dear. I hope you'll take good care of her. She's my pride and joy."

Tears sprang to Annabelle's eyes. "I love you, Mom," she said, grateful. It almost felt like before. These glimpses of her true mother came less and less these days, which made them all the more precious. Her mother started to speak again but stopped when a man in a white coat pushed the curtain aside and entered.

"Mrs. Morgan? I'm Doctor Blanchard. I understand you had a fall?"

"I don't remember falling. But my arm hurts."

James walked over to him. "Could we speak privately for a moment?"

They stepped away, and Annabelle took James's place next to her mother.

"He's a good one. Hold on to him," Miriam said, looking past her.

"How can you tell?" she asked, curious.

"His eyes are kind. He's a man who won't leave."

It was as though an arrow pierced her heart. Even in her current state, her mother remembered and was in pain over what Annabelle's father had done. At that moment, she hated him with every fiber of her being.

Annabelle

Monday morning, Annabelle was still thinking about Anita's party. First Juliana's comment about dreams, and then for the first charade challenge to have been a movie about dreams. She'd asked Anita later how the topics had been chosen. Anita told her that she'd written up a set for the opposite team, and Phil had written the ones for theirs. It had been completely coincidental. Annabelle was getting sick of that word.

She was getting dressed when she heard angry stomping on the stairs. The door burst open and James walked in.

"What the hell are these?" He was holding the pack of Marlboro Lights in his hand. His eyes were practically bulging from their sockets.

Annabelle took a deep breath. Why did she feel like a kid being caught by her father? "Why were you looking in my purse?"

"I couldn't find the ibuprofen and remembered you always carry some. But that's not the point." This was ridiculous. "What do they look like?"

He crumpled the pack in his hands. "I-I can't . . . I don't . . . ," he sputtered. "What are you possibly thinking. Smoking?"

"It's not a big deal, okay? Only once in a while. I've been stressed."

James walked toward her and put his hands on her shoulders. "This is why I've been telling you to make an appointment with someone. Polluting your lungs is not the answer!"

She pushed his hands from her shoulders, putting her own hands up in a conciliatory fashion. "I know, I know. Okay? I only have one occasionally, it's not like I'm smoking all day. And I told you, I'll call Monica and schedule something. But you have to stop treating me like a child. I'm an adult, and what I choose to put into my own body is my business."

He sat down on the bed, shaking his head. "I don't know what's gotten into you. I'm not treating you like a child, but you're acting like one. I'm a concerned husband who's watching his wife spiral. Drinking, smoking, letting her dreams influence what she does. Anyone would be worried!"

"Come on! You're making me sound like a mess! I'm not *drinking* and *smoking* all the time! It's normal to have a glass of wine at a party. And the cigarettes, okay, not great, but give me a break, James. I don't need this right now."

He stood up. "Promise me you won't smoke anymore. Please, Annabelle. If not for me, then for the kids."

She threw her hands up. "Fine. I won't smoke anymore. Now if you don't mind, I have to finish getting dressed and get to work."

He stood and left without another word. She slammed the door behind him, grabbed a pillow, and screamed into it.

ANNABELLE WAS STILL AGITATED WHEN she got to work but tried her best to put the argument out of her mind and concentrate on the file Riggs had emailed her about their new client. After reviewing everything, she began to make notes and outline a general strategy to discuss at their lunch.

Riggs walked into her office a little before noon. "Ready for lunch?"

"Yes. Is Chase here?"

"No. He's meeting us at the restaurant. Have you had a chance to look over the file?"

"Of course. His social media presence could use work. He's got a good following, but he's not posting enough. And his website is pretty bare-bones, only links to his podcasts and articles. If we want people to connect with him, some photos would be good, and maybe behind-the-scenes stuff. I listened to one of his podcasts, and it was good. He's got a great voice, and he's a compelling storyteller."

"Sounds like you're on the right track."

They continued their conversation in the elevator and went out to the sidewalk. Since the restaurant was only a few blocks away, they walked.

Riggs opened the door for Annabelle when they reached the restaurant. They were seated at a table.

"He's meeting us at twelve-thirty. I wanted to make sure we got here first."

Annabelle glanced at her watch. Great, they had fifteen minutes to sit here before he arrived. She missed Madeline. They ordered drinks—a Diet Coke for her and a club soda for Riggs.

"So how are you settling in?" Annabelle asked.

"Getting there. My wife's coming this weekend, and we'll start house-hunting. I'm not loving life in the corporate apartment. We could have stayed with my brother, but he lets his kids rule the roost. So—"

"Where are you looking?"

"Westport, Fairfield areas. How do you like Bayport?"

"We love it, but Westport is great too. If you're a golfer, you get access to Longshore, which is fabulous." She didn't want him living too close to her, and she definitely didn't want him to join their country club. She'd be seeing him enough at the office.

"I *am* a golfer. I'd heard about that, and the pool is great for the wife and kids."

Did he really just say "the wife and kids"?

"How old are your children?"

"Five and three. Girls. I'd like to have a son, but Gina wants to wait a bit. I don't agree. My philosophy is to get it all over with at once. Sure, it's a little crazy when they're small, but then we'll still be young enough when they're eighteen and out of the house."

Was he for real? "That's easy for you to say. You're not the one who has to carry the child for nine months and have your body go through all kinds of changes."

"Gina has easy pregnancies. And it's not like she has to work or anything. She's home full time. Sometimes I'd love to trade places with her."

Annabelle fought with every fiber of her being to find the restraint not to tell him what a complete asshole he was, but what was the point? "Good luck with that."

She picked up her glass to take a sip and looked up when the front door opened and a man walked toward their table. She watched in shock as he reached them. The glass slipped from her hand and crashed to the floor. The man standing in front of her was the man from her dreams.

33

The Wife

I've searched everywhere, but I can't find the key to his desk. He must have it with him. Frustrated, I turn on his desktop computer and am relieved there is no password protection. Of course, he could be keeping his secrets on his work laptop. I go to his email and look through it, but don't see anything suspicious. Next, I check his Google history, but it's empty. He's cleared it. I navigate to Amazon and check the order history. Bingo! He's forgotten to delete it. A book on sailing. Strange since we don't have a boat, and he's never expressed an interest. It was mailed to his office instead of the house. He must be learning about it as another way to connect with her. Does he have some warped fantasy that he's going to run off into the sunset with her?

34

Annabelle

"Are you okay?" the man asked, looking confused.

Annabelle did her best to recover. "I'm so sorry. I lost my grip on the glass." Someone came over and started clearing the area. She put a hand out. "Annabelle Reynolds. You must be Chase."

He shook her hand, and she felt herself blush as she looked into his eyes. This was a disaster. Her insides felt like jelly. *What the hell is happening to me?*

"Chase, please sit down," Riggs said, shooting Annabelle an annoyed look.

Annabelle felt like she was outside her body watching as they ordered lunch, discussed strategy, and outlined the next steps. She had to get off this account. There was no way she could work with this man.

"Annabelle and I were discussing your website and your socials. How would you feel about including pictures from your home life?"

Chase leaned back in his chair. "I don't know. My podcast draws people from all walks of life. I like to protect my privacy—especially for my family. It's the reason I do my podcasts under 'Chase Storm' instead of 'Sommers.' I get my share of death threats. I like to keep my professional and personal life separate."

"That's terrible. Must be frightening," Annabelle said.

"Comes with the territory. When you cover serial killers and murder cases, it's bound to rub some people the wrong way. Most of the time it's only people making noise, but I can't put my wife and son in jeopardy."

"If we do our jobs right, you're only going to get more popular. And if we get Hollywood interest, it will be difficult to keep you anonymous," Riggs said.

Chase laughed. "Hollywood? Let's burn that bridge when we get to it."

When their lunch finally ended, they all stood and shook hands again. As Annabelle's hand went into Chase's, the memory of her dream exploded in her mind. It was almost as if she were back on that beach running toward the surf with him.

"We'll be in touch soon. Thank you so much for entrusting your business to us. We'll get something set up for early next week in our offices," Riggs said.

Fortunately, Riggs hadn't noticed her discomfort. She didn't know how she had gotten through the lunch without revealing her distress. How was she going to get out of this, she wondered, thinking up excuses as they walked.

"Annabelle, I asked you a question."

"Huh?" She looked over at Riggs.

"What's up with you? First, you dropped your glass for no reason, and then you kept spacing out through lunch. Is everything all right at home? You seem like you're a thousand miles away."

Okay, so he had noticed. "I'm sorry. My oldest daughter is having some problems at school. I'm a bit distracted. Maybe you should reassign the client."

He stopped walking and stared at her, open-mouthed. "You can't be serious. You're the social media expert, which makes you uniquely qualified. You have all the skills that Chase is looking for. You can't let your personal problems interfere with your job."

Riggs had the empathy of a robot.

"I'm feeling a bit scattered lately. I want to make sure Chase gets the best service."

"Take the rest of the day off and go relax over the weekend. I'm not reassigning him."

Annabelle simply nodded, but she had a lot of thinking to do. She loved her job, although with Riggs as her new boss, she wasn't sure she would continue to. But this was not the time to switch companies: She'd been here for nine years, and her stock options matured in another year. If she left now, she'd be leaving a lot of money on the table. Even though James did well, it wasn't as though they had unlimited funds. And she knew all too well that all it took was an unexpected sickness to bring financial ruin. Could she afford to squander all that money because she was worried about a dream she had? Her actions were in her control. Just because she'd been attracted to the man in her dream didn't mean she was going to have an affair with Chase. If she quit and went somewhere else, maybe something worse would happen. What kind of a person was she if she couldn't resist a little temptation? And, besides, Chase was married too. She could always decide to quit if things did start to get out of control. But they wouldn't. Her dreams aside, Chase seemed like a decent guy, and he was in desperate need of a social makeover. She loved a challenge. At least that's what she told herself.

35

Before

Annabelle was exhausted. They'd spent over five hours in the ER last night. Fortunately, her mother hadn't required surgery, but they'd had to wait for the orthopedic surgeon to arrive to assess the break. James stayed with them the entire time. He had a calming effect on Miriam, and Annabelle had never been more grateful for his friendship. She couldn't stop thinking about her mother's comments about James and how she thought they were a couple. That must be why Annabelle had dreamed last night that she and James were married. Crazy. Randy was teaching an evening class and offered to come by after, but Annabelle told him it wasn't necessary. For some reason, the few times he'd come to visit her mother with her, his presence had agitated Miriam. She told him not to take it personally—there was no rhyme or reason to her mother's behavior these days.

At James's urging, Annabelle had taken the day off from classes. "You need your rest. All this stress isn't good for you or the baby," he said when they'd finally left the hospital last night. He'd insisted on following her home to make sure she arrived safely. He made her feel so taken care of, and she reveled in it. Unlike her friends, she had no experience growing up with a father looking out for her. She used to be so envious when other girls would complain about how their dads cross-examined every date, constantly making them check in, worrying about their safety and well-being. Her mother worried about her, of course, but it wasn't quite the same. It was nice to have James looking out for her. Sometimes she wished that Randy was more like him in that way. But she had other things on her mind. She'd been lucky to get an appointment at the law firm today. She looked up as the receptionist called her name.

"Mr. Gray will see you now," she said.

Annabelle followed her into his office.

"I have good news," said Preston Gray, a partner at Mitchell's law firm. His huge office, with oriental rugs and a gorgeous desk, indicated that he was high in the firm's pecking order. Preston exuded an air of wealth and success, from his custom-made suit to his salt-and-pepper hair. Annabelle made a mental note to send Mitchell a gift basket, to show her appreciation.

"You spoke with my father?" she asked.

He nodded. "He's not contesting any of it, and he's willing to make a lump sum payment for both the alimony and child support arrears."

She resisted the urge to ask if her father had expressed any interest in her life.

"I was also able to negotiate a ten percent interest penalty, even though, unfortunately, Connecticut doesn't mandate it. There is one caveat."

"What?"

"He wants to meet with you."

Annabelle shook her head. "Absolutely not!"

"Now, I'd urge you to consider. Ten percent of the alimony compounded almost doubles the amount. The same with child support. You'd be walking away from a number in the six figures."

"He can't buy me. I want nothing to do with him. He left when I was six years old. Never sent a card, never called, nothing. Why the sudden interest? It's not as though he's the one who initiated the contact. Does he think that this money absolves him of what he did?"

"I can't speak to his feelings one way or another. But I wonder, might it do you some good to see him, maybe put the past to rest? I can put a time limit on it, and I can insist that the meeting take place here if that makes you more comfortable. And don't forget that this money will help you to take care of your mother."

"What exactly did he say?"

Preston pressed the intercom button on his phone. "Margo, can you bring me the transcription from my call with Gerard Morgan?"

A moment later the door opened and an older woman entered with a folder. "Here you go, Mr. Gray." She withdrew from the room.

"Here it is, and I quote: *I should have gotten in touch years ago and made restitution. I'm happy to pay everything plus interest. But I want to see Annabelle. Even if she can't forgive me, I need the chance to tell her how sorry I am. I've changed. I really want the chance to prove it.*"

Annabelle stiffened. She didn't want to give him the opportunity to try to worm his way into her affections. She knew herself. She hated conflict. She never held a grudge—well, this was different. But she was afraid that if she met with him, she might be tempted to forge some sort of a relationship, and her father didn't deserve that. It was easy for him to say he was sorry now. And what about what he'd done to her mother? All the angst and misery he'd caused her. Maybe all that stress had contributed to her getting sick. He had his new family. He would have to live with his guilt—the same way she and her mother had had to live with his abandonment.

"No, I won't meet with him. And that's the only answer I want you to give him. A simple no. Forget the interest. If that's the only way he'll pay it, just collect the back alimony and child support. Then you'll see the kind of man he really is. If he has truly changed like he says, he'll pay the interest, even if I don't meet him. I appreciate all you've done for me, and I hope you can understand my position. I'm not trying to make things harder for you; it's only—"

"No need to apologize. You're my client. I want what's best for you." Preston paused, then tented his hands. "For the record, I wouldn't want to meet with the son of a bitch either."

Annabelle smiled. "Thanks."

"But . . ."

"I had a feeling there was a 'but.'"

"Let's say for a minute that he only wants to look like the good guy. He might figure that your initial reaction would be to tell him no. I say, let's call his bluff. Make him pay. That's a lot of money that could make a big difference for you and your mother. She's young. You don't know how long she's going to need that facility. I know that $450,000 sounds like a lot of money, and it is, but not when you factor in that you're paying over eight thousand a month for your mom's place. I'd rather see you get close to a million."

She nodded. "I see your point. Fine; call his bluff. But get the money first. Tell him you'll hold it in escrow until we meet. Does that work?"

"Yes, and you're making the right decision. You don't have to be nice to him. Hell, you don't even have to talk. You just have to show up. I'll put a time limit on it. One hour."

"Deal," she said, standing and extending her hand. "Thanks again. You don't know how much this means."

"I have two daughters. I do know. And I'm very sorry for what you've gone through. You deserved better."

Annabelle felt herself tearing up. It was probably due to the pregnancy hormones, but that didn't make what she was feeling any less real. She took a deep breath and nodded. "I appreciate that."

He walked her to the door. "I'll be in touch."

As she headed to the elevator, she was filled with a sense of anxiety. Was she making the right decision? What if meeting with her father opened up a Pandora's box?

36

Annabelle

I'm in a movie theater but no one else is here. It's dark, and I look around, wondering why I'm in this big space, all alone. The screen comes alive and a strange voice echoes throughout the room. WEL-COME TO YOUR LIFE. Fun house laughter gets louder and louder, and my heart starts to race. I need to get out of here. I stand, but my feet are stuck to the floor. No matter how hard I try, I can't lift my legs. Then a wind blows, and I'm knocked back in my seat. I gasp as I look up at the screen again and it's James's medical office. The camera zooms in on the house turned office from the outside, the white building with red shutters even though they are blue in real life. Then it zeros in on a clock. Seven A.M. I watch as the cleaning crew finishes vacuuming. A woman turns around and yells to another. "Do you smell that? Like rotten eggs." The other woman simply shakes her head. They finish and leave. The camera zooms in on the clock. It's noon now.

One of the nurses goes to the kitchen and pulls out a cake from the refrigerator. I watch as she puts candles on it, pulls out paper plates and napkins, all the while humming a tune I don't recognize. She goes into the hallway and calls everyone. "Cake Time." She stops by the receptionist's desk but Daisy, the woman who has been there for years, isn't there. A young woman I've never seen before sits at her desk.

"We always celebrate birthdays here. Daisy has a lighter in her top drawer. Can you hand it to me?"

The woman does and remains seated.

The nurse laughs. "You can come too. Just because you're a temp doesn't mean you have to miss out." A few minutes later, the entire staff is assembled in the kitchen. James is the last to arrive. The nurse hands a hat to James's partner. "You're the birthday boy. You know the rules."

He rolls his eyes and puts the cardboard hat on. Everyone laughs. She pulls the lighter from her pocket and flicks it. A loud boom! Fire engulfs the room. Black smoke everywhere. Windows shatter, debris flies, everyone is screaming.

I can't catch my breath. It's so horrible. And then the screen goes blank. Next. A news story. A gas leak in a local medical office caused by a crack in the gas line. No survivors.

I scream, tears running down my face. Nooooooooo.

Annabelle was startled awake by her own screams. Her hand went to her wet cheek and she wiped the tears.

"What's wrong?" The massage therapist jumped back, panic in her voice. Annabelle must have fallen asleep during her massage. She had taken the day off from work because she'd been so drained lately. "I'm so sorry! I guess I fell asleep and had a nightmare. I need to go!"

"You still have twenty min—"

Annabelle sat up. "I know. I forgot something."

"Okay. I'll let you get dressed." She withdrew from the room.

Annabelle jumped from the table, threw the robe on, then ran to the locker room. She had to warn James. She looked up at the clock. Shit. It was eleven-thirty. She called his cellphone but it went right to voicemail. Dressed, she bolted outside, calling behind her, "Add a twenty percent tip on my card."

James's office was a good fifteen minutes away with no traffic. She had to get there before noon. She called the main number.

"Neurology Associates."

"Daisy?"

"No, I'm temping for her today. Can I help you?"

"Yes, this is Doctor Reynolds's wife. I need to speak with him urgently."

"Um, he's with a patient. Can I have him—"

"No, get him now. It's an emergency. Interrupt him."

"Hold please."

Annabelle groaned as the hold music came on. Her eyes darted to the clock on the dash. Eleven-forty. She had twenty minutes. She honked her horn at the person in front of her doing twenty miles an hour. "Come on. I'm going to miss the light!"

The light changed and she floored it, narrowly avoiding a collision. Horns blared and her heart hammered in her chest as she changed lanes again, doing well over the speed limit. "Dammit." Why was she still on hold? A click then a dial tone. *What the . . .* she'd been disconnected. She called again and it went straight to a hold message. The minutes were flying by. It was eleven forty-five now. She cursed again and disconnected the call. Then called again. "Neurology Associates."

"You cut me off. Get my husband on the phone, now!"

"I'm sorry. Please hold."

More music. This was ridiculous. It was 11:49 now. She disconnected again then dialed 911.

"I need to report a gas leak. Please hurry!"

She pulled up to the office building right at noon and ran inside. The office closed for lunch from twelve to one so no one was in the waiting room. She ran to the kitchen. Everyone was standing around ready to light the cake just like in her dream.

"Stop!" Annabelle yelled, watching in horror as the nurse pulled the lighter from her pocket.

"Annabelle, what are you doing?" James cried.

"Everyone has to get out now! It's not safe."

James looked horrified. "Please excuse us." He put his arm around her and tried to lead her out of the room.

"No, you don't understand, there's a gas—"

She heard the click of the lighter before she could finish. And then nothing. No boom. No explosion. Everyone was staring at her now.

"I'm sorry. I don't—"

James shook his head. "Sorry, everyone. I'll be back."

They began singing "Happy Birthday," and then the shrill wail of a siren made them stop.

Next came the sound of heavy footsteps running in the building. The firefighters had arrived.

James looked at her in horror. "Oh my God, Annabelle. What did you do?"

Annabelle

James insisted that Annabelle go home. Hours later she was making dinner when he walked in.

"Where are the girls?" he asked.

"In their rooms."

"We need to talk. Let's go in my study. I don't want them over-hearing."

She turned the stove off and covered the pasta, then followed him down the hallway. She sat, and he shut the door.

He paced a few minutes, wringing his hands, then finally took a seat in a chair across from her.

"What happened today was unacceptable. We had to cancel all our afternoon patients, the fire department wasted hours on nothing, and you humiliated me in front of my staff. And all because you had a dream. Do you realize how insane that is?"

She swallowed and fought back tears. "I'm sorry. I really thought you were all in danger. I was right about the accident, and the bal-ance beam, and—"

"Annabelle! People have dreams all the time. I can't explain why some of the things you dreamed have come true, but that doesn't mean all your dreams will. And most important, you can't go around doing things like this!"

"But it was someone's birthday, the same as in my dream. And Daisy was out sick. I dreamt that too. But maybe the rest, I manufactured somehow. I don't understand what's happening, James, and I'm scared."

His expression softened and he moved next to her, putting his arm around her.

"Honestly, I'm a little scared too."

"So you believe I'm having visions of the future?"

"No. I'm afraid because you believe you are. You're incorporating things into your dreams and thinking you predicted them. That's not possible."

"James, I've done research—"

He cut her off. "This is just like when Scarlett was a baby. Remember, you saw danger everywhere. Don't you see? You almost put Olivia in danger because of your anxiety. If you'd left her at school, she wouldn't have witnessed that violence at the ice cream shop. You have got to get some help."

"You don't know that. What about my dream about the new client and Mitch going home sick? I didn't make that up. And if Olivia had stayed, it could have been *her* on the balance beam instead of Marguarite and she could have broken her arm." She didn't tell him about Chase. How could she explain that she'd been dreaming about being away with another man and then he'd materialized?

James stood and began pacing again. "*Could* being the operative word. And of course, you got a new client. You have a new boss. You could have guessed that. And maybe you noticed Mitch sniffling or not looking well. All that could have been manufactured by your subconscious. And then your anxiety put Olivia in the dream." He put a hand on her arm. "I think you should talk to someone."

"I don't need a therapist. I'm dreaming these things for a reason."

But his comment about her anxiety did get Annabelle thinking. Maybe not *all* the dreams were premonitions. No matter what James believed, though, some of them definitely were. How was she supposed to distinguish between them? If she had ignored the dream about the pickup truck, her husband and daughter would be dead. She knew that for sure. However, getting assigned a new client and seeing a co-worker go home sick were not earth-shattering events that she couldn't have picked up on and assimilated into her dreams. And the office having a birthday celebration was nothing new. She knew that they celebrated everyone's birthdays. Maybe she remembered that it was one of James's partners' birthday today. And maybe he'd mentioned that Daisy was out sick. The worry about the children—well, that had always been there.

Most people who'd watched a parent get sick and die well before their time were plagued with the fear of losing someone close to them. And of course, there was the other loss, the one that still haunted her. A constant fear of something bad happening to her children crouched in the back of Annabelle's mind. She knew the worst thing she could do was to cripple her children with her anxiety and so she forced herself to be more laid-back in her parenting style. James was different. He was overprotective, yes, but his concern for the girls wasn't overshadowed by fear. He expected that if he set down the rules and everyone followed them, all would be fine. But Annabelle knew all too well that tragedy could strike at any time, and that control was an illusion. All the overcautiousness in the world couldn't prevent the inevitable. She'd learned that the hard way.

"Annabelle, did you hear me?"

"Sorry, what?"

"I said, will you think about talking to Monica again?"

She'd seen Monica, her therapist, for a year after Scarlett had been born, when her anxiety had reached a place where she couldn't cope. She had been living in constant fear of something happening to Scarlett. Annabelle catastrophized every little ailment that came Scarlett's way, calling the pediatrician almost daily until the doctor gently recommended that Annabelle seek help. She'd learned how to navigate her fears to determine between those that were real and those that were imagined. She'd been doing fine, until now. These dreams were bringing it all back.

Annabelle nodded. "Yes, okay." Then another thought struck her. "You don't think I have a tumor or something?" She'd read that that could sometimes cause visions.

He closed his eyes for a moment, then opened them, pursing his lips. "No, of course not. Why do you always jump to the worst possible conclusion?"

She thought of her mother again. "Are you worried I'm going to end up like my mom? That maybe I'm already showing signs?"

James put his hands on her shoulders and looked into her eyes. "Annabelle, you're spiraling. I don't think anything of the sort. Besides, you were tested, and you don't have the gene."

"Those tests are not a hundred percent."

"Look, I think all this is most likely stress related. Talking to a therapist will help. In the meantime, please, stay off WebMD. I don't want you diagnosing yourself again."

"Okay, okay."

James stood. "And you'll make an appointment with the therapist, right? Make it a priority. You need to get yourself under control before things get any worse."

Annabelle took a deep breath, resisting the urge to reply with something snarky. She'd call Monica, but there was nothing wrong with her. She *was* dreaming things before they happened. She just needed to figure out why.

38

Scarlett

Scarlett was doing homework when her phone buzzed. It was Ben. She was surprised; normally they texted only in the mornings. She swiped.

Ben: My dad has to come to Connecticut on business

Right before Thanksgiving

He said I can come with him

Scarlett: Wow. That's awesome

Ben: His meetings are in Westport but I
thought maybe we could stay
near your house

We can meet before we get the parents involved

Scarlett: Good idea

Ben: What's your address?

Scarlett hesitated only a moment before typing it in.

Ben: Awesome. I'll tell him to find a hotel
nearby. We can talk about everything
and then I'll come meet your mom. Just
don't say anything to her until after
we meet.

                                        Scarlett: K. Can't wait!

Everything would be out in the open after Ben came to Connecticut. Together they would confront her parents, and then they'd
have to tell her everything. She'd have the courage to do it with Ben
by her side. She couldn't wait.

She was dying to tell Olivia but decided against it. She was hiding a lot from her sister, but maybe it was for the best. Scarlett hadn't
found exactly what she was looking for when she'd searched her
mother's closet, but she had found something. A letter in her mom's
handwriting. It sort of explained things. There were times when she
heard her mother crying in her room. She never knew why. She'd
taken a picture of the letter with her phone, and she looked at it now,
trying to discern its exact meaning.

My darling,

*You'll never read this letter. Fate has seen to that. But the love
that I feel for you transcends all time and space. Nothing has
the power to diminish it. How I wish that I could hold you.
That I could give you all the love that fills my heart so full it
feels as though it will burst. All I can promise you is that I
won't forget you. Though on the outside I may look as though
I've moved on and begun a new life, inside I will always be*

missing a part of myself. I can only hope that one day, against all odds, we may be reunited.

Scarlett wanted to know who her mother had written to. It was such a sad letter. Why had her mother let go of what sounded like the love of her life? She'd asked her mom in a roundabout way, but her mom had pretended that there hadn't been anyone special. This letter was proof otherwise. And it made sense now, why her mother cried by herself. It made Scarlett sad too. Did this mean that her mother was unhappy? Was she pretending when they were all to-gether sailing, or on family vacations? Did she wish that she were somewhere else, with someone else? And did her father know about it? She caught him sometimes staring at her mom with a faraway look, like he was trying to figure out what she was thinking. Did he worry that she was unhappy too? A terrifying thought came to her. Her mother wrote that she hoped they would be reunited. What if her mother decided she had to be with this person in the letter? What if she left?

39

The Wife

I don't even know how long it's been since we've had sex. Not good for a couple in their early forties. I need to do something about it. Even when we were intimate, there were never fireworks. But when you've been together for so long, maybe that's too much to expect. We've had our ups and downs like any couple; perhaps a few more downs than most, but we've weathered the storms together—most of the time. So maybe I have turned a blind eye to the cracks in our marriage, but hasn't everyone? The problem is that I'm beginning to feel like a fraud. I spend my days helping women in bad marriages to start a new life, so why am I so reluctant to examine my own? Our son isn't a baby anymore. He'll be off to college in a few years. High school graduations are often followed by divorcing spouses. Marriages anchored by children are common; our law firm sees a huge uptick in clients every June.

The harsh truth, though, is that many of the women I represent regret choosing to leave. I'm not talking about the ones in abusive situations, but rather the ones who've grown bored and complacent. They're looking to spice up their lives with romance. We all want romance, but the truth is, it rarely lasts. Every relationship eventually cools down. And what my clients often discover is that what they had is far better than what is out there. This is what gives me pause. Is a sexless marriage really the end of the world? We have companionship and respect for each other, and it's not as though we don't love each other. We do. Men have needs. I'm not excusing his behavior. But maybe if I try harder, we can fix this. I have to reignite the flame between us. Because letting him go is not an option.

40

Annabelle

I'm at the hospital, standing in front of a set of double doors that say "ICU" and I can't catch my breath. A gurney has whizzed past me and through the doors. On the gurney—Scarlett, bloodied and bruised. James comes running up to me, his face wet with tears.

"They wouldn't tell me anything on the phone. Is she alive?"

I start to answer, then James's parents, Charlotte and Art, come over. She's wagging her finger at me.

"It's all your fault, all your fault."

I try to get away from them, to go through the doors, but they won't open.

"Leave me alone!" I yell, but they surround me, all of them chanting the same thing. "It's all your fault. All your fault."

I push James aside and run in the other direction. But I stop, shocked. My mother is standing at the other end of the hallway, staring at me. I run toward her.

"Mom!" I yell. My heart lifts at seeing her. She looks like herself before she got sick. I can see the intelligence in her eyes.

"Oh, Annabelle. What have you done?"

I don't understand what she means. I grab her into a hug, but she pushes me away.

"It's all your fault. Scarlett may die, and it's all your fault."

"No!" I yell. Loud music is playing, and I cover my ears. I want to disappear. Everyone is so angry at me. The music gets louder and louder, its tempo fast and cheerful.

"Mr. Blue Sky" was playing. Her phone. James must have changed the alarm. Was that his idea of a relaxing way to wake up? Annabelle jumped out of bed and grabbed her phone from the nightstand, silencing the alarm. She went to her settings and changed her password. What the hell was he doing, playing around with her phone anyway?

He walked into the bedroom.

"Why did you change my alarm?"

"I told you. Waking up to a blaring sound isn't good for you."

"Neither is the song you picked. It's just as loud. Please, stay off my phone." She didn't want him snooping around on her phone.

James cocked an eyebrow. "Sorry. I was only trying to help. Someone woke up on the wrong side of the bed."

She rolled her eyes. She wasn't in the mood to be civil. "Stop being so *helpful* and worry about yourself for a change." She didn't know what was wrong with her, but something in her wanted a fight.

"What is going on with you? You're always on edge lately. Is everything okay at work?"

Contrition filled her. These damned dreams weren't James's fault. "I'm sorry. It's an adjustment, that's all. My new boss is not the best."

"Well, I'm sorry to hear that, but please don't take it out on me. You know you don't have to stay there if—"

"Really, James? You're going to tell me my job is meaningless, and that I should quit if I don't like my new boss? I get it. You make a lot of money, *Doctor* Reynolds. But I happen to get a lot of fulfillment from my job, and I'll be vested in another year, which will mean a lot of money in stock—since that seems to be all you care about."

His face turned red. "Now, wait a minute. That's not fair! I never said your job was meaningless."

"No, but you've implied it. How would you feel if I told you to quit your job when things weren't perfect? Just because I'm not a doctor doesn't mean that I haven't worked hard to hone my skills and make a name for myself at my firm."

"I can't talk to you when you're like this."

Annabelle went into the bathroom and slammed the door, leaning against it as tears ran down her face. Taking a deep breath, she held it and then released it, trying to talk herself down. The dream was caused by anxiety, she told herself. She definitely needed to call her old therapist and schedule a session. She was waking every day now with that horrible feeling of impending doom. Free-floating anxiety, Monica had called it. It was like a physical presence in the pit of her stomach.

Once she'd showered and dressed, her mood improved. The girls were finishing up their breakfast, and James was loading the dishwasher. She walked over to him.

"I'm sorry. I shouldn't have spoken to you like that. I'll do better."

He nodded, glancing over at the girls, then back at her. "Let's talk later." He gave her a peck on the lips. "Have a good day, everyone," he said as he walked out the door.

"All right, girls, leaving in ten?" Annabelle said.

"Okay," they answered in unison, getting up and gathering their things.

"My backpack's in my room. Be right back," Olivia said, running from the kitchen

"Oh, Mom," Scarlett called out.

"Yeah, hon?"

"Avery invited me to go skiing with her and her family this weekend. Can I go?"

Annabelle's dream flashed through her mind. "Um, I don't know. We haven't met her or her parents yet. I'm not sure I'm comfortable with you going away with people I don't know."

"Ugh, come on! You can always call her mom. What's the big deal?"

"Let me talk to Dad and—"

"He's worse than you are about this stuff. I finally found a good friend after Zoe turned everyone against me. I can't tell Avery you don't trust her family. Seriously, Mom."

"Just stop," Annabelle snapped, raising her voice.

Scarlett looked at her in shock. "What's with you? You're like psycho lately."

"That's quite enough, young lady. Now the answer is definitely no." The words seem to leave her lips unbidden.

"That's not fair!"

Annabelle closed her eyes for a moment, breathing deeply. "Nobody said life is fair."

Scarlett started to speak but then shook her head, grabbed her backpack, and opened the door to the garage. Olivia came skipping into the kitchen, oblivious to the tension in the air.

Scarlett didn't speak the entire ride, looking out the car window, ignoring Olivia's chatter until finally Olivia exploded.

"Why are you being so mean? I'm talking to you!"

Scarlett still didn't turn to look at her.

"Your sister's mad at me, not you," Annabelle said.

"Why?" Olivia asked.

"It's between Scarlett and me. Let her be, okay, sweetie?"

Scarlett turned to Olivia. "She won't let me go skiing with Avery because she's afraid her family might be a bunch of serial killers."

"That's not what I said at all. We'll discuss it tonight."

"Whatever," Scarlett said, opening the door and jumping out before the car had come to a complete stop.

Annabelle held herself back from calling after her. She smiled at Olivia. "Have a good day, honey. Love you."

"Love you too."

What a morning. She'd managed to fight with both James and Scarlett and had allowed her temper to flare to the point where she couldn't control her tongue. Regardless of whether or not these dreams were leading her somewhere, she needed some help dealing with them. It was time to schedule a session with Monica.

41

Annabelle

Before pulling out of the driveway the next morning, Annabelle went to Monica's contact and hit send. She'd take care of this before her day got too busy and she forgot. But instead of ringing, she got an automated message that the phone number was no longer in service. That was weird. Navigating to a browser, she typed in Monica's full name and the town. She was dismayed when an obituary came up. She'd died five months ago. The obituary didn't specify the cause. Annabelle's heart sank. The woman had been in her mid-eighties, but still, this was a shock. She looked across the street at Belinda's house and debated confiding in her, but she quickly decided against it. The last thing she needed was to get a reputation as some loony woman who thought her dreams were coming true. All the neighbors would be talking about her. Maybe she could call her doctor and ask for a referral to a therapist.

She dialed Kiera's number but got voicemail. As she pulled out of the driveway, a profound sense of loneliness filled her. How was it possible that she'd lived here for so long and in all that time, the only person she felt comfortable confiding in was a therapist she hadn't seen in years? From the outside, her life looked perfect. She was married to a successful doctor, had a great career, and two beautiful girls. They lived in a gorgeous house in a sought-after neighborhood with a busy social calendar. Sailing, tennis, parties. Their lives could be a commercial for the good life. Yet it all seemed so superficial. Their packed calendars kept them from thinking too deeply about anything. She didn't want time to think, because then she'd have to remember. Then she'd have to feel all those feelings that she'd tucked away in a little box, far out of reach. It was easier to keep busy and to focus on all the minutiae of their lives and their children's lives than to wonder if they were actually living a life of substance.

They gave back, sure. School charities, donations to needy causes, but it was easy; it came off the top. There was no true sacrifice, no going without to make someone else's life better. Any time things started to get too real—someone lost a job or had to move from the neighborhood because their circumstances changed—the conversation went quiet. What was she doing with her life?

Riggs was waiting for Annabelle in her office when she arrived. Could the morning get any worse?

"Wanted to catch you before you got involved in anything," he said as she walked in. She hated being ambushed. Throwing her tote on a chair, Annabelle crossed her arms and stood across from him.

"Everything okay?"

"Yeah, more than okay. Chase signed the contract and doubled the hours he originally requested. He was very impressed with you. That means he'll be your sole account for now."

"I don't understand. Why does he need so many hours?"

"He wants you to accompany him on some of his speaking engagements. You know, do some Facebook Lives, help with interviews, et cetera. You're going to California!"

"What?"

Riggs nodded, a toothy grin on his face. "I made some calls to my L.A. contacts. We've got him booked to do a talk at the National Crime Podcasters Conference."

"When is it?"

Riggs grimaced. "You need to leave the day after tomorrow."

"Are you serious? I need—"

He put up both his hands. "Look, someone canceled at the last minute and they had an open spot for him. It's too good of an opportunity to pass up."

Annabelle thought quickly. She supposed she could get Charlotte to come and stay with the girls, to help James out. "Okay, one night, or what?"

"Two, actually. You need to fly out on Thursday because his talk is early Friday morning. Then he's on a panel Saturday."

Great. Now she'd be gone for the whole weekend.

"Riggs, I don't understand why I need to be there. He's a big boy. What am I supposed to do, follow him around in between his talks?"

"Of course not. You'll be meeting with Ellen in our L.A. office. Chase's podcast has gotten some Hollywood interest. It's possible they might adapt some of his stories into a limited series. We're giving him the support of both agencies."

"That would certainly push him into the big leagues. He's okay with that? I thought he didn't want that kind of attention."

"Everyone wants that kind of attention. I had a long talk with him, and he's good with it."

She nodded. "All right, I guess that makes sense. What's Ellen's role?"

"I want you to work with Ellen to divide and conquer. She's got public relations experience, but she's newer to social media. You'll still be in charge of that, but she wants to work with you on connecting with some targeted influencers."

"Do I need to call to set up the meeting, or have you already done that?" She tried to keep the annoyance from her tone.

"I sent her Chase's schedule because, of course, when he gives his talk, you need to be there to take photos and help him network at the cocktail party. She'll email you some times to meet that work around his schedule."

"Well, I guess I'd better get myself organized for the trip."

"Dawn's already gotten your airline tickets. You're both booked for two nights in Santa Monica at the—"

Annabelle knew what he was going to say before he said it.

"Shutters on the Beach, right?" she asked.

Surprise played over his face. "How'd you know that?"

"Just a guess." She inhaled deeply, trying to stave off the feeling of dizziness that overcame her.

42

Before

The money from Annabelle's father was now in the law firm's escrow account. After her meeting it would all be transferred to her. She needed to be smart and invest it so that it would last. Her mother could live for many more years, and at the rate she was paying for her care, all the money would be gone. James had offered to introduce her to his family's money manager. Apparently, his parents were very well-off. Annabelle assumed his father did well as a surgeon, but it was his mother who brought the generational wealth to the table. Annabelle was beginning to understand that the world worked on connections, and that networking was more important than she ever realized.

She was meeting her father in an hour, and she was as nervous as a cat.

"Hey, baby, are you going to keep pacing until you leave? Come here." Randy opened his arms and gave her a hug. "Are you sure you don't want me to go with you?"

"No. I'm meeting him at the coffee shop in my lawyer's office building. I'm setting my phone timer to sixty minutes and leaving the second it goes off."

Randy raised his eyebrows but said nothing.

"What?"

"Maybe give the guy a chance. Hear what he has to say before deciding you're gonna bolt."

Annabelle gave him an incredulous look. "Seriously? What could he possibly say that would make what he did okay?"

"I'm not saying it's okay. But would it be so bad to have him in your life? Your mom—"

"Stop!" Her voice was harsher than she intended, and his eyes widened. "Sorry for snapping, but if you're going to say that I need a parent because of what my mom is going through—don't. She's not replaceable. I'm not looking for a switch. And it would be disrespect-ful to her, for me to even consider letting him back in my life."

"Didn't you tell me that your mom tried to contact him? Maybe she would want it."

Annabelle scoffed. "She tried a long time ago when I was little. All her letters went unanswered. I'm an adult now. I don't need him."

Randy threw up his hands. "Okay. I was only trying to help."

"I have to go. I'll see you after."

She left without kissing him goodbye, still aggravated. What was it with him? His parents were still together. He'd grown up in the same house and was close to all his siblings. He had no idea what she had gone through. And what did it say about him that he wasn't completely appalled by her father's abandonment? Did he think fa-therhood was optional? It made her a little nervous about his com-mitment to her. She pushed thoughts of Randy from her mind and rehearsed what she would say when she saw her father. He'd better not try to hug her. She would give him a cold hello, then take a seat and listen without comment. If he paused, she wouldn't fill the si-lence. She wasn't going to make this easy for him.

Annabelle parked her car and walked into the building and then into the coffee shop. It was close to five, and there were only a hand-ful of people scattered around. He wasn't here yet. She'd come half an hour early intentionally so she could be seated first and watch as he walked in. Her pregnancy wasn't showing yet, for which she was grateful. She didn't want him to know he had a grandchild on the way. She ordered a decaf latte and took a seat at a table in the back, facing the entrance. Her eyes trained on the door, she watched as several more people came in.

She froze when she saw him. He didn't see her right away, his gaze sweeping the room, resting on another lone woman for a moment. He walked over to the woman and spoke and she shook her head. Annabelle scoffed. He didn't even know what his own daughter looked like. Finally, his eyes rested on her. He moved toward her, and she suddenly felt flushed, the blood pounding in her ears. What was she doing? She didn't want this. But it was too late now.

"Annabelle?" he said. She was surprised that his voice sounded so different from the one in her memory.

"Hello." Her voice was flat.

He smiled at her, but she didn't smile back. Then he pulled out a chair and sat across from her. "I see you've already got a drink. Would you like something to eat?"

"No," she answered, avoiding his gaze.

He cleared his throat. "Thank you for meeting me. I can't tell you how much it means to me."

"You didn't leave me much choice."

He had the good grace to appear embarrassed. "How is your mother?"

"I'm not going to discuss her with you." She put her phone on the table, opened her timer, and pointed. "You've got sixty minutes."

"Fair enough. I won't insult you by making excuses for my absence in your life. I only wanted to explain. I was messed up. I took what I had for granted and chased the wrong things. It took me a lot of years, but I finally realized what matters in life. I know I can never make up for the past, but I'd love to be a part of your life now, if you'll let me."

She hadn't planned on saying anything, but her anger got the better of her. "You messed up and chased the wrong things? That's all you have to say? I thought you'd at least try to have a decent reason. Amnesia. Addiction. Jail." She rolled her eyes. "Pathetic."

"What do you want me to say? There's no good reason. I was foolish and immature. But now—"

"I don't want you to say anything. What makes you think I would have any desire to have a relationship with you? It's too late. I wish we didn't even have to take your money, but Mom deserves it, so I'm not even considering it *your* money. It's hers. Twelve years! You had twelve years to try to fix things. You could have at least honored your obligations and paid her. She worked her ass off to make sure I had everything. Did you know that? She took the night shift so she could be at home with me during the day. She had no life!" Annabelle clenched her fists. "I will never, ever, forgive you for what you did." She was panting, her heart racing, all her pent-up fury erupting.

"I guess I deserve that," he said, looking down at the table.

Annabelle crossed her arms, still fuming, but said nothing more.

He stared at her for a long moment, then spoke. "You don't have to wait for the hour to be up. I'll respect your wishes. But please know if you ever change your mind—"

"I won't," she said.

He put a business card on the table. "Just in case."

She stood and walked away, leaving the card on the table.

Scarlett

Scarlett was still so upset with her mother that she had barely spoken to her since she'd refused to let her go skiing with Avery. Now she was glad that she hadn't told her about Ben. Her mom was turning into a bigger control freak than her father. But luck was on her side. Her mom had just left for a work trip and would be gone until Sunday. Scarlett had never told Avery that she couldn't go, because she was going to do whatever was necessary to make sure she could. After they finished dinner, Scarlett jumped up and started clearing the dishes.

"Well, well, this is a nice change," her father said, arching an eyebrow.

She smiled at him. "I've been thinking about what you said about doing more around the house. With Mom away, I thought I should start now." She was laying it on pretty thick, but he didn't seem to notice. He started to get up with his plate, but Scarlett took it from him.

"I'll clean up here. Why don't you go relax."

"Who are you, and what have you done with my daughter?" he said, laughing. "All right, I'm going to go watch the news."

After he'd walked away, Olivia gave her a look. "What's up with you?"

Scarlett rolled her eyes. "Nothing. Can't I do something nice without everybody bugging out?"

"I guess."

After she'd finished loading the dishwasher and wiping down the table, she went upstairs and finished her homework. She didn't want to make the ask too soon and make him suspicious. Her dad knocked on her door at eight o'clock.

"Come in," she called.

He walked in. "Want to come watch a show before you go to bed, or are you still doing homework?"

"Sure. I'm finished. I have something I want to ask you."

He sat down on the bed. "What is it?"

She'd overheard her parents fighting about her mom having a dream and calling the fire department to go to his office. She decided to use it to her advantage.

"My friend Avery invited me to go skiing with her family this weekend in Killington. They have their own place there, and they go all the time. Avery said she has extra equipment, and I can take lessons. I've always wanted to go skiing. I asked Mom about it, and she like totally freaked out. Said she had a dream I crashed on the mountain, and she won't let me go."

His brow furrowed. "That's the reason she said no?"

Scarlett nodded, biting her lip. "She's been really weird lately. I don't know why, but it's not fair. I really want to go. Avery's my only friend at school, and I can't tell her that my mom won't let me go because of her dreams. She'll think I'm a freak."

"Your mother didn't mention the trip to me. And you know the rule, if one of us says no, you don't ask—"

"But Dad—"

He lifted a finger. "But, in this case, I'm going to override her. This is getting out of hand. I'll talk to your mom. You can go."

She threw her arms around him. "You're the best! Thank you."

"You're welcome. But I do want to talk to Avery's parents before-hand. I'll give them a call tonight."

"Okay, that's cool. I'll text Avery and get her dad's number for you. Don't tell him that Mom said no. I was hoping you'd say yes, so Avery thinks I already had permission. I was embarrassed."

"Hmm, I'm not gonna lie, I don't love that, but I guess I can understand. I won't say anything about that, but I can't let you go away with someone I've never even talked to."

"Of course. Thanks again, Dad."

Scarlett felt a little bit guilty lying about her mother's reasons, but her mom *was* acting strange lately, and she didn't have a good reason for saying no. Besides, she'd be home before her mother even returned from her trip, and then her mom would see she was being worried for nothing.

Annabelle

Annabelle opened the hotel door and was struck by a feeling of déjà vu. Chase's room was next to hers. Like in her dream. And the room was exactly like the one in her dream. She walked out onto the balcony and sat on the wicker chair, gazing out at the palm trees on the beach. The balcony looked a little different; the terra-cotta floor and white railing hadn't been in her dream. But the view was the same, and she couldn't shake the feeling that she was living in some sort of parallel universe. The sound of the crashing waves calmed her and she closed her eyes for a moment, savoring the breeze on her face and the smell of the salt air. She was meeting Chase in a few hours for dinner. Her phone rang, and she went back inside to get it. It was James.

"You arrive all safe and sound?"

"Yep. No issues. It's gorgeous here. Remind me again why we don't live in California?"

"Um, because my practice and my parents are in Connecticut."

"I'm joking, but, man, it's so nice to be out of the cold," she replied.

"Enjoy. So, listen. Scarlett told me about the ski trip."

Her stomach dropped. *Shit.* "Yeah, I forgot to mention it to you. I don't know Avery or her parents, and I'm not comfortable with her going away with them."

There was silence on the line.

"James?" She heard him sigh.

"This is about your dreams, isn't it?"

"I thought you didn't want to hear about my dreams."

"Annabelle, you can't put your anxiety on the kids. It's perfectly reasonable for Scarlett to want to go skiing with her friend. I spoke with Avery's father last night, and I'm comfortable with her going. She's not a baby, and you can't treat her like one."

Panic made her heart beat faster. Something terrible was going to happen to Scarlett. She knew it. Only now Annabelle was three thousand miles away and powerless to stop it. "James, please listen to me. I'm not treating her like a baby. I know she's going to get hurt if she goes skiing." The image of Scarlett's bloodied body from her dream came to her again. "Call it women's intuition, but please go along with me on this."

"I'm sorry, but I can't do that. One of us has to be reasonable. Did you make that appointment with Monica?"

"I tried, but I found out she passed away."

"Oh no! That's terrible. Well, I can ask around for some referrals."

"If I promise to make an appointment with someone, will you change your mind about the ski trip?"

"No. I promised Scarlett she could go. I think—"

She wiped away tears of frustration. "I gotta go." She cut him off and ended the call, throwing her phone on the bed. She started pacing, scrambling to come up with a way to stop Scarlett. Picking up the phone again, she called her mother-in-law.

"Annabelle? Is everything okay? James said you're away on a business trip."

"I am. Look, Charlotte, I need your help."

"What is it, dear?"

"Scarlett has plans to go skiing this weekend with a new friend, and I'm worried."

"Worried? About what?"

"I've never met the parents and it's a girl who Scarlett just started hanging around with. Scarlett almost got suspended for vaping, and it was connected to Avery." Her words were technically true, so she wasn't lying. She needed to make Charlotte concerned if this was going to work.

"That doesn't sound good. Did you speak to James about this?"

"That's the thing. I told Scarlett she couldn't go, and she waited until I left to persuade James to let her go. He feels caught in the middle. She's got him wrapped around her finger." Not exactly true, but Charlotte didn't need to know that.

"I don't think I should insert myself in the middle of this, dear. I'm sorry. But James has good sense, and I can't call his judgment into question."

Charlotte didn't seem to mind calling *Annabelle's* judgment into question in the past. She could see she wasn't going to get anywhere with her mother-in-law. "Okay, I understand. Please, don't mention this to James."

"All right, but I have to warn you, darling, being at odds over the children is not good for your marriage. You need to have a united front."

"That's what I'm trying to say. James is the one who isn't keeping a united front. I said no, and he allowed Scarlett to go around me."

"Again, this is between the two of you. I think you need to discuss it with James. It's not good to get others involved."

Annabelle wanted to scream. "I take your point. Will you please give me your word that this will stay between us?"

"Yes, of course. I'm always here if you need to talk."

Annabelle still had a day to try to figure something out. Scarlett wasn't leaving until tomorrow afternoon and wouldn't be on the slopes until Saturday.

*   *   *

CHASE WAS WAITING IN FRONT of the restaurant when Annabelle got downstairs. They were seated right away at an outside table facing the ocean. She inhaled deeply, trying to relax. Their drinks arrived, a vodka tonic for Chase and a glass of Sancerre for Annabelle.

"Cheers," Chase said, lifting his glass to hers. "Thanks for coming with me. I know it was short notice."

She took a sip of her wine. "It's not exactly a hardship. It's so beautiful here."

"Still, I'm sure it wasn't easy to line up help. You mentioned when we had lunch that you have two daughters."

She nodded. "I was going to ask my mother-in-law to come and stay at the house, but my husband was able to juggle his schedule a bit. Plus, we have a part-time nanny." His bringing up the girls made her think of the ski trip again. The pit in her stomach grew.

Chase gave her a concerned look. "Is everything all right?"

"My daughter is going skiing over the weekend, and I'm a bit nervous about it."

"Oh? Has she ever been before? Are you afraid she'll get hurt?"

Annabelle didn't know if it was because she'd dreamt of Chase, but it felt like he was someone she knew well, someone she could confide in. "Yeah, I guess. It's been a stressful few weeks. Some issues with my one daughter at school. Anyway." She sighed. "Maybe I'm being overprotective."

"I can understand why you'd feel that way. Especially being so far away. We do everything in our power to protect our kids, when the reality is, we have far less control than we think. But I'm sure she'll be fine."

She nodded. "You're right about that. I feel so powerless. But she was hell-bent on going, so whether I'm here or back home, there's not much I can do about it now. But enough about me. Tell me about your family. You have a son, right?"

His face lit up. "Yes, a great kid. A high school sophomore already. The time has flown."

"He's your only child?"

A look passed over his face that Annabelle couldn't discern, but he seemed sad. "Yeah."

Something told her not to press it. "Well, you're right about time passing so quickly. I feel like I blinked and they morphed from babies into little girls, and now I've got a teenager. Not loving the sass."

Chase laughed. "I get it. Are your daughters close?"

"Hmm, yes and no. They love each other, of course, but Scarlett's going through this stage where everything her sister says or does, she thinks is babyish. But Olivia adores her, and Olivia's my sunshine child. Nothing seems to get her down. They're both wonderful in their own ways."

"They're lucky to have such a great mom," he said.

She smiled. "Thanks. Not sure Scarlett would agree right now, but in all seriousness, we do enjoy our family life. It's just going a lot faster than I imagined."

"It does fly. I try to spend as much time as I can with Lucas. Course now that he's in high school, he doesn't want me around as much. But we're still close. Tara, my wife, thinks I dote on him too much, but I keep reminding her that he'll be off to college before we know it."

"My husband accuses me of the same thing. Says I let the kids get away with too much. I suppose it's good, though, that balance between the parents. Otherwise, the kids would get away with murder."

Chase nodded, but the expression on his face led her to believe that things might not be great between him and his wife. Before veering off into dangerous territory, she moved the conversation to a discussion of the conference tomorrow and what they wanted to accomplish. By the time they finished dinner, Annabelle felt even more at ease with him. Despite it being only a little past nine, it was close to midnight in her internal clock, and she suddenly felt exhausted. They walked back to their rooms.

"Thanks again for coming. I feel bad for pulling you away from your family over the weekend, but I'm glad to have you here."

She smiled at him. She still felt anxious about being so far away, but there was no need to make Chase feel bad. "It's fine. Maybe a change of scenery will do me good."

"Good night, then," he said, and went into his room.

Annabelle got undressed and plugged her phone into the charger. She noticed she had a text from James wishing her good night with a heart emoji. Her hand hovered over the phone, ready to answer, but she was still pissed at him. Regardless of whether or not she was overreacting, he had done the wrong thing by overruling her. And she still couldn't shake the feeling that something bad was going to happen, but she prayed she was wrong. The more she thought about the way he kept insisting she talk to a therapist like something was wrong with her, the angrier she got. Why couldn't he listen and be supportive, like Chase? It was the first time in her marriage that she was comparing James to another man. And he didn't compare favorably. Her text tone sounded again. Chase.

Chase: Thanks for a great night and for
coming with me. Sweet dreams

She hesitated for a moment and then she began to type.

Annabelle: Thanks for listening and not
making me feel silly for worrying

Chase: My pleasure. xx

She put the phone on the nightstand and turned out the light, a smile on her face.

Annabelle

My mother and I are shopping for baby clothes. She calls me over.

"Look how darling this is. We have to get it for Scarlett."

She's holding a toddler dress with yellow sunflowers on it.

I smile at her. "Very pretty. What size is it?"

Suddenly there are sunflowers popping up behind her. They shoot up from the floor and multiply as I watch. Despite their sunny appearance they seem menacing to me. "Mom, look. All these flowers are appearing." I point.

She doesn't answer me, but her eyes get wide and she puts a hand up to her mouth as though she's seen something horrible. She drops the dress on the floor.

"Mom, what's wrong?"

She backs away, shaking her head.

"She's in trouble. Big trouble. You have to stop her," she tells me.

"What do you mean? She's only a baby."

"No, no! He's lying. You can't trust him."

I'm confused. I don't understand who she's talking about. She disappears, and now I'm swimming in the dark. Someone's pool. Not ours. Where am I? I try to reach the other end but no matter how fast I swim,

I don't move forward. Why can't I move? I struggle, splashing, thrashing, but it's no use. "Help me! Help me!"

Annabelle's eyes flew open. Her shirt was wet with sweat, and her pulse was racing. Just a dream, thank God, just a dream. It seemed so real. Her mother, it was so good to see her, but then, the warning. What did it mean? She grabbed her phone to see what time it was. Six A.M. Nine at home. She pressed the contact for James.

"Hey, I was getting worried when you didn't answer my text, but I didn't want to call too early," he said.

"I just woke up. Everything okay at home?"

"Yeah, it's fine. Girls got off to school, and I'm in my office. How's everything there?"

She grabbed the bottle of water on the nightstand and took a long swallow. "Fine. Chase's panel is at ten, so I'll be there most of the morning, then I'll head over to meet with some folks at the L.A. office. What time is Scarlett leaving with Avery?"

"Right after school. You're not still worried about that, are you?"

"No more than normal. I mean, I'm always concerned for her safety. And she's never skied before."

"She'll be fine. She's athletic. And she'll have lessons. It's good for her to explore new things."

"I guess. I still wish she wasn't going." Annabelle didn't know why she was belaboring the point. Maybe she wanted to make her position known in case something happened, as wrong as that felt.

"It's going to be fine. You'll see. And we'll all be home together Sunday night. I miss you. It's very lonely without you here."

"Miss you too," she said automatically, even though she honestly didn't. "Well, I should go. Gotta get ready."

She hung up, a feeling of disquiet lingering. She went into the bathroom and turned on the shower, brushing her teeth while the water warmed up. Her text tone sounded, and she was surprised to see a text from Chase.

If you're up, want to meet for an early breakfast?

Smiling, she picked up the phone and typed back.

Getting in the shower now. Meet you in half hour downstairs?

Three dots appeared and she waited for the message, but they
disappeared and a thumbs-up emoji appeared next to her message.
She wondered what he had been intending to say. For some reason,
she suspected it had to do with her getting in the shower. She imagined some of the flirty responses he might have written. What was
wrong with her? She was being ridiculous. And completely inappropriate. They were both married, here on business, nothing more. She
wasn't looking to have an affair.

She couldn't put her finger on it, but there was something about
Chase that made her feel more like herself. She'd been living with an
ache in her heart ever since that terrible loss all those years ago.
James couldn't understand. He thought that he and the girls should
be enough to fill the void. But they weren't. They could never be.
And she couldn't make him see that. So she suffered in silence because it wasn't something she could share with him.

WHEN ANNABELLE GOT TO THE restaurant, Chase was waiting at a
table. She took a seat across from him. "Good morning," she said.

"Morning. How'd you sleep?"

"Tossed and turned a bit, and—"

"Still worried about Scarlett?"

She raised her eyebrows. "Guilty."

"I wish I'd known; I wouldn't have asked you to come. I feel
really bad."

"No, no. It's okay. Let's focus on you. I'm going to Facebook
Live your talk—I cleared it with the conference head, and she's fine
with it."

"I'm more comfortable behind the mic than the camera," Chase said, grimacing.

"Trust me, folks are not going to be disappointed when they see how good-looking you are." She put her hand to her mouth and felt the heat rise to her face. "Did I really say that out loud?"

He was staring at her, those blue eyes twinkling, the dimple by his smile drawing her eyes to it. "Um, thank you?" He chuckled.

"What can I say? Social media is a visual medium, it's my business to know what's going to sell. It can't be news to you that you're good-looking." What was wrong with her? She was trying to recover, but only digging herself a deeper hole. She had never behaved this way with a client before.

"Well, thank you, Annabelle. And if I may, I'd like to return the compliment."

She put a hand up. "Not necessary. We'd better finish breakfast and get a move on." She took a deep breath, trying to effect a professional air. But when she looked at him, her thoughts were anything but.

46

Annabelle

It was their last night in California. Yesterday had been jam-packed, between Chase's sessions, her meetings with the California team, and then the conference cocktail party and dinner. She enjoyed socializing, but a twelve-hour day with nonstop smiling and small talk was exhausting. She'd been checking in at home sporadically and was relieved to hear that everything was fine. Scarlett had survived her first day of skiing, with no broken bones.

Chase had finished his last panel, and they were in an Uber now, heading back to the hotel. A group from the conference were all meeting up for dinner, and Annabelle could have kissed Chase when he demurred, saying the two of them had to finalize a report.

"I hope you don't mind my bagging out of the group dinner, but I can't fake-laugh anymore today," he said, rolling his eyes. "Feel free to go if you want, but—"

"No, I was so relieved to hear you say that."

"So, listen, if you want to chill on your own, I get it, but if you're up for it, I was thinking maybe we could grab a pier burger, do the whole tourist thing. Unless you think that's too corny."

"I think it sounds perfect. I can't wait to change these heels for sneakers."

An hour later, they were sitting across from each other at a table by the window. Annabelle scanned the menu.

"What are you thinking?" Chase asked.

"Maybe the veggie burger."

Chase put his menu down and stared at her in mock outrage. "You're not serious? You know you want a juicy cheeseburger with fries on the side."

He was right. She was starving, and a juicy burger sounded great. It was James's voice in her head warning her of clogged arteries and trans fats that had influenced her first choice. "Twist my arm," she said.

When they got their food, they both dug in, and Annabelle was surprised that she actually finished all her fries. She dipped the last one into the ketchup on her plate and popped it in her mouth. She must have been even hungrier than she thought. "Shall we walk around the pier a bit?" she asked.

"Yeah. Then maybe a ride on the Ferris wheel?"

"Okay, but only after my food has digested." She was squeamish about heights, but it was a gorgeous night, and she bet the view from the Ferris wheel was spectacular. They walked in companionable silence for a bit, taking in the sights.

"Any word on your daughter?" he asked.

"Having a great time, and no broken bones, thank goodness." Although she wouldn't completely relax until Scarlett was home safe and sound tomorrow night.

"Glad to hear it."

"I guess my husband was right, and I let my dreams get the best of me." As soon as the words left her lips, she realized her mistake.

"Dreams?"

"Nothing. Not important."

"Annabelle, I know we haven't known each other all that long, but I feel like we're becoming friends. I'm pretty good at reading people—it's what I do for a living. You can talk to me."

She bit her lip. She would love to unburden herself, but he was a client. "I appreciate it, but . . ."

Chase stopped walking and looked in her eyes. "Can I be honest?"

"Of course."

"I wasn't that impressed with Riggs. The only reason I'm with the company is you. Investigative reporters stick their noses in other people's business, but I'm not digging for a story. I just want to help if I can. I'm good at keeping a confidence. Part of the code."

They walked over to a bench and sat.

She looked at him, then plunged ahead. "I've been having some strange dreams, and some things in the dreams have come true." Annabelle watched Chase's face closely for a reaction. So far, he merely looked interested. She told him about the plane crash and the accident with the pickup truck. "Anyway, um, I had a dream that my daughter was in the hospital, and I can't shake the feeling that something bad is going to happen while she's away skiing." Once she started, she couldn't seem to stop. "I said no, but then she talked to James, and he said yes, and now I'm here, and I can't stop it and . . . You must think I'm unhinged."

Chase reached out and put a hand on hers. "I think nothing of the sort. There's a long history of people seeing the future in dreams. I don't know what your dreams are or what might come true, but I think we can definitely get messages from the universe, warning us. But let's break it down. What exactly did you see with your daughter?"

A wave of relief overcame Annabelle, and gratitude that finally someone was listening to her. "Nothing specific. More like quick images where she's lying still, eyes closed. And then I'm in the waiting room in the hospital, and everyone is blaming me."

"Okay, so, if something were to happen on the ski trip, you are the one who said no, so no one would blame you, right?"

She considered that. "I guess, yeah, maybe you're right."

"Sounds like some of what you're dreaming are visions, and maybe some are regular, from your imagination."

She thought about the fiasco at James's office. She nodded. "I need to distinguish the dreams my worries and anxiety concoct from these other dreams about the future."

"The trick is how to tell the difference, I would think," he said.

"Exactly. Maybe some *are* coming from me, like the ones about my kids. But others are showing the future, like the plane crash and the pickup truck. I haven't figured out why." She wasn't ready to tell him that she'd dreamt about him. She didn't want to freak him out.

"It must be scary," he said.

Annabelle felt herself tear up. Chase wasn't making her think something was wrong with her, the way James was. "It is. I don't understand why this is happening to me."

"People have been having visions in their dreams for centuries."

She tried to lighten the mood. "I'm no prophet, but I guess you're right about that. Thank you for not making me feel foolish, and for listening."

"Of course. What does your husband say?"

"That I should see a therapist."

He raised his eyebrows. "I don't know much about this kind of thing, but it doesn't sound to me like you need a doctor. Maybe try to find someone who knows more about it."

"I've done some research, and apparently it's not all that uncommon. There are people who specialize in visions and dreams, but some of their methods seem a bit out there." Annabelle decided to tell him a little more. "I dreamt I was here, weeks before any of this was set up. I even dreamt I stayed at this hotel."

He stared at her. She was mesmerized by his eyes as she flashed back to her dreams of him. Not wanting him to probe further, she stood. "Shall we take that Ferris wheel ride now?"

"Okay." He smiled, and her eyes were drawn again to the dimple by his mouth. Why did he have to be so damned cute?

They got their tickets and took a seat. Her stomach did a flip-flop as the wheel began to turn and they rose higher. The view was magnificent as the sunset painted the sky a vibrant orange over the blue Pacific. "It's so beautiful here," she said.

"It is. I've always felt like I could live in California," Chase said.

"I can see why. Beautiful weather, palm trees everywhere, sun. It makes me wonder why we stay somewhere where the weather is only nice half the year, if that."

"Would you ever consider moving? Working out of the L.A. office?"

"No. My husband's practice is in Connecticut, and so are his parents. He wouldn't leave."

"What about your parents?"

"My mom died eleven years ago, and I don't talk to my father."

"I'm sorry to hear that. Do you have any siblings?"

She shook her head. "Nope. Just me. My father left us when I was a kid, and he screwed my mom over. It's a long story, but I don't want to have anything to do with him. James's parents are good grandparents, and I wouldn't want to move the girls away from them."

"It's hard. Once you have a family, you lay down tracks. It's not easy to uproot everyone."

They were both quiet for the rest of the ride, seemingly lost in their own thoughts. When they got off, Annabelle thought it best to end the evening. "I'm beat. Think I'll head back and call it a night."

"I'll walk you back, I—"

"It's okay. Enjoy the pier. I'll see you in the morning." Annabelle walked away before Chase could protest.

When she got to her room, she washed up and changed. She brought her laptop over to the bed and navigated to Facebook. Her text tone buzzed, and she picked up her phone. From Chase. It was a photo of his hand holding a glass of wine, the moon and ocean in the background.

Thanks for a great night. Hope your dreams are only sweet ones xx

She started to type, then erased it and simply hearted the message. Since his room was right next to hers, if she went out on the balcony, she would see him. Shaking her head, she went back to her laptop and typed *Tara Sommers* into the search bar. Several profiles popped up. She clicked on the first one, but quickly realized it couldn't be Chase's wife when she saw it was a much older woman. Two more Taras were too young, and then finally she found a profile under Tara Winters Sommers. A beautiful blond woman who looked to be in her forties. Annabelle went to the *About* section and places lived. Fairfield, Connecticut. Bull's-eye.

Annabelle clicked on a recent picture showing Tara at a restaurant with two other women. She was holding a martini glass and smiling. There were some political posts, some feminist memes, and a few more of her with other women. Tara seemed to be involved in a variety of causes. There were fundraisers for a shelter, and posts asking for donations to school lunch programs. She was dressed to the nines and perfectly made up in each picture. She was much more glamourous than Annabelle; she felt a little intimidated by how beautiful Tara was.

Her social posts revolved around parties and events—nothing at home or with their son. Annabelle wondered if that was because they didn't spend a lot of time together, or if she was simply keeping her family life private. She thought of Chase's comments about his wife thinking he doted too much on his son. She kept scrolling and came to a series of posts from the holidays the year before. The first looked like a Christmas party, and they were with a group of friends. Chase had his hand on the shoulder of a guy sitting down, and the other arm by his side. Tara's arm was linked through Chase's possessively. The next post was the two of them in evening wear for a New Year's party. Again, Tara's arm was linked through Chase's, but his hands were clasped in front of him. She studied picture after picture, looking for a clue to their relationship. He didn't seem into his wife. Or maybe that's what she was hoping to see. It was odd that there were no family photos, and that the last ones of Tara and Chase were from almost a year ago. All recent posts were of Tara with friends.

Annabelle's own Facebook page was full of family outings and photos, special occasions, and shout-outs of significant accomplishments. She realized, of course, that so much of social media was smoke and mirrors. She knew from her job how people curated their online profiles. And how often had she seen a friend posting about how wonderful her husband was, only to file for divorce a few months later?

The recent activity on Tara's page could belong to a single woman. It was weird. But what bothered Annabelle the most about Chase's current absence from his wife's Facebook page was that she was happy about it.

47

Before

The semester was almost over, and Annabelle was beginning to feel optimistic about her future. She had the resources to ensure that her mother would continue to be well taken care of. She and Randy were getting along great, and his excitement about the baby was contagious. Two weeks ago, she had moved in, and it was nice coming home to him every night. James had moved out a week ago, after buying a house near the beach in Fairfield, but still came over often. She had a feeling his parents had contributed, but she didn't ask. And in another week, she would be starting a position as a digital marketing associate for a public relations firm. By law, she wasn't required to disclose her pregnancy, but she did nonetheless, and it hadn't negatively impacted her chances.

She was showing now, which made it all the more real. As she was getting dressed, she caught a glimpse of her body in the mirror and was suddenly struck by the miracle of it all. She ran her hand over her swollen belly. "Hi, baby. It's your mama," she said, feeling a little bit silly. But then she felt something. It was like a flutter— a brand-new sensation she couldn't describe exactly. Then she realized it was a kick. Was her baby responding to her voice? Tears sprang to Annabelle's eyes, and for the first time since learning the news, she felt a connection to her unborn child. She used to think those moms who read to their stomachs were goofy, but now she realized there might be something to it. She picked up her phone, ready to dial her mother—an instinct that still hadn't died—but then her elation deflated. It wasn't fair. This should be a joyous time to be shared with her mother. She sighed and texted Randy instead.

> They're delivering the crib this afternoon.
> I have class so making sure you're still
> going to be home from one to four. I've
> got a lab today, so I won't get home
> till closer to 5.

He texted that he'd be there. She got dressed and was about to head to the door when she got a text from James.

> I packed your lunch last night when I stopped over. It's in the fridge. Candy
> bars from the vending machine don't cut it!

Annabelle laughed and went to the kitchen to retrieve the brown paper bag with her name and a smiley face on it. She *did* need to pay more attention to her nutrition. The prenatal vitamins were not enough on their own.

After her morning classes, she ate her lunch and then decided to take a walk around campus before her afternoon lab. It was a gorgeous May day and she breathed deeply, enjoying the sensation of the sun on her face. It was hard to believe that in a little more than three months, the baby would be here. She needed to start interviewing nannies. She and Randy had decided to wait to find out the sex. People kept asking her what she hoped it was. She thought that was the silliest question; she was going to love this child no matter what it was.

She was about to go back inside when her phone lit up with a text from the university. Her afternoon class and lab was canceled.

This was a nice surprise. Now she could be there to make sure the crib was set up properly and didn't have any damage. Even though she'd asked Randy to make sure, she knew he wouldn't be as careful about it as she would. She walked to her car and drove home.

Annabelle called out to Randy when she walked into the hallway, but he didn't answer. She could hear music coming from upstairs. She called his name again as she climbed the stairs to their bedroom.

"Randy?"

The door was shut, and she pushed it open. The first thing she saw was the UConn sweatshirt on the floor. As her eyes moved toward the bed, the second thing she saw was a naked woman lying next to Randy. She froze. Her mouth dropped open, but no sound came out. This couldn't be happening!

"What the hell?" she finally managed, her voice strangled.

"I thought you said she wasn't going to be here," the woman said in a calm voice. Annabelle realized it was Darlene, the girl from last semester who'd come by the house.

"Annabelle. I thought you had class." Randy looked panicked. Annabelle turned around and ran down the stairs. "Annabelle, wait!" he called after her, but she flew down the hallway and out the door.

She jumped in her car and drove away. How long had he been cheating on her? If her class hadn't been canceled, she would never have known. What a snake! What was she going to do now? She'd moved out of her house; she had nowhere to go. Tears streamed down her face.

James. He would know what to do.

48

Scarlett

Scarlett loved skiing! There was nothing like the feeling of whooshing down the mountain with the wind in your face. It was like flying. She'd taken lessons in the morning, and by the second day, she had advanced to the intermediate slopes. Even though Avery could have skied the harder trails, she stayed with Scarlett the whole time. She couldn't remember when she'd had such a fun weekend.

Avery's parents pulled up to Scarlett's house and stopped the car.

"Thank you so much. I had an awesome time!" she said as she grabbed her bag and got out of the car.

"You're a natural," Mrs. Draconis said, smiling. "We'll do it again soon."

"I'll FaceTime you later." Avery gave Scarlett a hug, then got back in the car.

Scarlett opened the front door and called out, "I'm home." She threw her bag on the floor and hung up her coat, then went to the kitchen where her dad was at the stove stirring something.

"Hi."

He turned around and enveloped her in a hug. "So how was it?"

"Great! Why haven't we ever skied? It's so much fun. I can't wait to go again. Avery's mom said I'm a natural."

James smiled and pointed to his leg. "Trick knee. Don't need to make it worse, and then I wouldn't be able to hop on and off our sailboat. I'm glad you had fun. Your homework all done?"

"Yeah, we did it on the drive home. I'm gonna go unpack."

She went upstairs, still on a high from the weekend. Her phone pinged. Ben!

Ben: How was skiing?

Scarlett: Awesome! How was ur wknd?

Ben: Boring. Have good news tho

Scarlett:?

Ben: Dad's trip got moved up Coming next Friday

Scarlett: Wow!

Ben: Yeah, mite b late. Meet Sat?

Scarlett: Cool

Ben: I'll text a time

A knock on her door made her look up. "Can I come in?" her dad asked.

"Yeah."

Scarlett: GTG

She put the phone down. "What's up?"

"I wanted to double-check about sailing to Newport next week-end."

Shit. She'd forgotten about their trip. "I promised Avery I'd help her with something next Saturday. Can you go without me?" She hoped she sounded convincing.

His brow creased. "We've had this planned for a month. What does she need help with?"

Scarlett thought fast. "It's a fundraiser project for school. We're making T-shirts and selling them at the fair the following weekend. It's important. I get credit for it too."

"Let me talk to your mom about it. I'll have to see if Gram and Grandad can come stay with you. I don't want you to be home alone overnight."

That's the last thing she needed. "I can spend the night at Avery's."

"Okay. I guess. I'm disappointed though. What if we went Sunday instead?"

She thought about it. Scarlett didn't know how long Ben was going to be in town, and she hated the idea of not being able to see him both days if he was still going to be here. "You're treating me like a baby. Like Mom does. Just go, and I'll go next time."

He stood up and pursed his lips. "You're growing up too fast. Dinner in half an hour."

As soon as he left the room, she called Avery.

"Hey, I need a favor."

Annabelle

It was after ten by the time Annabelle got home, and all she wanted to do was go to sleep. Their flight from Los Angeles was supposed to have left at eight A.M. but was delayed for four hours due to some mechanical issue. When she got home, James was watching a documentary in their bedroom, and the girls were in their own rooms. He looked up as she came in.

"You must be exhausted," he said, then got up and gave her a kiss. "Missed you."

"It's good to be home," she answered. "I'm going to go say hi to the girls."

She went to Olivia's room first, but when she opened the door, she saw that she was asleep, a book open on her chest. Annabelle smiled. She closed the book and pulled the covers up to her daughter's chin, then kissed her forehead and turned off the light. She rapped lightly on Scarlett's door and opened it after Scarlett's "Come in."

Scarlett's phone was in her hand. She put it facedown on the bed and looked up at Annabelle.

"Hi. How was your trip?"

"Good. How was skiing? I'm happy to see you home and in one piece."

Scarlett rolled her eyes. "I told you I'd be fine. It was awesome. They said we could go again soon."

Annabelle nodded. "I'm sorry I was heavy-handed about it. I've been a little stressed lately, and I shouldn't have put that on you."

Scarlett smiled at her. "It's okay. All's well that ends well."

Annabelle laughed. "Quoting Shakespeare now."

"Hey, listen. Did Dad tell you about next weekend? Newport?"

"No, we haven't caught up yet. I came right up to see you girls."

"Well, I volunteered to work on a charity project with Avery, so I'm not gonna go. I'll spend the night at Avery's."

"Oh. Well, we can postpone—"

Scarlett shook her head. "No, you've been looking forward to it. I'll be fine. Besides, Olivia's excited to go, and she's bringing Sophie. I'll go next time."

Annabelle felt backed into a corner, but she didn't have a logical argument for her daughter, so she simply nodded. "All right. As long as Avery's parents are okay with having you another weekend." She paused. "Such an imposition." She grinned.

"Yeah. I'm the worst!"

"All right. I'd better go and see what Dad's up to. Love you." She kissed Scarlett on the cheek and left.

As Annabelle approached the bedroom she heard James's voice. She didn't know why, but something made her hang back and listen, her back to the wall next to the bedroom door.

"This is all your fault," James hissed, sounding angry. Who was he talking to? A few seconds later he spoke again. "You'd better figure something out and fast! And don't call me when I'm home."

She walked in. "Hey, were you on the phone?" She made her voice breezy.

He looked up, startled, then smiled. "Hi, babe." He waved a hand.

"A patient with a question. So tell me about your trip." He clicked the remote and turned the television off.

She was sure he would never speak to a patient that way. "You sounded angry, James. What's going on?"

He stood up and pulled her to him. "It's nothing. Boundary issues, that's all. Welcome home. Come sit."

Annabelle looked at him a moment longer. Whatever it was, clearly, he wasn't going to tell her. "Let me go wash up first."

James was reading when she came out, and she took a seat on the love seat in their room. He put his book down and gave her his attention. "I don't like it when you're gone over the weekend. Seems like you're working more now that you turned down the promotion than you were before. Maybe you should take some time off."

"What are you talking about?"

"I don't like you jetting off with some man. I looked him up. He looks like a player."

"What the hell is that supposed to mean? And I wasn't *jetting off* with some man. It's work. What's up with you? You're not normally the jealous type." Annabelle had to fight to keep her tone even.

His voice rose. "Things are falling apart here. The girls need you. I can't do everything around here."

"I don't even know what to say to that. What happened to 'you'll support me whatever'?"

"You're gone too much. It's like you don't even care about the family anymore." James stood up and began to pace, his breath coming in short spurts. "I've been patient and supportive. But I'm at my wit's end! Take a damn break! It won't kill you."

Annabelle's mouth dropped open. What was going on? He'd never spoken to her like this before. "James, calm down. It was one weekend! You're gone a hell of a lot more than I am."

Like a switch, he deflated. "I'm sorry. The truth is, *I* need you. You've been distant lately. I guess I'm feeling a little insecure."

"Well, it's not attractive." She knew her words would wound him, but she didn't care. "If I've been distant, maybe it's because you did an end run around me with Scarlett. We're supposed to be on the same team." Why was she using sports metaphors now? Riggs must be rubbing off on her.

He clenched his jaw. "Not this again. You can't blame me for that. You were being unreasonable. All I'm asking is for you to take some time off. Let someone else follow this guy around the country."

The heat rose to her face. "Enough, James. I'm not taking time off right now. I'm beat. I'm going to sleep." She wanted to end the conversation before it got heated again. His extreme mood swing made her think again of that horrible dream, and there was a part of her that was nervous.

Suddenly he was the old James again, conciliatory, protective. "I'm sorry, babe. I just worry about you. How's your anxiety?"

Annabelle tensed. "Just because I was worried about Scarlett's trip doesn't mean I'm anxious. Some people worry a bit more than others. It's not abnormal. Stop treating me like I'm one of your patients." She got into bed and turned on her side away from him. Then she sat up again. "Scarlett told me she's not joining us next weekend. That's a shame. I was looking forward to some family time."

"I was, too, but she's getting older, and we can't expect her to spend all her weekends with us. Besides, it's for school, and that's important."

"Let's do Port Jeff instead. That way it can be a day trip. To be honest, the last thing I want to do right now is spend another night away from home."

"That sounds fine," he said as he slid in next to her and turned off the lamp. He moved toward her and began to stroke her arm. He must be kidding.

She pushed him away. "I'm exhausted, James."

"Got it," he said, moving over to his side of the bed.

She closed her eyes and drifted off.

I'm on a roller coaster and it's going around in circles, faster and faster. I'm laughing, and my hair is flying in the wind. I turn to my left to see who's on the ride with me, but I'm alone. The car goes up the track and I stifle a scream. It's almost vertical, and I worry that the car will roll backward. "Let me out!" I shout, but no one can hear me. The car rises almost to the top, then I feel it slipping back and I scream, but everyone else is laughing. Just when I think it's not going to make it, I reach the top, and then I'm in a tunnel. It's not a roller coaster any longer, but a haunted house.

"Isn't this fun?" Randy asks.

Randy! How is he here? He smiles at me and my heart melts, but then I remember what he did. "What are you doing here?" I demand. The car whips around, and I gasp as something reaches out and grabs my hair. I turn to see what it is but nothing's there. When I turn back around to talk to Randy, he's gone, and James is there in his place.

"I don't like this ride. I want to get off," I tell him.

He smiles at me, but it's not a real smile. His eyes are cold. "You can't get off. You're stuck. You have to see it through."

"What do you mean?" I yell, but we're suddenly plunged into dark-ness. A screen emerges in front of me and a movie starts to play. It's Olivia and Scarlett as little girls. Home movies of all of us. First, we're at the zoo. Then at the pool. Then the beach. I hear the sound of film playing, and then it sounds like a broken cassette and the video dis-solves. Scarlett's face appears, and she's looking at the camera. Her face is splattered with blood.

"Why didn't you save me? Now it's too late." She begins to cry, then turns around and walks down a long road until she disappears.

"What movie is this?" I ask James. But he's gone now. My mother sits in his place. She stares straight ahead, saying nothing.

"Mom. Mom, what is happening?"

She turns to me. "He's lying. It's all his fault. You can't trust him."

"Who is lying?" I'm yelling now, but it's as if she can't hear me. "Mom, Mom!" The ride goes dark again, and I feel myself fade into

nothing. I jump out of the car and run, trying to escape from the ride. I feel like I can't breathe. Finally, I burst through the door and into the blessed light.

Annabelle gasped and sat up. She glanced at the window; still dark. Slipping from the bed, she grabbed her robe and went downstairs. Parker followed behind her. Three A.M. *The witching hour,* she thought. Why was she dreaming about her mother so much lately? And Randy! She had done her best over the years to erase him from her memories, but obviously that was never going to happen. She thought back to all those years ago when she believed that her future was planned out. She had such hope for them. They were soulmates who would spend the rest of their lives together. But it didn't work out that way. The family that she thought she'd have with him wasn't meant to be. That was when she'd learned that fate was a cruel mistress, waiting until happiness was within your reach to snatch it all away.

She grabbed a fleece blanket and curled up on the sofa. Parker jumped up and settled on her legs. "My good boy. Thanks for keeping me company," she said, reaching out to pet his head. Grabbing the remote, she turned the television on low and stopped at an old episode of *Frasier.* She did her best to concentrate and put the disturbing dreams out of her thoughts. After a while, she felt sleepy and closed her eyes. The last image in her mind before she finally fell back asleep was of her mother making a slicing motion across her throat.

50

Before

Annabelle had been staying at James's house for two weeks. He'd been her rock, listening to her rail against Randy one minute, then dissolve into sobs the next. She didn't know what she would have done without him. Randy showed up at James's house, but she refused to see him, and James ran interference for her. She ignored all Randy's calls and texts, too, until finally he stopped trying. She'd barely been able to concentrate on her finals, but somehow, miraculously she'd passed, and her college career ended. She'd let the administration know that she didn't plan to walk at graduation, so they would mail her diploma.

She was sitting at the kitchen table at James's house, picking at the roast chicken he'd made for dinner. He was standing by the counter, still in his scrubs, a look of concern on his face.

"Are you sure you don't want to walk? It's a rite of passage."

"What's the point? My mother won't be there. Randy and I are through. There'll be no one there to cheer."

"I will."

"I know you would. But I don't want to parade across the stage with my stomach out to here." She rolled her eyes. "It's fine. Plus, I don't want to run the risk of seeing Randy."

"Now that you brought it up, I have to ask. Are you sure you don't want to talk to him? No matter what, he is the father of your child. He's begged me to try to talk you into seeing him."

"Absolutely not! There's nothing he can say that will make me ever want to have him in my life again. I need to be with someone I can count on. The fact that he cheated on me, especially now . . ." Annabelle shook her head. "It's unforgivable. He was probably seeing her on the side all along. It shows you his lack of character. I could never trust him again. One man already let me down; I don't need another."

James pursed his lips. "I understand. I honestly don't know how he could do what he did. I thought he was better than that. I'm so sorry that you're going through this."

"I wish he didn't even know about the baby, but I don't suppose I can keep him away forever."

James tilted his head. "I don't blame you. I'm happy to be Uncle James and to support you, but are you sure Randy doesn't deserve the chance to be a father?"

"I don't know. I need space right now. No matter what he asks, tell him to stay away from me."

"Okay, you got it."

"I still can't believe I gave up my apartment, and now I have nowhere to live. Mrs. Miller already rented to someone else."

James walked toward her and took a seat at the table. "Move in here."

"What?"

"I'm serious. I have plenty of room, and I like having you here."

"I don't know, James. You've already done so much for me. I feel like I'm taking advantage of you."

"I wouldn't offer if I didn't mean it. Come on. I'm hardly ever here with my schedule at the hospital. You'd practically have the place to yourself. You just started your job and you don't need the added stress of finding a new place. Plus, your stuff's already here." He smiled.

"But what about after the baby comes? You don't need an infant waking you up at all hours of the night. Sometimes I can't help but wish I could turn back the clock and prevent this from ever happening."

James gave her a long look. "The baby is as welcome as you are. It's not an imposition, really."

"What if you start dating someone? How're they going to feel that you have a single mom living here with you?"

"This imaginary girlfriend will have to understand. Any other objections?"

She bit her lip. "I guess not, if you're sure. But I want to pay you rent then."

"That's not necess—"

"I insist. I'd be paying somewhere else."

He nodded. "Okay. Welcome home."

"Thank you!" She heaved a sigh of relief. James made her feel safe and taken care of—a feeling she hadn't felt since before her mother got sick. He was right; the last thing she needed was to be trying to find a new place to live on top of everything else. She appraised him objectively. He was nice-looking in a quiet way. The dark glasses gave him a studious look, but she'd noticed how pretty his eyes were the few times she'd seen him take them off. He didn't have the startlingly good looks that Randy had, but she could tell he was one of those men who would get better looking with age. Tall and fit, with a strong jawline, he'd engender crushes in his patients. Doctors had a certain cachet, and that would add to his appeal. This wasn't the first time that she wondered if his feelings for her were deeper than friendship, but it was the first time she'd wondered if hers could be.

51

The Wife

I took the day off work today and am sitting outside his office building, waiting for him to leave. When he does, I go inside carrying lunch for him and tell his assistant I came to surprise him. She apologizes and says he's not in. I ask if I can leave it for him in his office and she says yes, although she looks at me a bit suspiciously and tells me she doesn't know when he'll be coming back. I rarely come to the office, and I've never brought him lunch. But I'm getting desperate for answers, and this was the only plan I could come up with to see if he's hiding anything here. I shut the door and go straight for his laptop. I quickly scan his email, but it all looks like business emails. He is a stickler for cleaning out his inbox, so there aren't too many. Next, I open some folders on his desktop here and there, one eye on the door, hoping she doesn't come barging in to see what's taking me so long. I open his browser and search the history. I scroll down and stop when I see the link for the marketing firm. I click it, and the company address comes up. I write it down. I go down the rest of the list, and my hand freezes. He's been searching legal statutes for custody. If he thinks he's going to take our son away from me, he's crazy.

52

Annabelle

"Hey there, wake up." James's voice roused Annabelle, and she opened her eyes.

"Morning," she said, pushing herself to a sitting position. "What time is it?"

"Six-thirty. What are you doing down here?"

"I couldn't sleep, so I came down to watch TV."

"You know that's not good. You don't want to develop insomnia. Studies have shown that screens are bad—"

She turned away so he didn't see her roll her eyes. "James, it's way too early for a lecture. Please." She got up, pushed past him, and climbed the stairs. Why couldn't he just chill for once? As she got dressed, the dream came back to her in full sequence. She could hear James's shower still going in his bathroom. She was grateful that the previous owners had had the foresight to attach separate bathrooms to the main bedroom. She loved having her own space, and not having to chat with someone when she was first up. Besides, James was meticulous and had to have everything in its exact place. Annabelle had a tendency to let things pile up.

When she was dressed, she went downstairs and pulled out the ingredients to make pancakes. Both girls loved them, and she wanted to do something special since she'd been away all weekend. By the time they came downstairs, the delectable aroma filled the kitchen, and a plate was piled high with chocolate chip pancakes.

"Yummy!" Olivia shouted. "Thanks, Mommy!" She walked over to Annabelle and helped her set everything up on the table.

"Thanks, doll. Where's your sister?"

Olivia sighed dramatically. "On her phone, where else?"

Annabelle laughed. "Do me a favor and let her know breakfast is ready."

"Okay," Olivia said as she skipped off to call her sister.

"Something smells good," James said, smiling at her. "Wish I had time to stay." His text tone sounded and he grabbed the phone from the counter and put it in his pocket without checking it.

"Listen, sorry for snapping earlier. You know how I am before I have my coffee," Annabelle said.

"No worries. I should know better by now. But in the future, if you can't sleep, try to read, or meditate. I've seen too many patients with sleep disorders that start out innocently enough."

"I get it, but we've talked about this. You can't compare us to your patients. Sometimes a sleepless night is nothing more than a sleepless night."

"Message received." James gave her a kiss and left.

Where were the girls? Annabelle walked to the hallway and called up the stairs. "Come on. We've got to leave in fifteen. The pancakes are getting cold."

"Coming!" Scarlett yelled, then ran down the stairs and blew past her. Olivia walked down, looking at Annabelle with a frustrated expression. "She wouldn't open her door until finally, I banged so loud, she had to. You should take her phone!"

"Okay, okay. She doesn't need another parent." Annabelle shooed her toward the kitchen.

"Thanks for making these, Mom," Scarlett said as she poured some syrup on her pancakes. "I'm glad you're home. I missed you."

Annabelle smiled. "I missed you, too, honey. How about we watch that new Halloween movie Friday night?"

Scarlett nodded. "Great!"

The girls gobbled their pancakes. Annabelle picked at hers but couldn't summon an appetite.

"Who are you texting this early?" she asked Scarlett.

Scarlett didn't look up to meet her eyes. "Just Avery."

"Not a boy?" Annabelle pressed.

Scarlett's head shot up. "Nope." She had the look of someone caught doing something wrong.

"How are things on Instagram? Better?"

"Yeah, it's all good."

Still, Annabelle couldn't shake the feeling that Scarlett was hiding something.

SHE WAS ABOUT TO GO to her office after grabbing a coffee, when Riggs stopped her in the hallway. "Can you come by my office?"

"Okay, everything all right?"

"Yes," he said, walking away. She followed him, annoyed.

She took a seat and he shut the door. "I know you just got back yesterday, but I need you to go to L.A. again."

"Seriously?"

"Yes. Ellen has set up a series of meetings with some producers who are interested in adapting Chase's podcast on female serial killers."

Annabelle couldn't believe this. "When are the meetings?"

"Thursday and Friday."

That meant she wouldn't get home until Saturday for all intents and purposes, even if she took a red-eye. So much for her Friday movie night with Scarlett and their sailing trip on Saturday.

"Is it really necessary for me to be there?"

"Chase requested that you go with him. We want to keep the client happy, right? Look, I know he's been taking up a lot more time than expected. I've already talked to Michael. He's agreed to pay you a bonus for all your hard work."

"I appreciate that, but it's not just about the money, Riggs. The reason I didn't take the promotion was so that I wouldn't be away from my family so much, and now I'm away more than you."

"I can't force you to go, but—"

She put her hands up. "I'll go, I'll go. But you need to let Chase know that I'm not at his beck and call."

Riggs nodded. "I understand. I'll talk to him. I'm asking you as a favor, go this time. He trusts your opinion, and he's going to have to decide who to get into bed with. He doesn't have experience with these kinds of folks. You do."

"Yeah, but not as much as the L.A. office does. He'd be better off with Ellen."

"Like I said, he trusts you."

"Fine. I'll make it work."

"Thanks." He turned toward his computer and started typing.

"I guess we're finished," Annabelle muttered as she got up and left. She returned to her office and pulled up the calendar on her phone. James wasn't going to be happy about her being gone another weekend—especially with Chase. She started to make notes on what she had to rearrange. She was still on edge because of these terrifying dreams about Scarlett, but she was beginning to think those were all about her anxiety and not any sort of warning. Instead of feeling irritated about the trip, she found she was actually looking forward to it. The weather was getting colder here, and the sun was hardly making an appearance. It would be great to be back in the sunshine.

She couldn't help but wonder if a bigger part of her excitement had to do with going away with Chase again. She thought about her dream on the balcony, with the two of them drinking wine. That hadn't happened last time; neither had the swim in the ocean. Was this upcoming trip fated to be the turning point in their relationship? But no, that was totally in her control. She wouldn't allow things to take a turn she would regret.

But a little voice inside her whispered, *Maybe you don't have a choice.*

53

Before

By late August, Annabelle felt enormous, but James continued to tell her that she was glowing and beautiful. He was so earnest and sincere that she almost believed it. She knew in her heart that his feelings for her had grown. It was obvious in the way he looked at her a moment too long, or the way his fingers grazed hers when he'd hand her something. He fussed over her, treating her like a princess, and she let him. He checked to make sure she remembered to take her prenatal vitamins. He made dinners with a variety of vegetables and insisted she eat them. It had been so long since someone took care of her that she reveled in it. He'd also begun to go with her when she visited her mother. His presence had a calming influence on Miriam, who continued to act as though they were a couple. And he never missed a doctor's appointment. It felt like they were a couple in every way except that they each went to their own bedrooms at night.

Annabelle began to wonder if James was her destiny. Was it possible that he was the one meant for her all along? The only thing holding her back was that she didn't feel the same attraction to him that she had with Randy. But maybe that was a good thing. She would never take Randy back, although she had debated calling him to discuss how they would co-parent. But then James handed her the letter that changed everything.

"Randy asked me to give this to you. He got a job offer to teach at the University of Arizona."

She was stunned. "Arizona? I guess that answers my question as to how involved he wants to be." Hot tears sprang to her eyes, and she blinked to stop them. She opened the letter and read.

Annabelle,

I wish you the best and hope that one day you will find it in your heart to forgive me. It was a stupid mistake, and I'm sorrier than you know. But it's too late for explanations and excuses. I'm grateful that James is there for you. He's a better man than I am. I hope you'll be happy, and I'm sorry I couldn't be the one to be there for you. I'm leaving next week. Please take good care of yourself and our child.

Randy

She crumpled the letter and threw it on the floor. History repeating itself, only her child wouldn't know his or her father at all. How was she going to explain his absence? She knew firsthand that no matter how she tried to spin it, the child would take the rejection personally. And how could it not? The most primal of instincts was to protect your young. After what Randy had done to her, she shouldn't be surprised that he'd so easily walk away from his child, but she was. She was devastated. She could never take him back—trust was vital to her, and he'd proven that he wasn't worthy of it. But she had hoped that he would prove to be a good father. And it tore her in two that he was moving so far away. Just because someone breaks your heart doesn't mean you stop having feelings for them. Randy's abandonment would have far-reaching consequences on the happiness of her child, and there was nothing she could do to prevent it. Now she would have to tell her precious child that its father didn't want it. Unless . . .

Annabelle

The meetings had gone well. They finished the last one and were headed back to the hotel. The agency had arranged a car for them, and Annabelle felt herself relax for the first time that day when she climbed in the back and rested her head against the seat.

"They really know how to make you feel like a star," Chase said, laughing. "If you hadn't prepped me on Hollywood-speak, I might have gotten a big head."

Annabelle smiled. "They definitely lay it on thick, but all kidding aside, they seem very excited to work with you. Any team you felt more of a connection with than the others?"

He nodded. "I liked the first two groups. We still have that last meeting in the morning though. By the way, were you able to book an earlier flight out now that the afternoon meetings are canceled?"

"No. My two o'clock at our L.A. office is still on. It's fine. I'll sleep on the flight and be home in the morning."

They made small talk on the drive. It was close to six when the driver dropped them at the hotel.

"Feel like grabbing a drink?" Chase asked.

She had already decided that she wasn't going to allow any opportunity for things to progress between them. "I'm pretty beat. I'm going to order room service and make it an early night."

"Oh," he said, his disappointment obvious. "No worries. I'll see you in the morning."

When Annabelle got to her room, she kicked off her shoes and called James.

"Hey you," he answered.

"Thanks again for rearranging your schedule to accommodate my trip. What's going on?"

"The girls are in their rooms. Parker's at my feet, and I'm about to watch a crime drama on BBC."

She was suddenly homesick. "Wish I was there."

"Me too, babe. Only one more night."

"My meeting tomorrow goes until four, so I'll have to take the red-eye. I'll get in at seven A.M."

"I'll be there."

When Annabelle ended the call, she sent a text to each of the girls telling them good night, and then called room service and ordered a glass of wine and a scallop entrée. While she waited, she sorted through her work emails. She got up when she heard a knock on the door, expecting room service. When she looked through the peephole, she was surprised to see Chase. She opened the door.

"Hey, what's up?"

He was dressed casually in shorts and a T-shirt and was beaming from ear to ear. In his hands he held a bottle of champagne. "We just hit half a million subscribers!"

She broke out into a wide smile. "Seriously?"

"Yep! I just found out. You have to have a celebratory drink with me."

She was about to answer when she saw the room service cart coming toward them.

"I'll wait on the balcony," Chase said. Before she could respond, he walked past her.

After the food was left, Annabelle stood still, indecision filling her. Another dream coming true. But what could she say to him? She took a deep breath and joined Chase outside. He'd already poured a glass for each of them, and he handed her one.

"Thanks for everything you've done to help. This is a dream come true. Cheers."

"Cheers," she said, touching her glass to his and taking a sip. Her eyes lingered a moment on his mouth, and she found herself wondering what it would feel like to kiss him. She brought the glass to her lips and took a gulp, forcing herself to look away. They sat down in the chairs facing the beach, and she was overcome once again with that same sense of déjà vu. She tried to shake it off. "Congratulations. It's quite an accomplishment."

"Thanks, I can hardly believe it myself. This should help with the adaptation discussions."

"Definitely! Your family must be thrilled."

A cloud came over his face. "My son is psyched, but Tara doesn't really get it. The only comment she made was that she hoped this didn't mean I'd be gone all the time now."

Annabelle didn't know what to say. Was this the classic "my wife doesn't understand me" schtick? "I'm sure she'll come around. And it *is* hard when someone has to travel a lot."

"I'm sorry. I must sound like a real jerk; I don't mean to complain about her. Do you ever wish you could go back and change things that you had no idea at the time would have such a profound effect later?"

She thought back to that last year in college. She blew out a breath and turned to him. "Like what?"

"All I ever wanted was a family. Maybe it's because growing up, I didn't have much of one. Like your situation, my dad took off when I was young, and it was only my mother and me. I always dreamed about having a big family."

"I didn't know that. Why didn't you say anything before?" she asked.

"I guess I didn't want to sound like I was comparing my heartache to yours."

She took another sip of her champagne. "I'm sorry you went through that too. Do you ever hear from him?"

"No. I don't even know where he is. And I have no desire to."

"I get it," she said.

"I feel like you get a lot of things about me. It's the strangest thing, but I feel like I've known you forever."

Annabelle was tempted to tell him that she'd dreamed about him, but hesitated. "I know what you mean. It does seem like we've known each other in a past life or something." She forced a laugh. She didn't believe in past lives but didn't know what else to say.

"Maybe we did."

"Actually, I have something to tell you." She bit her lip and looked down at her feet, too shy to meet his eyes. "You know those dreams I told you about? Well, you were in some of them."

He touched her arm, sending a frisson across her skin. "Really? Tell me more."

She looked at him. "I dreamed about us being here. And drinking wine on the balcony." She laughed. "We even took a dip in the ocean, which obviously hasn't happened."

"Were these dreams before or after we met?" Chase asked.

"That's the thing. Before. That's why I dropped that glass the day at lunch when I saw you. I'd already seen you in my dreams."

Chase whistled. "That's wild. What else?"

She shook her head. "That's it, essentially. Us here. Talking. Nothing inappropriate," she hastened to add.

He cocked an eyebrow. "That's a little disappointing."

Now she felt uncomfortable again. "Obviously, we're both married and not looking for anything. I think we're meant to be good friends. So tell me. Did your wife want a big family as well?" Annabelle needed to steer the conversation in a different direction.

Chase leaned back in the chair. "Tara and I got married right after college. I thought we wanted the same things. Both her parents are still together, she's also an only child. I don't think her desire to have kids was as strong, but still, she agreed that we'd try for three or four children."

Annabelle didn't speak, letting him continue.

He swirled his glass, quiet for a moment. "She got pregnant before we were married. The truth is, I had been ready to break up with her, but then I thought I could make it work for our child. Then in her fifth month, she lost the baby."

"I'm so sorry."

"We tried again, and same thing. Five months, and a miscarriage."

"That's terrible. How devastating." She reached out and put her hand on his, squeezing gently.

"We had more losses, and it became too much. She didn't want to try anymore, and I understood. I talked about adoption, but she refused." He stopped and took a sip of his champagne. "I don't want you to think this is a come-on. I feel so comfortable talking to you. I hope it's okay that I'm being so transparent."

Annabelle didn't know if it was the champagne getting to her, or the intoxicating way Chase was starting to make her feel, but she wanted to know more. "Please, go on."

"It took a toll on our marriage, which was never that solid to begin with. I was about to leave her, and then she got pregnant again. This time it took. And then we had Lucas. He's our miracle child, the light of my life. I'd do anything for him."

"How are things between you and Tara now?" She was in dangerous territory, but she couldn't seem to stop herself.

He raised his eyebrows. "Not good. She's erratic, gets angry easily. Lucas and I both walk on eggshells a lot. But once he came along, I couldn't leave her. She would fight me for full custody; she has a vindictive streak. Honestly, I never felt okay leaving Lucas with her. I'm the peacemaker in the house."

"Are you saying she's abusive?" Annabelle was horrified at the thought.

He shook his head. "Not abusive exactly, but emotionally unstable. She would never intentionally hurt Lucas, but she's not a great mother. I do the lion's share and try to make up for what she lacks. I guess life takes us on paths we don't expect."

Annabelle didn't know what to say. Chase looked so vulnerable that it broke something open in her, and she told him all about Randy. He listened quietly, letting her get every detail out. Then she told him about the other loss. The one that still defined her. With each word, she felt herself unburden a little bit more. It felt so healing to share what had happened. Her tears flowed as she spoke. When she was finished, a peace came over her, unlike anything she'd known in years. They stood up, and he embraced her. They stayed that way for a long time, holding each other as if they were mending all the broken parts inside each of them.

The Wife

I've been reading his texts. He's become very close with her. She's besotted, I can tell. But she has no idea who he really is, or what he wants from her. He's lying, manipulating her. I still can't believe what he's been keeping from me, and the lengths to which he's gone to guard this terrible secret. I don't know where to turn or who to trust. I have to do something, but I don't know what. If I go to the authorities, it will destroy our family. And our son, our poor son, when he finds out that his father isn't the man he thought he was. It will kill him. I'll lose everything, and it's not fair. I need to stop him before he does something that will alter our lives forever. I'm running out of time.

56

Scarlett

One more day until she would see Ben. It was so hard for her to concentrate on her classes that Friday when all she could think about was her meeting with him. Lucky for her, her mom's flight got in tomorrow morning, and her dad and Olivia were going to the airport to pick her up. She told Olivia to ask their parents to take her out to breakfast. She didn't want to risk them getting home before she left. She was meeting Ben at a coffee shop downtown, a few blocks from her house, at nine tomorrow morning. She would ride her bike there. The only one who knew about it was Avery. They walked together now to the cafeteria.

Avery frowned. "Are you sure you don't want me to be there in case there's a problem? I can sit at a table and pretend not to know you." Avery's hair was pulled back into a ponytail and as usual, she wore a T-shirt with a slogan over a pair of jeans. This one was black and on the front in white letters were the words BE REAL NOT PERFECT.

"You're such a worrywart. No, that'll just make me nervous. I'll be fine."

"What's his dad's business?"

"I don't know. Who cares?"

"We could, like, look him up, make sure it's all legit," Avery said.

"I told you, he is who he says he is. I have proof."

"What kind of proof?"

Scarlett had promised Ben that she wouldn't tell anyone about what the two of them had discovered, until they met and figured it all out together. "I can't say, but you have to trust me."

Avery narrowed her eyes. "I hope you know what you're doing. Can you at least text me to say everything's okay after you meet up?"

Scarlett nodded. "I will, but don't expect it immediately. I don't want to be on my phone as soon as I meet him."

Scarlett wished Avery didn't overthink everything so much. But she guessed that was what would make her a good journalist one day. She smiled at her friend.

"Don't worry. I'll be fine. Promise."

57

Annabelle

Annabelle leaned back against the airplane seat and closed her eyes. James had transferred his airline points to her so that she could up-grade to first class, and she was grateful for the extra room and the fact that no one was in the seat next to her. She wanted to sleep on the flight, so that she'd be present for her family for the rest of the weekend. It bothered her that she'd spent the last two away from them. She thought about her evening with Chase last night and all that they had shared with each other. It scared her to think of what might have happened if James hadn't FaceTimed her, prompting Chase to make a hasty retreat. They hadn't had the time to talk this morning, as he had to rush off to catch his flight after their meetings.

She wished she could talk to James the way she had with Chase. But when she tried to share that particular pain with her husband over the years, it seemed too much for him, and he was always trying to somehow make up for it. Her lingering grief seemed to be an af-front to him, as though she was ungrateful for the life they had built or holding on to broken dreams of the past. But there were so many times when she'd glance at a photo of the four of them and think to herself that there should be five. She carried that regret with her every day of her life. A year didn't go by when she didn't imagine what her son would be like as another one of his birthdays passed.

At first, she and James would honor him together, go to the cemetery, and talk about what might have been. But after a couple of years, James had stopped. Said it was maudlin, and they needed to move on. He begged Annabelle not to tell Scarlett and Olivia about him, persuading her that it wasn't fair to make them grieve a brother they would never know. She agreed. To protect them, but also because she didn't want to share the grief. It was hers and hers alone. And she would never let it go. A part of her was buried deep in that ground along with her son. Chase had been so kind and tender. It had felt so liberating to pour out her sorrow to him.

Annabelle slipped AirPods in her ears and put on some soothing music, breathing deeply, hoping sleep would come. The cabin lights were turned off, and she pulled a blanket up to her chin. Feeling drowsy, she gave in to the pull of sleep.

I'm holding my newborn and feeling so happy. I can't believe I'm a mother. My own mother told me that I'd feel a rush of love the minute I held my baby, but I never understood it until now. A doctor comes into the room. He's wearing a mask, and all I can see are his eyes. Why is his mask black? My stomach tightens as he comes closer and I back away, shielding my baby. The doctor comes closer, menace exuding from him like cologne.

"What do you want?" I want to ask, but no words come out. He says nothing, just strides over and grabs my baby. I try to hold on, but I can't.

"No, no, what are you doing?" I yell. I try to swing my legs to get out of the hospital bed, but I can't move. I don't feel my legs. Why can't I move? I'm screaming and crying, "Bring my baby back!" But he's gone.

James walks into the room, looking at the floor. His eyes won't meet mine.

"Where's the baby?"

He looks up and shakes his head sadly. "Dead."

Annabelle woke with a start and swallowed, wiping the saliva from the corner of her mouth with her hand. She was filled with a terrible sense of doom. She needed to get home and be with her children, but she was stuck thirty thousand feet in the air. There was no way she could go back to sleep. She couldn't rest until she was home and saw with her own two eyes that her girls were fine.

She picked up her phone and joined the airline's Wi-Fi, holding her breath in anticipation of some terrible message. She breathed a sigh of relief when she saw that she had no texts from James or the girls. She was itching to call home, but it was the middle of the night in Connecticut, and she didn't want to alarm them. What did these dreams mean? The ones she'd had about Chase were all coming true. Maybe not all; she hadn't gone swimming with him. But he had been on her balcony drinking champagne, not wine. And they had embraced, just like in her dreams. She thought most about the ones of Scarlett. Were her dreams warning her that she was about to lose another child?

She needed to distract herself, so she scrolled through the movie options and settled on a comedy she'd seen several times, forcing herself to banish the distressing dreams from her mind. She'd be on the ground soon, and then she'd see that everyone was fine. She found herself wishing that Chase was on the plane with her. She could use his steadying presence right now.

When they landed and she took her phone off airplane mode, a bunch of texts appeared. James assuring her that all was well and he couldn't wait to see her. She felt better immediately. She smiled when she saw one from Chase and clicked on it.

> Hope you got home safe and sound and that everything's okay there. I can't stop thinking about our conversation last night. Thank you for sharing all that you did. You made me feel less alone. Sorry we couldn't fly back together. See you Monday at lunch. Xx

Her eyes rested on the two x's, and she felt butterflies in her stomach. She was acting like a teenager. Not good. She typed back a quick reply.

Just landed. I feel the same way. I didn't even realize how much I needed to talk about it all. I'm really grateful for our connection. See you Mon xo

Annabelle closed her eyes, reliving the prior evening, and took a deep breath. It had felt so right unburdening herself to him, and he to her. She wasn't naive enough to believe he could be her soulmate— if there even was such a thing. Their relationship had built-in guard-rails, which made it easier to open up to each other. But she couldn't deny that she was attracted to him, and that there was a connection between them. Of course, they couldn't be a couple, and she had to rid herself of that notion once and for all. Men and women could be friends, she assured herself, even as the old line saying that they couldn't from *When Harry Met Sally* popped into her mind. But this was real life, and Chase had become important to her. It would all be fine. She deleted the text chain between her and Chase and put her phone in her purse.

James was waiting outside for her, and he got out of the car as she exited the airport. He pulled her into a tight embrace. "Welcome home. I missed you." Olivia jumped out of the back seat and ran to her mother.

"Hi, Mommy!"

Annabelle squeezed Olivia and gave her a kiss on the cheek.

"Missed you guys too," she said as James took her suitcase and put it in the back of the vehicle. "What's going on?"

When they were all in the car, James handed Annabelle a bottle of water. "I figured you might be thirsty."

She took it gratefully. "I am. Thanks."

"Did you get any sleep on the flight?" James asked.

"A little. It's okay, I'll catch up later."

"Can we go out to breakfast?" Olivia asked.

"Your mom probably wants to get home and—"

"It's fine." She turned to James. "It'll be nice."

"Okay, we'll go to the diner before heading home," James said.

Olivia cheered. "Sophie's coming over later and spending the night. Daddy said she could since we had to cancel sailing."

"Sounds good, sweetie." She turned to James again. "How's Scarlett?"

"Fine. She's going over to Avery's in a bit for that project. She's spending the night there."

Annabelle was disappointed. What she wanted more than anything was everyone under one roof so she could sleep soundly. But she had to accept the fact that her children were growing up and had their own lives. She pulled out her phone and sent Scarlett a text.

I'm back. Miss you and can't wait to see you tomorrow. Have fun at Avery's. xoxo

Scarlett didn't text back but hearted the message. Annabelle supposed that would have to be good enough. At least she knew everyone was safe and sound. She pushed her dream to the back of her mind. There was nothing to worry about.

58

Scarlett

It was eight o'clock. She was leaving the house in half an hour to meet Ben. Olivia had just texted her to say they were going out to breakfast, so she probably had more time, but she didn't want to risk it. She couldn't believe she was finally going to see him in person! She hoped that he would like her as much after he met her. It was so much easier to try to sound cool on text than in person. She didn't want him to think she was a dork or something. What if she said something stupid? She took a deep breath, trying to calm herself. Everything would be okay. He cared about her; that wasn't going to change once they met. They had a connection, and nothing could break it.

She stood in front of her mirror and brushed her hair. Should she put it in a ponytail or leave it down? Grabbing a scrunchie, she pulled it back, but then decided it made her look too young. She turned around and peered over her shoulder to see how the jeans looked. They were okay, but the shirt was too baggy. She went to her closet and picked out a more form-fitting tee. That was better. Taking one last look, she decided she was ready. She ran down the stairs, grabbed her backpack, threw her phone and wallet in it, and went into the kitchen. Parker got up and came over to her, nuzzling her hand with his head.

"Hey, boy. I'll be back. You be good." She grabbed a treat from the canister on the counter and gave it to him.

She went out to the garage, got on her bike, and took off.

The Wife

Things are ramping up. It sickens me to see the things he writes to her. He tries to be so cute in his texts, and she's eating it up. Does he really think she'll love him when she learns the truth? He's delusional. I need to make her stay away. It's time to put an end to this.

Scarlett

Scarlett arrived at the coffee shop and looked around for Ben. She must have gotten here first. She walked over to an empty table and sat, her eyes trained on the door. She had butterflies in her stomach and inhaled deeply, trying to calm down. The door opened again and her heart sank when she saw it was just another man. What if Ben stood her up? Then the man walked over to her table and stopped.

"Scarlett?"

"Who are you?"

He pulled a chair out and sat. "I need to explain something—"

Oh my God, oh my God! Avery was right. Was this some creep pretending to be Ben?

"How do you know my name?"

"I know you thought you were meeting Ben, but I can explain."

She stood up. "Get away from me!" she whispered. She didn't want to make a scene. Humiliation filled her when she thought about all the things she'd texted to this weirdo pretending to be Ben. What did he want? She ran toward the door and he got up, calling after her.

"Wait!"

The blood pounded in her ears as she flung the door open and looked around. She needed to hide. He was coming. She ducked around the corner and hid behind the dumpster in front of the alley, watching as he spun around looking for her. Finally, he walked over to a white BMW parked on the street and got in. Once he pulled away, she ran to her bike and jumped on it. She had to get home! As she cut down the alley she heard a car behind her. Glancing over her shoulder she screamed when she saw it was the white BMW. It was coming right at her. She pedaled faster and faster, her heart racing. She looked over her shoulder again. It was getting closer. Before she could figure out what to do, she felt a hard jolt and went flying over the handlebars. Then everything went black.

Annabelle

"Are you going to have any more pancakes, or are you ready to go?" James asked Olivia, whose eyes had been bigger than her stomach.

"I'm done," she said.

"I'm finished," he corrected her.

"Me too," she said, giggling. Annabelle delighted in her younger daughter's ability to let everything roll off her back.

They paid the bill and left the diner. Annabelle's lack of sleep was beginning to get to her. It was not quite eleven o'clock. She didn't know how she was going to stay awake until evening, but she knew better than to sleep now and throw her system off entirely. When they got home, she went upstairs and was about to unpack when she heard their doorbell ring. Must be Sophie, she thought as she looked out the bedroom window. Her heart skipped a beat when she saw the police car. Dropping the skirt in her hands, she flew down the stairs. James was standing there with a police officer. The officer looked up as she approached. James turned around.

"I was about to call you," James said.

"Mr. and Mrs. Reynolds, can we take a seat for a minute?" the officer asked.

"What's happened?" Annabelle said, panic making her feel faint.

"Is Scarlett Reynolds your daughter?"

"Yes," Annabelle and James answered in union.

"I'm afraid there's been an accident. Your daughter was on her bike downtown, and she was struck by a car. We found your address in her wallet. It was on her country club membership card. She's on her way to Norwalk Hospital."

"No! What are you talking about? She was at her friend's house," James said.

"How badly is she hurt?" Annabelle asked, grabbing James's arm to steady herself.

"I'm not sure, ma'am. Would you like me to take you to the hospital?"

"Yes!" She ran past James and out the door. "Call your mother to come stay with Olivia. You can meet me there."

She jumped in the passenger seat of the police car and struggled to get a breath. "Where was she? Who hit her? She wasn't even supposed to be on her bike."

"It was a hit-and-run. There were no witnesses. There'll be an investigation, of course."

It didn't make any sense. Avery lived on the other side of town. Scarlett was in downtown Bayport. What was she doing there on her bike this early in the morning? "I don't understand," she said to herself as much as to the officer. Then she had an idea. She called James. "Text me the phone number to Avery's house. I want to see if she knows anything."

"Okay. My mother just got here so I'll meet you at the hospital. I tried to call, but I couldn't get any information." He sounded as frantic as she felt.

She ended the call and waited for the text. As soon as the number came through, she hit call.

"Hello?"

"Is this Avery's mother?"

"Yes, who's this?" the woman asked.

"This is Annabelle Reynolds. I'm Scarlett's mom. She told me she was going to your house today, but she was hit by a car down-town. Do you have any idea where she might have been going, or does your daughter know anything?" The words came out in a rush.

"Oh my gosh, that's terrible! Is she okay?"

"I don't know. I'm on my way to the hospital now."

"Hold on, let me get Avery. As far as I know, she had no plans with Scarlett today."

Her heart dropped. Scarlett had lied to them. What could she be hiding? A few minutes later, Avery's mother was back.

Annabelle felt sick to her stomach as Avery's mom told her that Scarlett had been conversing with a boy named Ben that she met online.

"Avery said they were meeting at the coffee shop downtown today."

"I've never heard of this Ben. Do you know anything else about him?"

"Let me put my daughter on."

"Mrs. Reynolds?"

"Avery, what is going on? Who is Ben? How long has this been going on?"

She could hear Avery crying. "I'm sorry. I covered for her. She said she knew she could trust him. I tried to get her to find out more about him. All I know is that his name is Ben, and he lives in Chi-cago. He said he was coming here with his dad, who was in town for a business trip. I've seen his Instagram. I can send you the link."

Annabelle tightened her hands into fists, doing everything she could not to scream. "Yes, please send it." When she ended the call, she turned to the officer. "I think she met a predator online. She must have been trying to get away from him." Her whole body was shaking now, and she hugged herself to try to stop it. She clicked on the link Avery sent, and it took her to Instagram. It was a good-looking young kid. Model good-looking. The kind of picture a cat-fisher would use. The name was generic—Ben Smith. "Can you get a warrant to see who the Instagram page belongs to?"

"Yes, definitely. When we get to the hospital you can give the information to the detective meeting us there."

Annabelle wiped the tears from her cheeks. Her dreams had warned her, and she had dismissed them. "Can you go any faster?" she pleaded. "Please. Hurry!"

62

Annabelle

The police officer escorted Annabelle into the Emergency Room and was able to get her taken up to the Intensive Care Unit right away. "What's happening with my daughter?" she asked at the nurses' station, banging on the glass to get someone's attention. A woman looked up and met her eyes. She walked around to Annabelle.

"Are you Scarlett's mother?"

"Yes. Where is she?"

"She's being evaluated. She was unconscious when she was brought in, and the doctors sent her for a CAT scan. Please come sit down." She led Annabelle to the small waiting room adjoining the unit. "I know this is scary, and I promise that as soon as we have more information, we'll update you. We're taking good care of your daughter."

Annabelle collapsed onto the sofa, numb with shock. This couldn't be happening. How had her perfect life turned into this nightmare? It took her a moment to register that a man was standing in the corner, looking at her. He walked over to her.

"I'm Detective Stanton. Officer Blake said that your daughter was meeting someone. Do you know who?"

"Some boy named Ben, according to her friend."

"My partner questioned people at the coffee shop. They said she was talking to a man. Conflicting descriptions, unfortunately. The only consistent thing was a white male in his thirties or forties, average height and weight."

Annabelle's heart sank. So it *was* some predator masquerading as a boy. She pulled her phone out and went to the text from Avery, showing it to the detective. "This is who Scarlett thought she was talking to. It's the first I've heard of him. Her friend said they've been texting for a couple of months now."

"I have her phone. It was in her backpack. Do you know her passcode?" the detective asked.

Annabelle nodded. He gave her the phone, and she typed in the code. The phone opened. She handed it back to the detective with a shaking hand.

After a few minutes, he looked up. "I don't see any text chains with a Ben. Only some between her and Avery, some texts from you and your husband and an Olivia."

"Maybe she erased them?" Annabelle said.

"Probably. I'll give this to our tech folks and they'll be able to tell." He went back to swiping the phone. "Hmm. She has WhatsApp. I wonder if they used that."

Annabelle looked up, surprised. "She wouldn't have known about that app. He must have suggested it." Annabelle knew people used it when they wanted their texts to be encrypted and not easily hacked. Who in the hell had Scarlett been communicating with?

"Are the messages there?"

The detective nodded "Yes. They go back quite a ways."

She jumped up and held out her hand. "Let me see."

"Hang on a second."

She was about to grab the phone out of his hand, but before she could, the elevator opened and James came running toward her. "Any news?"

"No, the doctors are evaluating her. They said they'll come update us as soon as they know anything."

The detective introduced himself to James and briefed him on what he and Annabelle had discussed. James's face turned red. "Who is this son of a bitch messaging her? He had to have done this!"

The doors to the unit opened, and Annabelle stood as a man in a white coat approached them.

"Mr. and Mrs. Reynolds?" he asked.

"Yes. How's our daughter?" Annabelle asked.

"She's stable. I'm Doctor Jenkins. She's suffered a blow to the head and has a closed brain injury. No other injuries, other than contusions on her arms and legs. Scans showed no bleeding, which is good. But we're concerned with brain swelling, so we've put her in a medically induced coma to let her brain rest. She hadn't regained consciousness before we did so. We'll be keeping her in ICU where we can keep a close eye on her."

"Oh my God! Is she going to be okay?" Annabelle asked.

"She's on a vent?" James asked.

The doctor nodded. "Yes, we've intubated her and have her on midazolam. We'll continue monitoring her vitals and her neurological status, including intracranial pressure."

"I'd like to see her scans and take a look at her pupils too," James said, then stopped. "Sorry, you don't know me. I'm Doctor Reynolds, a neurologist. Nothing against you, Doctor Jenkins, but I want Matthias on this." He turned to Annabelle. "He's the chief of neurosurgery." He looked back at the doctor. "I want his assessment before we go any further."

Dr. Jenkins nodded. "I understand. I'll have Doctor Matthias paged."

"Can we see her?" Annabelle asked.

"Yes. Someone will be out shortly once we get her settled in a room."

Annabelle burst into tears again, and James put his arms around her. "She's going to be okay. Everything's going to be okay," he whispered.

But Annabelle took no comfort in his words.

63

Annabelle

It had been a week, and Scarlett was still in a coma. Dr. Matthias had taken over. It killed Annabelle to see her baby lying there so still, with a tube down her throat. She was improving, but the doctor wanted to give her more time. Annabelle hadn't left her side, spending the nights in a recliner by her bed.

James walked into the room with two cups of coffee. He came every morning before work.

"Any updates?" he asked.

"Doctor Matthias will be by after nine. He said he hopes they can lighten the sedation soon."

"You look exhausted. Why don't you let me come and stay tonight? You should go home and get a good night's sleep."

"No. There's no such thing as a good night's sleep until she's awake, and I know she's okay." Her voice broke, and she took a deep breath. This unending nightmare was taking a huge toll, but there was no way she would step foot outside the hospital until it was time to take Scarlett home. Ironically, her sleep had been dreamless all week. She was losing hope.

"You won't do her any good if you get so run-down that you get sick. Just one—"

"Stop it, James. I'm not leaving, and that's final! Maybe if you hadn't tried to make me think I was crazy with those dreams, this could have been prevented. Something was warning me that Scarlett was in trouble, but you chalked it up to anxiety. So stop telling me what to do and what to think."

He was momentarily speechless. "You're blaming *me* for this?"

She threw her hands up. "No, no, of course not. I'm just saying, stop micromanaging me. I feel like you're always hovering and lecturing. Our daughter has been reaching out to a stranger because we weren't paying attention. I just want you to leave me alone right now." She had read through all the texts over and over, looking for any clue as to who this Ben might be. It was clear to her how cleverly he had found out where Scarlett went to school and where she lived. She had no idea what the texts about her and James hiding something meant. The detectives said they could tell that some of the texts had been deleted and were working on recovering them. The man must have manufactured some sort of lies about them. Annabelle was so upset with herself for not monitoring Scarlett's phone—for foolishly elevating her privacy over her safety.

"There's obviously a lot going on right now. This is clearly not a good time for a discussion." James handed her one of the cups. "Here. I'll get out of your hair. I'll be back later this afternoon."

Annabelle couldn't bring herself to respond and merely stood watching as he walked away. *Was* she blaming him? A little. But she was also blaming herself. When did she stop listening to her own instincts and allow James to run her life? She was a smart, capable woman, yet she kowtowed to him in too many ways. Scarlett had been acting so distant, angry even, and Annabelle had ignored it. She'd told herself that it was normal teenage sullenness, when it had been a cry for help. All those questions Scarlett had asked her about true love and love at first sight—she should have read between the lines and realized that Scarlett was asking for a more personal reason. Instead, she'd let some predator into her life, who'd then almost killed her. Annabelle needed answers. What was she supposed to do next?

Her phone pinged: a message from Chase, asking how Scarlett was. He'd been so supportive, checking in every day, even arranging to have lunch sent to her on a couple days, with a note telling her she needed a break from hospital food.

The police hadn't been able to find the owner of the Instagram account. It had been deactivated and had been set up using an un-traceable Gmail account. They were waiting on a warrant to get in-formation from Instagram about the IP address of the deactivated account. They had questioned Avery at length, but she didn't have any other helpful information. The poor girl felt guilty for keeping the information to herself, but Annabelle didn't blame her. That's what best friends did. She'd certainly kept her own share of secrets over the years.

This mystery man was out there somewhere. What if he tried to come to the hospital and hurt Scarlett? The police didn't think that was likely and wouldn't agree to station anyone outside her room. But it was another reason that Annabelle wouldn't leave. She didn't trust anyone else to keep her daughter safe.

Scarlett uttered a soft noise, and Annabelle jumped up and stood next to the bed.

"Sweetie, can you hear me? It's Mom. I'm right here."

She took Scarlett's hand in hers. "You're safe now. No one can hurt you." She tried to make her voice sound confident, but in her heart, she didn't believe the words coming out of her mouth.

64

Scarlett

Everything hurt. Where was she? It was dark and cold. Scarlett tried to open her eyes, but it was like they were glued shut. There was something on her arm squeezing it now and then, and beeps and hissing sounds all around her. She tried to speak, but it was like she was underwater. Her throat burned too. And she was tired. So tired. What had happened? She tried to remember. Ben. She was meeting Ben. But he wasn't there. A man. A man who knew her name. It was all wrong. She'd run from the coffee shop and he called after her. She'd jumped on her bike. She pedaled faster and faster, cutting through the alley for a shortcut. That was the last thing she remembered.

Her mom was talking. She strained to make out what she was saying, but she could only catch a word here and there. Her body felt so heavy. Was she dreaming? Maybe it was sleep paralysis. She'd heard about that before, maybe even had it happen once or twice. That terrible feeling when you want to move, but it's like invisible bricks are on top of you. That's what this felt like. She didn't like it.

Her mom was talking again. No, she was reading. Oh, she was reading Scarlett a story. Like she used to at bedtime. Why was she reading to her, and why couldn't Scarlett move? Think, think. Her bike. Trying to get away. From Ben. No, not Ben. A man who was pretending to be Ben. But why? She tried to remember, but only snatches of visions came to her. She recalled waiting in the coffee shop, excited, anxious, looking at the door every time it opened, expecting to see him. Then that man walked over to her table and sat down. Avery had been right. He was preying on her. She had to get away from him. This liar. A weirdo.

She felt someone touching her, rubbing her arm. "I love you, Scarlett. I'm here."

Her dad. She wanted to tell him she could hear him, but she couldn't speak.

"I'm so sorry, Scarlett. This should never have happened." Her dad's voice sounded funny. Was he crying?

65

Annabelle

Annabelle and James both stood up as Dr. Matthias came into the hospital room. He said hello, went straight to Scarlett, and lifted an eyelid, flashing a light in it. He did the same with the other eye. He then inspected the intraventricular catheter site and reviewed the readings on the external monitor.

"I'm pleased to see her pupils are reacting to light, and her ICP pressure is down significantly at seventeen. We need to get to fifteen before we can start to wean her off sedation. Have you noticed any movement?"

"Not much. Some moaning, but that's about it," Annabelle said.

"That's okay. We're getting there. We need to stay the course. Her vitals are good. Blood pressure's still a little elevated, but we'll keep an eye on that. How are Mom and Dad holding up?"

James merely shook his head. Annabelle could see that he was fighting tears. "We're hanging in there. Thank you for taking such good care of her."

"Of course. I'll be back to check on her again later this afternoon. And you have my cell if you need anything at all."

Once he left, they sat back down. "You should get to the office. It won't do for both of us to neglect our work," Annabelle said.

"It's okay. I pushed my appointments to the afternoon. Why don't you go home for a few hours to get a change of scenery? You haven't left the hospital in ten days." James had been bringing her changes of clothing, and she'd been showering and getting dressed here.

She shook her head. "No, I can't." She couldn't make him understand that something was telling her if she left, Scarlett would die. Annabelle knew it was an irrational fear, but she wasn't about to test it. She'd made a promise to Scarlett that she wouldn't leave until she woke up, and Annabelle was determined not to break her promise.

James turned to look at her. "I know you don't want to hear this, but we have to face facts. Scarlett could be in this state for a long time. There's so much we don't know about the brain. The fact that she didn't regain consciousness after the accident is not a good sign."

Annabelle wanted to reach out and slap him. "Why are you telling me this?"

"I'm only trying to prepare you. You can't live in the hospital for months."

She stood up, furious. "She's not going to be here for months. Dr. Matthias said her pressure is almost back to normal, and they'll bring her out of this soon. Why are you being so negative?"

"Sweetheart, just because they lessen the sedation doesn't mean she'll wake right up. She's had a traumatic brain injury. There's no telling when—" He put a hand on her arm. "Or *if,* she'll recover."

"Get out!"

"What are you saying? Annabelle!"

"I mean it. How dare you say that to me! I don't care that you're a neurologist. In this room, you're her father and that means you cling to hope with everything you've got."

"Don't you think I want more than anything in this world for her to get out of that bed?" He was crying now. "I'd change places with her in a minute. But I can't. I can't do anything but sit here helplessly, hoping and praying she'll be okay. But at the same time, I'm watching my wife barely holding on, making herself sick, not getting any sleep. I won't lose you both!"

She stood up and wrapped her arms around him. Of course, he was suffering as much as she was. "I'm sorry. I'm scared too. But I can't leave her, James. I can't. Please try to understand."

"Okay," he whispered. "We'll get through this. We can't let it tear us apart."

She nodded, but in her heart, she knew it already had.

Scarlett

She was feeling a little better. Her body didn't hurt so much anymore, although her throat was still sore, and she still couldn't move. But she could hear more of what was going on around her. The doctor had been in and told her mother that she was doing better. That's how Scarlett knew she was in the hospital. Her mother's voice sounded so scared. She wanted to tell her that she was fine, and not to worry, but the words wouldn't come. After the doctor left, it was quiet. Then she heard a phone ring and her mother say hello.

"Chase, hi. Yes, she's doing much better. They're going to decrease her sedation, starting tomorrow. Yeah, I forgot to change the address with the printer, and they sent the promo pieces to the house like I originally asked. I had James drop them off when he came by the hospital this morning. Can you come by and pick them up?"

She was getting tired again, and her mother's voice faded.

SOMEONE WAS TALKING AGAIN. IT wasn't her mom, but someone else. Who was in her room? She strained to listen. No, it was her mom. She was talking to someone.

"Hi, thanks for coming to pick these up."

"No problem. I'm so sorry for all you're going through. What are the doctors saying?"

The other voice belonged to a man.

"They're hopeful, but until she wakes up—" Her mother stopped talking, and it sounded like she was crying. A few minutes later, she spoke again. "Thanks for checking in so often. Your texts always brighten my day. I'm so sorry to leave you in the lurch, but hopefully, Riggs is taking good care of you."

"Don't give it a second thought. You need to be here with Scarlett."

Scarlett's heart began to beat faster. The voice. It was his. It was him! What was he doing here? *Mom, Mom!* she wanted to shout. *That's the man from the coffee shop!*

67

Before

It was time. Annabelle woke up at midnight to unbearable pain. No one had told her how awful contractions were. The baby was coming. She was still two weeks away from her due date. She called the hospital to have James paged, as he was working the late shift.

"Everything okay?"

"My water broke."

"I'm on my way. How far apart are your contractions?"

"Twenty minutes."

"Hang tight. I'll be there in fifteen."

"Don't speed. It won't help if you get into an accident. It's raining like crazy out there. I'm not going to deliver in the next hour."

"Okay, okay. See you soon."

She winced, doubling over as another contraction racked her. This hurt like a bitch. She was definitely asking for drugs. After it passed, she went upstairs and got her little bag from the bedroom.

Everything was going to change. Her baby was finally coming. Annabelle was suddenly terrified. What did she know about being a mother? She always thought she'd have a child in her early thirties, not twenties. She had no family support, a sick mother who needed her, and a job that barely paid the rent and expenses. There was the money from her father, but she wouldn't touch that. Her mother was still young, she could live for many more years, and Annabelle had to make sure she had the resources to keep her mother where she was. And she couldn't live with James forever. He'd made it clear that he had feelings for her, but as much as she liked and respected him, she wasn't in love with him. He had asked her to marry him. Said he didn't care if her feelings weren't as strong as his, and that she'd come to love him in time. It was tempting to give in, let him be a father to her child, a partner to her. It would make everything so much easier. But it wasn't fair to him or to her. Even though Randy had turned out to be a snake, she'd been in love with him, and she wanted to feel that again. She wasn't going to settle.

She sat on the bed to slip her feet into the loafers James had left next to it. But when she tried to put them on, they were too tight. She raised her legs to get a look at her feet and was shocked to see that they were swollen. Maybe she'd been standing too much. Even though she was nervous about the baby's arrival, she couldn't wait until her body went back to normal. She walked over to the closet and, with her toe, pushed a pair of flip-flops out. They would have to do.

Annabelle returned downstairs and put her bag and purse next to the door. Then she realized her cellphone was in the kitchen, so she went to retrieve that and put it with her things. *That's everything,* she thought. Now she just had to wait for James to get here.

She looked up as the door opened and James rushed in, his hair soaked and raindrops dripping from his jacket.

"Ready?"

She shook her head. "Not really. I'm scared. Is it too late to turn back time?"

He gave her a smile and took her hand. "You're going to be fine. I know it's scary, but I'll be right next to you. Grab an umbrella."

When they went outside, the wind was blowing so hard that it turned Annabelle's umbrella inside out. She ran to the car and slid in. "I'm not scared about the labor—well, I am, but I'm talking about motherhood. I still feel like a kid myself. I'm not ready for this. I mean, I never even babysat. I don't have any nieces or nephews. I don't have the first clue what to do with a baby. Do you think all first-time mothers feel this way?"

"I don't know. Probably. Change is scary, and this is a big one. But I'm sure you're going to be a great mother."

"How do you know? What if I'm not? I can't cook. I can barely sew."

"Cooking and sewing are not prerequisites for motherhood in the twenty-first century." He laughed. "The only reason I had a decent meal growing up was thanks to our housekeeper."

Annabelle was quiet the rest of the drive, her thoughts racing. She wondered if Randy had already left for Arizona. Did he even think about the fact that his child was soon coming into the world? Sorrow overcame her, and she began to weep.

"Hey, you okay?"

"Not really," she sniffed. "I know I said I was glad Randy was out of the picture, but I'm sad that he doesn't care about his own child. I don't know how I'm going to do it. I barely make any money. I can't afford a nanny. I should be interviewing for a full-time job now and working toward my dreams. This is a nightmare."

"I'm sorry, Annabelle. But you're not alone. I told you, I'm here for you."

"I appreciate that, but it's not the same."

His jaw tightened. "Do you really want to be back with Randy, after what he did?"

"No. This isn't about me wanting to be with Randy. But one day this child is going to want to know where their father is. And it's going to hurt. No matter how much I love this child, it will always feel the rejection of its biological father. I know this because it's what I feel. And I'm really sad to pass on that legacy."

"Maybe you don't have to. I would—"

Another contraction made her scream. "They're coming faster now. Something feels wrong. My head is killing me." She cried out again as the pain intensified. "I'm gonna be sick."

"Almost there."

He sped up and pulled into the parking lot, stopping the car in front of the emergency doors. Throwing it in park, he leapt out and opened her door. Before he could help her out, she vomited. She looked at her hands. Why were they so swollen? "What's wrong with me?" she cried.

James helped her into the building. "She needs to be admitted to OB right away." He showed his ID. "I think she might be preeclamptic."

"Right away, Doctor Reynolds."

The next thing Annabelle knew, she was in a wheelchair and being raced down the hall to the elevator, with James keeping pace beside her.

"It's going to be okay, honey. It's okay."

She started to shake, her whole body vibrating, and then everything faded from sight.

68

Annabelle

Annabelle and James stood on one side of Scarlett's bed, waiting. The team's assessment had determined that it was time to decrease her sedation. Dr. Matthias was getting ready to extubate her now. Scarlett's eyes were open, and she still had enough of a sedative in her system to keep her calm. She indicated that she understood what he was saying when he explained what was about to happen. Annabelle held her breath as she watched the doctor extract the tube, and Scarlett begin to cough.

"Doing okay?" Dr. Matthias asked once the tube was out.

"Yeah," Scarlett croaked, her hand going to her neck reflexively. "Throat hurts."

"It will for a while. So glad to see you're back with us, Scarlett!"

James and Annabelle each took one of her hands. Annabelle wiped the tears from her face with her free hand. "Sweetheart, thank God you're awake." She wanted answers, but the doctor had warned them to go easy at first.

Scarlett looked at Annabelle. "Him. It was him!"

James and Annabelle looked at each other quizzically.

"What are you talking about, sweetie?"

Her mouth opened, but no words came out and she yawned. Her eyes closed again. Panic seized Annabelle. She looked at the doctor.

"Is she going into a coma again?"

He glanced at the instruments by the bed, then back at Annabelle. "No, she's just exhausted. There's still some sedation in her system. She's just sleeping."

Annabelle breathed a sigh of relief. "When can we take her home?"

"We'll need to monitor her for a while. I want her to have some respiratory therapy as well, since she's been on a vent all this time. We'll have to play it by ear."

After Dr. Matthias left, Annabelle turned to James. "What do you think? Is she in the clear?"

He nodded. "I think so. They'll do some cognitive tests when she's fully awake again, but her scans and vitals all look good. Looks like there was no damage to her brain, thank God."

She exhaled. "Okay, okay. What do you think she meant about *him*? Do you think she was referring to the man she met?"

"I don't know. She could be confused. We're going to have to wait for answers, as hard as that is. I can't believe the police have made no progress at all. If only that damn alley had cameras."

"It burns me up. Do you think the person who hit her was the same one she met? Or maybe she was trying to get away, and someone else hit her?"

"We may never know that. They did say it was a white vehicle; that much they could tell from the paint transfer. But that's not very helpful, is it?" James said.

She shook her head. Why couldn't she dream about *this*? That would be helpful. But since Scarlett had been struck, Annabelle hadn't had any more dreams—or at least none she remembered.

Her phone buzzed, and she picked it up from the chair where she'd been sitting.

"Hello?"

"Mrs. Reynolds?"

"Yes?"

"It's Detective Stanton. We have some new information. We've tracked down the IP address of the person who set up that Instagram account."

"Who is it?"

"I can't disclose that yet. But the IP address allowed us to trace it to the physical address where the computer is located. We're waiting for a warrant now. Hoping to go in shortly. I'll keep you posted."

"Why can't you tell me who it is?"

"I'm sorry, ma'am, I promise to give you that information as soon as I can. I know you've been frustrated with the lack of progress, so I wanted to let you know we were making headway."

"Please let me know as soon as you have more information."

"What was that all about?" James asked when she ended the call. She filled him in.

"Let's hope they find this bastard," he said, his face red. He looked at his watch. "I need to go pick up Olivia from play practice. I'll bring her back with me and grab some dinner for us all on the way."

"Sounds good." She rose on tiptoes to kiss him.

Her phone buzzed, and she saw it was Kiera.

"Hi."

"How's she doing?"

"She woke up. I was so scared! She's resting now. Thank you for the beautiful flowers, by the way."

"Of course. I've been worried sick. We're all praying for her and for you. Any idea who the hell this guy is that was texting her?" Kiera asked.

"They think they found the address of the person on the Instagram account, so fingers crossed."

"Well, keep me posted. I'm sorry I couldn't get there, but with my girl's flu, the last thing I wanted to do was bring germs to your house."

"Of course. I'll talk to you later."

After she ended the call, Annabelle texted Chase to tell him that

Scarlett was finally awake. He'd been so sweet and solicitous, checking in with her several times a day. He texted her back.

> Something's happened that I need to
> talk to you about. I know you don't
> want to leave the hospital, but can
> you come out to the parking lot
> for a few minutes? It's important.

Now that Scarlett was out of the woods, she supposed it would
be okay. She typed back.

> Ok. When?

> I'm on my way.

Before

Annabelle heard voices yelling all around her. Her vision was blurry, but bright lights overhead and the cold temperature alerted her that she was in an operating room. James was holding her hand, telling her everything was going to be fine.

"Stay very still. We need to deliver you via C-section," he told her. "They're going to give you a spinal block."

"Why? What's happening?"

"Your blood pressure is too high. You have preeclampsia, but you'll be fine once the baby is delivered."

"Stay still, Annabelle," another voice commanded.

She held her breath as a cold cloth swabbed her back.

"You're going to feel some pressure," the same voice said.

She closed her eyes and tried not to think of the large needle going into her back.

"Okay, all set."

"Where's Doctor Pappas?" Annabelle asked.

James squeezed her hand. "He's away on vacation. You weren't due for another two weeks, remember? They're trying to get the doctor on call, but he's not here yet. There have been a bunch of accidents, power out everywhere. I don't know if something happened to him or what. We can't wait. I'm going to have to deliver you."

"Are you sure? Have you done a C-section before?"

"Yes, don't worry. I've done quite a few. You'll be fine."

The next hour was a blur of voices as she went in and out of consciousness. Finally, she heard the cry of her baby, and she wept in relief.

She watched as they rushed the baby over to a table to be examined.

"Let me see," Annabelle called out, holding out her arms. After a few minutes, James came over to her and placed the baby on her chest. It was the most exquisite emotion she'd ever felt. Overwhelming love washed over her, and she knew in that moment that she would lay her life down for this precious child.

"Hi there, my sweetheart. Mommy loves you. Mommy—" She started to shake again, and James quickly picked up the baby. "I can't, I can't—"

The last thing she heard was James's voice shouting, "She's seizing!"

WHEN ANNABELLE WOKE UP AGAIN, she was alone in a hospital room. It was dark. She felt around for the call button and depressed it. A few minutes later, a nurse came in.

"Where's my son?" she asked.

"Let me find out."

"Do you know where Doctor Reynolds is?" she asked, wondering if James had left.

"Your husband went upstairs to get a cup of coffee," the woman said.

Annabelle started to correct her, but let it go. "Okay, please. I want to see my son."

The nurse nodded and left the room.

She tried to remember what had happened. She remembered

having the C-section and holding her son in her arms. But that was the last memory she could summon. What had happened? And why wasn't her son in the room with her?

"Hey, you're awake," James said, walking in, a coffee cup in one hand.

"Where's my son? I don't remember anything after I held him."

He pulled a chair close to the bed and sat, reaching for her hand. "You had a seizure. We treated you with magnesium sulfate, a central nervous system depressant. You've been out for almost eighteen hours."

"Why did I have a seizure?"

"Remember how swollen your hands and feet were?"

She nodded.

"You had preeclampsia, a condition that sometimes occurs with pregnancy. Your blood pressure shot up, and you had a seizure. Fortunately you had no organ damage, and we were able to get everything under control."

"What caused it? Did I do something wrong? Did I hurt the baby?" She was starting to feel like she couldn't breathe.

"It's not your fault. Nothing you did. There are lots of potential causes. Genetics, immune system reactions. But nothing you did caused it."

Annabelle realized James still hadn't answered her question about the baby.

"Is the baby okay?"

He stood and came over to the side of the bed. "He went into respiratory distress. It happens sometimes. We tried, but . . ." He reached out and took her hand in his. "I'm so sorry, Annabelle. He didn't make it."

A sob tore through her and she pulled her hand back. "I want to see him."

"I don't think that's such a good—"

"Get me my son. Now!"

"Okay. I'll be back."

She continued to sob, holding a pillow to her chest, her body heaving as though she were being hollowed out. How could this have happened? Was she being punished for her ambivalence about the pregnancy? The arrogance of deciding whether or not she wanted a child? And now the only thing she wanted was her son. She wished she had died too. Because she knew there would be a part of her that was forever missing. And she would never, ever, be truly happy again.

70

Annabelle

She hadn't seen Chase since he'd stopped by last week, and Annabelle realized she missed him. She went to the bathroom and looked in the mirror, pinching her cheeks to put some color into them. She had to admit she looked pretty grim. When she came out, she touched Scarlett's arm lightly to see if she'd rouse, but she merely moaned and turned to her side. Annabelle leaned down and kissed her cheek. She sat and picked up the magazine she'd been reading, trying to distract herself from her racing thoughts. Finally, her phone pinged, and she saw that Chase was there.

"I'll be right back, honey," she said as she left the room.

Chase was waiting in the visitor parking lot. Annabelle's spirits lifted when she walked toward his car, and he smiled at her. He opened the car door and got out, embracing her in a hug.

"How's she doing?"

"She's out of the coma. Resting now. She started to talk to us but fell back asleep."

"She hasn't told you what happened yet?"

"Not yet. But the police think they've identified the house where the messages came from. They're close to finding out who's behind this. So what's going on? You said it was important."

He looked down at the ground. "I have to talk to you about something. Do you think we could go for a quick drive? I need to show you something."

"I can't leave. Scarlett could wake up—"

"I promise we'll be quick. But it's really important."

"Just tell me, Chase. What is it?"

He blew out a breath. "It's about your son."

She went cold. "What are you talking about?" The blood began to pound in her ears, and her whole body felt like it was going numb. "What about my son?"

"He's not dead."

Scarlett

Scarlett opened her eyes and looked around the room. She wondered where everyone had gone. She turned toward the window and noticed it was beginning to get dark. She was about to call for a nurse when her father and Olivia walked in. Holding a teddy bear, Olivia ran over to Scarlett.

"You're awake!" She reached out to hug her sister, but their dad's voice stopped her.

"Easy, honey. Your sister's still hooked up to an IV."

"A what?" Olivia asked.

Her dad walked over and pointed to the tube coming out of her arm. He looked at Scarlett tenderly. "You had us really worried, kiddo. How are you feeling?"

"Okay, I think. Still pretty tired, but I'm glad I can talk. I could hear you guys, but I couldn't move. It was really scary."

He took her hand in his. "I'm so sorry. Do you feel up to talking now? Do you know how you ended up in the hospital?"

She shook her head.

James sat down in the chair next to the bed and patted the one next to him for Olivia. "Someone hit you while you were on your bike. What were you doing downtown? Do you remember?"

She did, but she was afraid he would get mad if she told him. But she needed to warn her mother about the man. Her father must have sensed her hesitation.

"Honey, you're not in trouble. We already know you were texting someone. We just want to find out what happened. Please."

Tears came to Scarlett's eyes as she recalled her humiliation at finding out that all this time, she'd been texting someone only pretending to be Ben. She couldn't tell her dad everything yet, though. She needed to talk to her mom first. "Ben was supposed to meet me, but a man came instead."

"What man? Had you ever seen him before?"

"I don't know. Where's Mom?"

He gave her a strange look. "Isn't she here? I figured she went to get a coffee or something."

"I woke up, and she was gone."

"I'm sure she'll be right back. She hasn't left your side since you've been here. You don't know who the man was?"

She swallowed. "I think he knows Mom."

"What do you mean?"

"I heard his voice here talking to Mom. I don't know why he was here, but it was him."

"That seems impossible. Are you sure?"

Scarlett nodded. "I can't remember his name, but I recognized his voice. It was definitely him."

Her eyes started to close and her body felt heavy again. "Tired."

"Okay, sweetheart. You rest. Olivia and I are going to go up to the cafeteria to see if your mom is there."

72

Annabelle

Chase put a hand on her arm, but she swatted it away. "I don't know what kind of sick game you're playing. My son died the night he was born!"

"Annabelle, please listen. My son, Lucas. I found out he's not mine. I think our babies were switched at birth."

Her knees felt weak, and dizziness overcame her. Chase closed the distance between them and caught her before she fell. "How is that possible?"

"Come with me. I need to show you."

Still numb, Annabelle got into Chase's car, and he drove out of the parking lot. Her mind exploded with memories from that night. Holding her son right after delivering him, feeling his heartbeat next to hers. And then the cold reality the next day brought. James telling her he had died. Could it be true? Her son, alive? "Where are we going?"

"My house. I have all the proof there."

"What proof?"

"My son, Lucas, gave blood at a blood drive over the summer. A few weeks later, he mentioned that his blood was type A."

"What does this have to do—"

"Hear me out. My wife and I are both O. I thought she had cheated on me. I told you . . . our marriage was not great. So I tested him with 23andMe, but I put it under a fake name. I elected to be contacted if there were any blood relatives and gave a Gmail account under the fake name. It came back with a maternal match to a sibling. I realized that Tara couldn't be his mother. That's when Scarlett emailed me."

"How? Scarlett didn't do the DNA test. James didn't let her."

"Well, she must have taken it anyway. The results show that she's a maternal sibling match to Lucas. I emailed her back pretending to be him and told her that I needed to talk to my parents before going any further. I was trying to buy some time to figure things out."

"I don't understand. How could Scarlett be your son's sister? That makes no sense."

"The baby that you lost. His birthday was September third. Right?"

A chill ran through her. "How did you know?"

"That's the same day my wife delivered. You were both at the hospital the same night. I can show you the report."

"Why didn't you just bring it—" Her phone rang and she glanced at the screen. It was the detective.

"Hello?"

"Mrs. Reynolds. We're at the house where the Instagram account originated. We've located the phone that was texting your daughter. It belongs to a man named Chase Sommers."

She had to bite her lip to keep from crying out. She saw Chase glance over at her from the corner of her eye. "Are you sure?"

"Yes, quite sure. Not only that, but we found your daughter's backpack in the house as well."

Annabelle's pulse raced. "So that means—"

"It appears as though Chase Sommers is the one who hit your daughter."

73

Scarlett

Dad and Olivia hadn't found her mother. Her dad kept trying her mother's cellphone.

"Maybe she went to get you something special," he said to Scarlett. Before she could answer, her grandparents walked into the hospital room, and she smiled as they approached the bed.

"Darling," Gram said. "Thank goodness you're awake." She kissed Scarlett on the cheek. Her grandfather went to the foot of her bed, picked up her chart, and read it. "Looks good," he said to James, then came over to her.

"You had us very worried, young lady!"

"Sorry, Grandad."

"Mom and Dad, would you take Olivia up to the cafeteria and get her something to eat?"

"Oh, okay," Gram said, looking surprised.

After they left, James pulled a chair up next to her. "Scarlett, I know you wanted to wait for Mom, but you need to tell me what happened. Who was this boy you thought you were texting? Who did you think you were meeting?"

She started to cry. "My brother."

"What are you talking about? You don't have a brother."

"Dad, I did the 23andMe test. I forged your signature on the waiver. It came back with a match to a sibling on Mom's side. She had another child before me. Did you know that?"

He was looking straight ahead, not speaking, a look of pure shock on his face.

"Dad? Did you know that?"

"It must be a mistake."

"I have the report. But it wasn't Ben at the café. It was some man. I don't understand. But there is someone out there who's my brother. I guess Mom gave him up for adoption or something."

"Your mom didn't give a baby up for adoption. But—" James stood up and started pacing. "The baby died."

"Why didn't you ever tell us? What happened?"

He sat back down on the bed and took her hands in his. "It was before your mom and I were married, and um . . . it was complicated. We were friends at the time. I was with her when she delivered. The baby died."

Scarlett shook her head. "That's just it. He couldn't have died. I found him!"

He put his head in his hands. "Oh, Scarlett. What have you done?"

Annabelle

It took everything Annabelle had not to react to the news that Chase was the one who had hit Scarlett. She had to get out of this car! But they were on the highway and she couldn't just jump out. She had to pretend everything was okay. She modulated her voice and acted as though she was talking with James. "I'm with Chase now. I'll ask him to bring me back to the hospital, James." She didn't end the call but turned the volume down. Maybe they could track her phone and find her. Or maybe she'd watched too many police shows on television. "That was James. I need to get back to the hospital right away. Something's going on with Scarlett," she bluffed.

She couldn't get a breath. She put the window down and leaned out to get some air. This couldn't be happening. How could she have so badly misjudged Chase? He'd made her feel so comfortable. She had poured her heart out to him, told him things she'd never even told James.

"Take me back, now!"

"Okay, okay. But we still need to talk about Lucas."

It took every ounce of restraint to keep her rage from spilling over and screaming at Chase. But she couldn't risk it. He'd manipulated his way into her life, and then tried to kill her daughter. He was capable of anything. She had to pretend that she didn't know. But he must have realized that once Scarlett was awake, she would tell Annabelle all about him. Was he going to hurt *her* now? She had to stall. *Think, think.* "Chase, why are you telling me this now about my son? And why did you go through the effort of hiring our company and getting to know me first? I don't understand."

"I wanted to make sure you were a good person before I told you. I love Lucas. Just because I found out he's not my biological son doesn't change the way I feel about him. But I didn't feel right not looking into it. I mean, he has a right to the truth, as much as it pains me."

How could she believe a word he said, knowing what she knew now. What kind of crazy person had she let into her life? Maybe the reason he was drawn to all those stories about psychopaths was because he was one.

She saw a flash of lights before she heard the siren. Gripping the seat, she did her best to appear unaware of what was about to happen. Chase adjusted the rearview mirror, looking behind him. "Was I speeding?"

He pulled over to the side of the road and two police cars pulled up behind them. An officer got out, approached the car, and indicated Chase should put his window down.

"What's wrong, Officer?" Chase asked.

"Please step out of the car, sir."

"What did I do?"

"Out of the car."

Chase opened his door and stepped out. Immediately the officer handcuffed him. Annabelle jumped out of her side and stood watching.

"Chase Sommers, you are under arrest for Evading Responsibility, Assault in the Second Degree with a Motor Vehicle, and Reckless Endangerment in the First Degree."

Annabelle's fear was suddenly replaced with rage and she stormed over to the other side of the car and stood in front of Chase.

"You hurt my daughter, you son of a bitch. How could you? I trusted you!"

"Annabelle, wait—"

She rushed toward the second police car, and the officer opened the door so that she could get in. "Are you okay, ma'am?"

She nodded.

"I'll take you back to the hospital now."

Annabelle was shaking as the implications of what she'd just learned hit her. The important thing was that Scarlett was safe now. But what if Chase was telling the truth about his son, and he was really *her* son? Had her son been living with a monster all these years?

Annabelle

James jumped up from his chair when Annabelle walked into the hospital room.

"I've been so worried! Where were you?" His eyes widened when he saw Detective Stanton walking in behind her.

"I'm fine." She looked over at Scarlett and back at James. She didn't want to frighten her daughter. "You're awake. How are you feeling, honey?"

"Okay."

"Detective Stanton wants to ask you a few questions. Is that okay?"

Scarlett nodded. The detective approached the bed and held out his phone. "Is this the man who you met at the café?"

"Yes, that's him."

"Can you tell me what happened after you met him?"

Scarlett looked up at the ceiling for a moment. "He knew my name. I realized he must have been pretending to be Ben. He had messaged me to meet him there on the same text chain we'd been using all along. So I guess I was never really talking to my brother. I freaked out and left, and he chased me. That's the last thing I remember."

"Chase Sommers is the man you believe was texting you?"

"I guess, if it wasn't my brother."

"Why were you using WhatsApp instead of regular text?"

"He emailed me and said we should move our chats to that app so it would be more secure. I thought I was talking to my half brother, and that he didn't want his parents to know that he knew the truth." She rubbed her eyes and yawned.

Annabelle was worried the questioning was taking a toll on her.

"Detective, I think she's had enough for now."

He nodded. "Okay, one last question. Did he threaten you in any way?"

"I don't know. It's kind of a blur."

"Okay, thank you. I'm very sorry for all you've been through." He turned to Annabelle and James. "Can I talk to you outside for a moment?"

They followed him out, and Annabelle closed the door to Scarlett's room.

"Mr. Sommers is being booked right now, but he'll most likely make bail. To be safe, I'm going to have a police officer stationed outside her door tonight. When is she being released?"

"We're not sure yet. But I'm staying here until she is," Annabelle said.

"Okay, good. This goes without saying, but please, if Mr. Sommers tries to contact you, don't speak to him."

"Of course she won't," James said, a vein bulging in his temple. "I'd like to kill that bastard!"

"James!" Annabelle shot him a look. What a thing to say in front of a police detective! "He doesn't mean that," she said.

"I understand," Stanton said. "Both of you keep your distance. Let us handle it."

"Detective Stanton, how do we find out if Chase's son is my biological child? Scarlett thinks his name is Ben, but it's Lucas. One way or the other, I have to know if my son is alive. Scarlett says she has a DNA report that shows she has a half brother."

The detective exhaled. "You should start by contacting the hospital. If you have evidence or a strong suspicion that it was intentional, we could open up an investigation."

"Okay, thank you."

After he walked away, James turned to Annabelle. "I cannot believe this is the man you've been flying off to California with! How could you not know he was a fraud? It's insane!"

She felt like she'd been punched. "Are you serious? How could I know? What are you accusing me of?"

He shook his head. "It's beyond . . ."

"Listen, I don't want you to say anything to Scarlett about Chase being the one who hit her. Let's wait until everything shakes out and she's stronger."

"What the hell? Are you protecting him now?"

"Of course not! I'm just saying, there are a lot of moving parts here, and we need to untangle them first. Including figuring out what the hell happened the night I gave birth. You were there. I don't understand how it's possible that my son is actually still alive."

"For all we know this guy hacked into the DNA site and made it look like he was a match to Scarlett. This whole thing could be an elaborate scam that targeted Scarlett," James said.

But something told Annabelle that James was wrong. She searched her memory about that night. The hospital had been short-staffed. The doctor on call had never arrived. Could James have been so overwhelmed that he put the wrong bracelets on the babies?

"Annabelle, did you hear me?" James's voice brought her back to the present.

"What?"

"I was talking to you."

She crossed her arms. "I don't think Chase made this up. He was going to show me his own test. Someone switched our babies."

"If you're right, then it must have been a mistake."

"Aren't there procedures in place to prevent that kind of a mistake? I distinctly remember an ID bracelet was put on him before he was brought to me. This had to be intentional. Do you have any idea who could have done this?"

James merely shook his head, but Annabelle could see it in his eyes. He was lying.

Scarlett

Her parents came back into the room. Her mom sat on the edge of the bed and took Scarlett's hand in hers. "Sweetheart, I wasn't truthful with you when you asked if there was someone special before Dad. There was, and I got pregnant. But he turned out not to be a good person. He lied to me and cheated on me. Your father was there to support me during the pregnancy, and we fell in love."

Scarlett felt sick to her stomach. Even though she already knew her mother had had a child before her, somehow it wasn't real until she heard it from her mother's mouth. It rocked her to her core. "So, you did give up a baby? How could you?"

"I didn't." She glanced at James. "I had complications and ended up with a C-section. Your dad actually delivered the baby."

"What? Dad's a neurologist."

Her mom shook her head. "He was an OB resident at the time. What ended up happening, well, it made him change specialties. I held my baby, and then I had a seizure. I had something called preeclampsia. When I came to again, that's when I learned that the baby had died." She blew out a breath. "Or so I thought."

"So did Chase steal your baby?"

"No, honey. I think he just found out too. I guess he was worried about losing his son, so he hired me to promote his podcast to get to know me first. Or at least that's what he told me."

"I can't believe you have another child. That I have a brother. I do have a brother, right?"

"We don't know, Scarlett," James answered. "This could all be some sort of scam. I don't know what that man wanted from you or why he was texting you, but the police will sort it out. I think we have to assume he's lying."

"But then why did I match with someone on the DNA test?"

"That's a very good question," her mom said. "We're going to find out, but for now, I want you to rest. And I'm sorry that you had to find all this out in this way."

"Why did you keep it a secret? Were you ashamed that you had sex before you were married? It is the twenty-first century, Mom."

"I wasn't ashamed, sweetie. I didn't see any reason to tell you, or at least not until you were older. I thought my son was dead. It was my own sorrow, and I didn't want you to have to bear it."

Scarlett guessed that made sense. Now she understood why there were times her mother seemed sad or far away. She realized it was always in the fall; that must have been when she had the baby. She thought of something else. "I found a letter you wrote. I thought you wrote it to an old boyfriend. Was it for your son?"

"Yes. I needed some sort of closure, I suppose."

She looked at her father. "Dad, it's kind of weird that you changed specialties because of what happened?"

He got a look on his face that Scarlett couldn't read. Her mother answered for him.

"It wasn't Dad's fault. He performed the C-section perfectly, but maybe he felt some sort of guilt over the baby dying, since he was the only doctor there. Is that right, James?"

His face turned red. "I don't want to revisit that horrible night. This isn't good for any of us to dredge up." He stormed out of the room.

Annabelle and Scarlett looked at each other. Scarlett rested her head back on the pillow.

"I wish it had been Ben I'd been texting. He seemed super cool. It's really creepy that it was his dad."

"His name is Lucas, not Ben. Chase used a fake name on the report until he could figure out who his son's biological parents were."

"I told him things I thought I was telling my brother. I feel really yucky now."

"I'm sorry, honey."

"Are you going to meet Lucas?"

"First things first. We need to figure out if he really is your brother."

Annabelle

Scarlett was being discharged that afternoon, and Annabelle had left and gone to the store to pick up all her favorites. James's parents were at the hospital with Scarlett and would wait there until Annabelle came back to pick her up. At their house, she grabbed the mail from outside and brought it in with her. After she unloaded the groceries, she sorted through the pile of mail and frowned when she came to a plain white envelope with her name and address. It looked as though the letters had been cut out from magazines or newspapers—like the ransom notes you see on television. She slid her thumb under the flap and opened it. A folded white paper was inside. She sucked in a breath when she saw what it was. A receipt printout from the Phoenix Motel for one night, paid in cash. The same place she'd dreamed she saw James with another woman. She looked at the date. A little less than a month ago. Did this mean that James *was* cheating on her? She was still holding the paper in her hand, trying to make sense of it all, when he walked in.

"I thought you had appointments this morning?" she said, surprised to see him.

"I had them rescheduled. I wanted to go with you to bring Scarlett home." He looked at her hand. "What's that?"

"Why don't you tell me?" Annabelle thrust it at him.

He took it from her. His eyes widened and then his face became a mask. "I have no idea. Where did you get this?"

"Someone mailed it to me. Are you having an affair? Because I dreamt that you were there with some woman."

"Come on, Annabelle. This is beyond getting old."

"I'm serious! What the hell is this? Did your girlfriend send it?"

"This is absurd! I have no idea who sent this. Someone paid cash for a room and mailed you a receipt. It proves nothing! I have no idea why you would dream it or who would send it. Someone is clearly trying to gaslight you. We've been through hell. Scarlett is finally coming home. Let's not fight."

She stood there, frozen. Why would she have seen him at that motel in her dreams? Something had to be going on. But she had no real proof. Anyone could have sent this. And as she'd learned, her dreams didn't always translate literally. But still, what did that motel have to do with them? James came closer and put his arms around her.

"I love you, Annabelle. You're my whole world. It's been so lonely here with only Olivia and me. I want my family back under one roof."

But her family was not complete. She moved back out of his arms and looked at him. "I can't stop thinking about Lucas. I've gone over that night in my head so many times, and it still makes no sense. Once I get Scarlett home and settled, I'm going to that hospital to figure out what happened."

"What good is that going to do? What's done is done. Isn't it more important to see where we go from here?"

Annabelle looked at James in perplexion. "What's done is done? What are you talking about? Someone has to be held accountable. My son was taken from me. How can you be so cavalier?"

He heaved a heavy sigh. "I was the doctor in charge that night. So whoever made the mistake, it's all going to come back on me. We've talked about this—it was a crazy night. It was a mistake, Annabelle. Let's just move forward. This could negatively affect my practice."

She stared at him for a long moment. She distinctly remembered watching them put the bracelet on her son. She'd even looked at it, a thrill running through her when she read the date. It was her mother's birthday. It had seemed like a good omen at the time. The only way the babies could have been switched was if someone had done it intentionally. "James, someone did it on purpose. There's no way that bracelet slid off."

He didn't answer.

Another thought occurred to her. "When Scarlett was born, you said something that struck me as odd, but I dismissed it." Her pulse quickened. "You said, *I'm happy to be the man who made you a mother.*"

"I don't remember, but if I did, so what? That means nothing."

"No, no. You were worried I'd take Randy back. You kept asking me about it. And then, after what happened, you took over, made me depend on you."

"Just let it go." His hands were balled into fists.

Annabelle's stomach tightened. It was all becoming clear. "Tell me the truth. It was you. Wasn't it?"

"You're crazy."

"Tell me the truth! I have a right to know!"

James scowled. "You were so ambivalent and worried about being a good mother. You kept talking about a do-over. How it wasn't the right time for you to have a child. You didn't want it! And they had lost so many children. They were dying for a child, and all you could do was whine about how you didn't think you'd be a good mother. I did it for you. And for us!" He was yelling now.

Her blood rushed to her head, and all she heard was a pounding in her ears. "How could you give them my baby?"

"Once I did it, there was no turning back. I thought, you know, you'd get over it. It seemed like fate. The Sommers family came in on the same night. She'd had so many miscarriages. They were so excited that she finally went full term. And then I delivered her baby, and I could tell he wasn't going to make it. I tried my best, but he died soon after he was born. Then you had that seizure, and you were out. They were both in the nursery, and something told me to do it. You weren't ready to be a mother, and she wanted nothing but to be a mother. Your mom was getting sicker, and she needed you. It wasn't the right time for you. Between taking care of your mother and trying to start a career, you were overwhelmed. It seemed like it would be a clean slate for you to start your life. And I knew you could have more. This was their last chance."

Annabelle was speechless. Immobilized. Almost outside of herself. But then she exploded. "How could you? You stole my child from me. You ripped my heart out, do you know that? Do you have any idea of how many nights I've cried for him? How empty I still feel? You can't decide to *give away* someone else's child. But you did! You had no right!" She pushed James, fury filling her as she looked at him, this man she'd spent all these years with, and realized he was a total stranger. "You comforted me. Swooped in and made me depend on you. You proposed shortly after, and I was so devastated and lost that I said yes. You took advantage of me!"

His face turned red, and his eyes bulged. "I saved you! You had nothing. I took you in, took care of you after that asshole cheated on you, and yet you still pined after him. *I* was the one who loved you, who wanted to give you a good life. But you were never grateful! I changed my career because of you! Everything I've ever done is because I love you, but all you can do is mourn the past. I've given you a wonderful life! I've given you the life you always wanted."

"No! It's the life *you've* always wanted! And now we almost lost Scarlett because of you. You're horrible! All these years, living with me, seeing what it did to me, and the whole time, you knew?" Annabelle was screaming now. "Get out! Get out! You're going to pay for this! I can't bear to even look at you!"

"I'm not going anywhere! This is my house. My family. You're not going to take it all away. You can't throw away our marriage over one mistake."

She scoffed. "Mistake? It was a deliberate act. You've deprived me of my child for all these years. How could you possibly think that I could stay with you after that?"

His demeanor changed again and James softened his voice. "Annabelle, please. I know it will take time, but you have to forgive me. Yes, I did a horrible thing, but I really thought it was the right thing at the time. And I've given you two other children."

Her mouth dropped open. "What are you saying? That it's okay that you took one child from me, because you replaced him with two? Are you out of your mind?"

"No, of course not. I'm just saying that I love you and our family, and I don't want to see you destroy everything over something that I deeply regret."

"I'm not the one who's destroyed everything. What you did is criminal. I've looked into it, James. Not only could you lose your medical license, but you could be arrested for kidnapping."

"Kidnapping! What are you talking about?"

"Yes, kidnapping. You kidnapped my baby when you took him and gave him to someone else."

"You can't be serious. You'd actually have me arrested? You can't do that! I'd lose my license, my liberty, everything. After I've dedicated my entire life to taking care of you . . . you would . . . you would do that?" The look in his eyes hardened. "I won't let you destroy everything I've worked so hard for."

"You're a monster. And you're going to pay."

He moved toward her and the menacing look on his face made Annabelle shrink back. His hands encircled her throat before she even registered movement. She was pinned between him and the counter. His fingers dug into her neck, cutting off her air.

"James! S-s-stop," she sputtered.

But it was as if he couldn't hear her. His fingers tightened, and she began to choke. She couldn't breathe. Frantically, she reached behind her and pulled a knife from the butcher block and swung her arm around ready to stab him. His eyes widened and he dropped his hands, backing away from her.

Her hands came up to her neck as she massaged it and continued to cough. He turned and walked out of the house.

The dream that started it all. Now she understood. She needed to call a lawyer.

Annabelle

James had been gone for two days and despite his pleas, Annabelle refused to see him. He'd begged and cried, swearing he had no idea what had happened to him to make him put his hands on her. But it had scared the hell out of her. She had no idea who he really was. How had she lived with him for all these years oblivious to his duplicity? She had already contacted a lawyer and asked him to draw up a separation agreement. She was going to use the threat of turning him in for kidnapping as leverage to get full custody. There was no way she was going to allow him to be alone with their children until she could be sure he wasn't dangerous. She could still feel his hands on her neck. It was surreal! She hadn't told the girls the truth, but they knew that something terrible had happened between their parents. The atmosphere at their house was somber.

Chase's wife was on her way over to talk to Annabelle. She had called Annabelle last night, and they'd talked for over an hour on the phone. Chase was out on bail, and Tara had told Annabelle she'd asked him to move out.

The doorbell rang. Annabelle took a deep breath and walked into the hallway. She opened the door and looked at the woman standing there. Tara's pictures hadn't done her justice. She was stunning and exuded an effortless elegance. Silky blond hair framed her face in loose waves down to her shoulders. The stylish black frames she wore only accented her cornflower-blue eyes. Clad in dark jeans and a form-fitting top, Tara looked like she could grace the cover of a fashion magazine.

"Come in," Annabelle said, not sure how to greet this woman who had been raising her son.

Tara held out a slender hand, and Annabelle gave it an awkward shake. "Shall we go to the kitchen? I made a pot of coffee."

"Sure," Tara said, following her.

"Thank you for coming over," Annabelle started. "I know this is a difficult situation for everyone. I don't quite know where to begin." She brought a tray over with the coffee, cream, and sugar and poured a cup for Tara.

Tara pursed her lips. "It's been a nightmare. I haven't told Lucas the truth yet. It's been enough trying to deal with Chase being arrested and—" She pulled a tissue from her purse and dabbed her eyes, sniffing. "I'm sorry. I'm still grappling with all this myself."

"Of course. Did Chase say why he hit Scarlett? What did he hope to gain?" Annabelle still couldn't understand how he could have done it. "Was it intentional?"

Tara put the tissue back in her purse and leveled a stare at Annabelle. "My husband is not a good man."

Annabelle's eyebrows shot up.

Tara shook her head. "I really thought he had changed. I'll bet he charmed you. Made you feel like he understood you like no one else. He's good at that."

"Well, I—" Annabelle didn't know how to respond.

Tara put her hand up. "It's okay. It's not your fault. He's a master manipulator. He's done it before, with another woman he worked with a few years back. We almost split up, but he swore he would devote himself to Lucas and to me. In my line of work, I see what divorce does to families." She took a sip of her coffee. "Were you in love with him?"

Annabelle was taken aback. Had she been? "I don't know. I mean, nothing happened. We were just friends, but I felt like he understood me in a way no one has in a long time."

"Emotional affair?"

"Does it matter now? The man almost killed my daughter." Annabelle felt herself getting angry. "I didn't have an affair with your husband, okay? I never would have. We bonded over our shared grief. Losing children." She shook her head. "Or at least I thought we had. Now I know he's a con man. Is it even true that you had those late pregnancy losses?"

Tara bit her lip and looked down at the table. "He was telling the truth about that. But I don't think he really cared. I went through the grieving process with no support from him." Annabelle wanted to ask her how she could have stayed with a man like that, but she refrained. "You have a family law practice, right?" Annabelle asked instead, even though she had looked her up and knew she did.

Tara nodded. "Yes. I only represent women. I've got a reputation for making men pay. So, Chase knew that. I will say, the only thing he cares about is Lucas. He said that your daughter was going to ruin everything. His plan was to seduce you into being with him, and then disclose the truth. That way he could keep Lucas. He wouldn't have to worry about me fighting for custody. Since Lucas is your biological child, you'd have the right to custody. Chase was trying to string Scarlett along to keep her quiet until he made you fall for him. But Scarlett kept texting that she wanted to ask you about it. He was afraid she would tell you everything before he had time to fully work his charm on you."

Annabelle was aghast. "He admitted that to you?"

"Our marriage is over. And he doesn't care about me. I see now that the only reason he stayed was because of Lucas."

Then Tara went on. "He claims that he didn't mean to hit Scarlett—he was going after her to try to convince her to keep his secret. But I mean, the fact that he just left her there—"

Annabelle felt her rage bubble up again. "He left her to die.

What if no one had seen her and called 911? He's a monster." She found it hard to believe that Tara could have no idea what kind of man Chase was. "You must have seen signs. A normal person doesn't behave that way."

"It was hard to live with the cheating, but I loved him. He's got this ability to make you feel like you're the most important person in the world. I've known him since college, and he's always been able to charm his way out of anything. I had no idea he was capable of this kind of subterfuge. Pretending to be someone else, stringing your poor daughter along."

"Where is he now?" Annabelle asked.

"I would have let him rot in jail, but my parents insisted on paying the bail for Lucas's sake. He's staying at a hotel for now."

"I hate the fact that he's out there."

"Well, the reason I wanted to come over is about Lucas. I know you want to meet him, but for his sake, I'm asking you to give me some time to break this to him."

"Yes, of course. I want only what's best for him. But you have to understand how hard this is for me. How long are you thinking?"

"I don't know, Annabelle. I really need to talk to his therapist first. He's already traumatized by his father's arrest. I'm sure you don't want him to have a breakdown. Lucas suffers from anxiety already."

"He's in therapy?"

"Yes, as I said, for anxiety. It's very common with young people these days. Anyway, I need to find the right time and the right way. You're a mother; you understand."

"Are you sure keeping him in the dark is the right approach? I would think explaining the reason why his father did what he did would make things a bit easier for him, rather than thinking his dad tried to hurt some random girl. How have you explained it to him?"

Tara pursed her lips. "I haven't really. I take your point. Give me a day or two. Can you do that?"

"Yes, of course."

Tara stood up. "One more thing. Lucas's biological father. Do you know where he is?"

Randy. She hadn't spoken to him since the day she found him in bed with that woman. He had no right to Lucas, had bowed out when she was pregnant. If he had any desire to see his child, he would have gotten in touch a long time ago.

"The father's not an issue. He didn't want to be involved."

"Well, that's something at least. Have you told your daughters that James switched our babies, speaking of disclosing the truth to our children?"

"No. I—we, I guess—have to figure out what we're going to do. If I report him, then of course I need to tell them. But I need a little time to figure it all out."

"I'll follow your lead. You're the more injured party. As devastating as this is, if James hadn't done it, I wouldn't have had these years with Lucas."

It hit Annabelle again. How much she'd missed. How different her life was from how it should have been. She began to cry. What a mess this all was. Thinking about telling her own children the truth shone a light on Tara's concerns. And poor Tara, she couldn't even imagine how she must be feeling. She was Lucas's mother. Just because he wasn't biologically hers, she was no less of a mother to Lucas than Annabelle was to Scarlett and Olivia. Even so, Annabelle had mourned her son all these years and knowing he was alive and well, there was nothing that could keep her from wanting to know him. "I think you're right. We all need some time. I want you to know that I have no intention of trying to take Lucas from you. When you're ready to tell him, I don't want him to be afraid to meet me. You can let him know how much I've missed him, and that I just want to meet him and hopefully forge a relationship. I'm not going to do anything to hurt him. Or you," she added.

Tara blinked away tears. "The courts will likely agree that he's old enough to make a custody decision on his own. He's thriving and happy with us and they'd be reluctant to uproot him. But I'm happy to hear that you're not thinking of a legal battle. I can't tell you how much that means to me."

Annabelle was taken aback. So Tara had already thought this all through. And being a family attorney, who would know better? Annabelle had no intention of fighting for custody but she didn't like the way Tara made it sound like she had no rights at all. She couldn't bear the thought that now that she had found out her son was actually alive, she could lose him all over again.

79

The Wife—Tara

"I want to go see Dad," Lucas says for the tenth time. What is it with this kid? His dad gets arrested, and he still thinks he hangs the moon. I'm so tired of Chase being everyone's darling.

"Let's sit down. I wasn't going to tell you this yet, but I think you have a right to know."

His brow furrows as he pulls up a chair at the kitchen table.

"Your dad hit that young girl with his car and left her there to die."

Lucas shakes his head. "You're lying! Dad told me he didn't have anything to do with that. He swears he only went to talk to her."

I reach out to take his hand, but he snatches it back. "Lucas, listen to me. The police found her backpack in his home office. He had a phone where he was texting her, pretending to be you."

Confusion fills his face. "No. That doesn't make any sense. Why would he do that?"

It was all going to come out soon, so she may as well get it over with. "There's no easy way to tell you this. Something happened the night you were born. There was another woman there that night. She thought her baby died, but it turns out that our babies were switched. The girl Dad was texting is your half sister."

I can see him trying to process my words, but I'm not sure they're sinking in. He shakes his head. "Wait, you mean, you're not my real mother?"

"Of course I'm your mother. I raised you, and I love you. But, no, I'm not your biological mother. Dad found out when you gave blood. Your blood type is incompatible with ours."

The sixteen-year-old sitting across from me regresses to the child he used to be and begins to cry. I stand up and put my arms around him. "Dad and I love you. That's never going to change."

"Will I have to go live with someone else? I don't want to!"

"No, I've spoken to her. She's not going to pursue any legal action, and you're old enough that the courts will respect your wishes. But she does want to meet you when you're ready."

"I don't know." He's sobbing now. "I don't know."

"Shh, it's okay."

"I want to talk to Dad."

I bite my lip before I can say something I'll regret. "Okay. Go call your dad."

80

Annabelle

It had been two weeks since Tara had come to the house. Annabelle had thought of nothing else but Lucas.

She was tired of waiting. She picked up her phone and called her.

"Hi, Annabelle," Tara answered.

"Tara, I'm trying to be patient, but this is killing me. I need to see my son."

She heard a sigh on the other end of the line. "I was going to call you. I've spoken to Lucas. He doesn't want to meet you."

Annabelle's breath caught. "What did you tell him?"

"The truth. But he says he's not ready. I'm doing my best to talk him into it, but his therapist says I need to let him go at his own pace. His entire world has been thrown upside down. I promise I'll keep trying."

What could Annabelle say? She wasn't about to force Lucas. She hadn't told the authorities that James had switched the babies because she wanted to protect Scarlett and Olivia. She didn't want her children to see their father in prison, so she would go along with the lie that it had been a hospital mix-up. She thought of Lucas having to deal with Chase's arrest. Tara was right: It was too much. She had to give Lucas time.

"Can we meet for coffee?" Annabelle asked.

"Um, okay. I'll meet you at Sugar's in an hour."

After getting off the phone, Annabelle scrolled through Lucas's Facebook page again, riveted to the images in front of her. He was a beautiful boy. *Her* beautiful boy. Her heart ached to know him. Light brown hair and brown eyes specked with gold—like her mother's. He had Annabelle's nose, Randy's smile. Tall and lanky, yet with none of the typical teenage awkwardness. He seemed like a popular kid, but not stuck-up, at least from what she could tell on his page. She'd been surprised he even had a Facebook account, but Tara told her that he had one so he could access his basketball team's page where important info was shared. He also had an Instagram, but it was set to private, so Annabelle couldn't see what he posted there. She suspected he was much more active on that platform, as most kids were these days. He didn't post often, but there were pictures of him with basketball teammates, friends at a barbecue at the beach, as well as some family photos with Chase and Tara. She stopped at one of the three of them celebrating Lucas's most recent birthday at a restaurant and felt a pain in her chest. He should have been celebrating all those milestones with her.

Chase's image made her seethe. It all came rushing back—the way he'd drawn her out, making her feel like they had so much in common. How he'd faked his grief over losing those babies. All a facade. He must have ice in his veins. To be the reason Scarlett was in the hospital and then call every day to check on her. It was mind-boggling. She was so full of anger, and she had nowhere to put it.

Taking a deep breath, she tried to calm herself. Annabelle closed her laptop and left the house to meet Tara.

* * *

TARA WAS ALREADY SEATED, LOOKING at something on her phone when Annabelle arrived at Sugar's. She put the phone down on the table and stood up as Annabelle approached, leaning over to give her a hug.

"I got you a coffee and a muffin. You look like you need to eat something," Tara said, smiling.

Annabelle sat down. "Thanks. I haven't had much of an appetite lately. How're you doing? I saw the article in the paper about Chase. I hope it hasn't negatively impacted you too much."

Tara shrugged. "Some of my clients have dropped me, but what can you do? Everyone loves a salacious story. They're making him out to be some sort of pedophile with the texting thing. It's been hard." She sniffed and brought a tissue to her face, dabbing at her eyes. "I don't care for myself so much, but poor Lucas."

"I'm sorry. This is so unfair. People can be so cruel."

Tara's lip trembled. "I'm grateful that I've found a friend in this." She grabbed Annabelle's hand and squeezed it. "Your support means so much to me. And I can't tell you how much it takes the pressure off, your deciding not to do anything official in terms of Lucas." Annabelle had spoken to her lawyer, who had strenuously advised her to seek legal status as Lucas's biological mother, but she didn't have the heart to do it. She kept imagining how she would feel if the situation were reversed, and she had to give up legal custody of Scarlett or Olivia. Or how Lucas would feel if he had to leave the person who'd been his mother all these years. And Tara seemed to have been a good mother. It wasn't her fault that James had switched the babies. Both their husbands had done horrible things, and it wouldn't do any good for them to be at odds with each other. They needed to stick together. "We've both been betrayed by our husbands. We have to support each other."

Tara took a sip of her coffee. "I appreciate that. This has been particularly hard on Lucas. All this publicity has caused problems at school. Honestly, I'm thinking it might be wise to move."

Annabelle's heart skipped a beat. "Move? Where?"

"Oh, not move. Just take a little break. My parents have a house in Paris, and I was thinking maybe I'd take him there for the rest of the school year. To let him get away from all this and get a reset. Homeschool him."

"Um, that seems extreme." She couldn't let Tara take Lucas out of the country. "Tara, listen, I know I said I wouldn't take any legal action, but I don't think it's a good idea for you to take him to Paris right now. Surely you can understand that."

"It was only a thought. Living in such a small town makes it even harder. You must understand how awful this is for Lucas."

"It's awful for all of us. But you can't run away from the problem."

Tara was about to speak when a woman rushed by and knocked her tote bag from the back of her chair. All the contents were scattered across the floor. Tara's face turned red, and she jumped up. "Watch where you're going!" she yelled, then murmured under her breath, "Idiot."

Annabelle was taken aback by the comment. She leaned down to help her.

"Are you okay?" Annabelle asked.

"Yeah, fine. Just wish people were more careful." She gave Annabelle a bright smile.

They sat back down. "Where were we?" Tara asked, her good humor seemingly restored.

"I was saying I don't think you should go to Paris right now."

Tara waved a hand. "Oh, right. Don't worry, it was just an idea."

But Annabelle was worried. She had a bad feeling. She had to be careful, though. Even if she decided to assert her claim, it would take time. And if she made Tara angry, nothing was stopping her from taking Lucas and leaving the country. "I'm sorry. I'm being insensitive. Maybe some time away would be good, but can you wait a little bit? I'd really like to meet him before he's away for an extended period. Could you try again with him?"

Tara smiled. "Of course."

They finished their coffee and walked outside, saying goodbye. Annabelle went to her car and slid behind the wheel. The next thing she did was make another call to her lawyer. There must be something she could do.

81

Annabelle

Ever since her coffee date with Tara yesterday, Annabelle had been uneasy. Her lawyer was ready to initiate the paperwork to compel a legal DNA test to assert Annabelle's parental rights. The DNA test that Scarlett had taken should be enough to convince the court to do the test. If not, then she would have to implicate James and tell the court that he had admitted to switching the babies. That would bring criminal charges against him, which would be terrible for Scarlett and Olivia, but in the end, Annabelle would do whatever she had to do to prove that Lucas was her son. He had a right to know her, just as she did to know him. And she couldn't sit back and do nothing while Tara took him away.

Their first move was to file a motion prohibiting Tara from taking Lucas out of the country. After Annabelle's meeting with the lawyer this afternoon, everything would be set in motion. She had a splitting headache and decided to lie down for a while. Stretching out on the sofa, she pulled the fleece blanket up to her chin and closed her eyes.

I'm inside someone's house, in a large hallway. It's a big house; everything is white, and nothing is out of place. My heels click on the marble floor as I walk from the hallway into a living room where large

French doors lead out to a stone terrace. I glance at the walls. Black framed professional photos: Chase, Tara, and Lucas. I'm in their house. I walk over to one wall to peer more closely at the picture, my heart clenching as I drink in the image of Lucas. I hear a woman's voice, and I walk toward it, up the stairs, down the hall, to a room that looks like a home office.

It's Tara. I call out to her, but she doesn't hear me. I approach her, but she can't see me either. She's on a laptop, and I peer over her shoulder. She's searching for how to purchase a prepaid smartphone. It takes her to a link. I watch as she puts in Chase's name and credit card information. Everything goes dark. I blink and she's holding a phone, texting. She's texting Scarlett. She begins to laugh.

"Stupid girl. So gullible."

The scene changes. I'm outside a rental car agency. I follow Tara in and watch as she completes the paperwork. I glance at the contract. It's in her name. She goes out and gets into a white BMW, the same model Chase drives.

Another transition. Now we're sitting in the car outside the coffee shop. Scarlett runs out, crying, and jumps on her bike. We follow behind her and when she turns down the alley, we speed up. We're going to hit her. I yell, Stop! Stop! But Tara ignores me. We get closer, and I shut my eyes before I feel the impact of the car slamming into my daughter.

Annabelle sprang up. It was Tara all along! She placed a call to Chase's cellphone.

"Annabelle?"

"Chase! It was Tara. She set you up!"

"What? What are you talking about?"

"I saw her. In a dream. She rented a car just like yours. We can get the rental receipt. There would have been damage to the car. We need to stop her! She's threatening to take Lucas to Paris."

82

The Wife—Tara

It does my heart good to see Chase suffering. I act like the devoted wife, sitting by his side at the defense attorney's office as he professes his innocence. He keeps claiming he has no idea how that backpack got into his office, or where the phone with all the incriminating messages came from. He swears all he did was answer Scarlett's initial email when she first got the DNA report, and the next time he had contact with her was when he got an email from her asking to meet him at the coffee shop. Of course, he doesn't know that the email asking him to meet her was really from me posing as Scarlett. It's so easy to make a Gmail account in anyone's name.

I nodded along, holding his hand, telling him I believed him and would stick by him through this terrible ordeal. Because of course, I do believe him. I know he's innocent. Well, innocent of the charges against him. But not innocent of betraying me and our family.

Ever since Chase almost left me all those years ago, I regularly monitor his emails and his texts. He uses the same tired code: Lucas's birthday month and day. So, when I saw the email that Scarlett had sent him saying she was a DNA match, I started digging. This time it was worse than I feared. Not only was Chase sidling up to another woman, but the idiot had gone and done a DNA test on our son. If he hadn't done that, Scarlett would never have known she had a brother. But Chase ticked the box allowing contact from any matches. It didn't take me long to dig through all his research into the hospital and see what he had discovered—the babies had been switched. Why hadn't he come to me first? I knew he must have been devastated. The way he fusses over Lucas, constantly considering him before anything else, makes me sick. The two of them, peas in a pod, so happy together; they're always laughing at the same jokes, sharing the same taste in food and sports. I always felt like a third wheel. It's why I never wanted kids. *I* was supposed to be the most important person in Chase's life, the sun around which he orbits.

I couldn't tell him that though. A child was the carrot I used to get Chase from the beginning. I faked my pregnancy right before college graduation, when I could tell he was getting ready to break up with me. I knew he'd never leave his child—not the way his father had left him. It wasn't hard to pretend to have morning sickness, to buy a fake bump, and then to have that devastating miscarriage at five months. I acted like I hated my body getting bigger and couldn't bear for him to see me naked, so it was easy to fool him. He was so sympathetic afterward, worried about my well-being and happiness— as he should have been. But then he wanted to try again, and I had to pretend to be sad each month when I got my period even though I was on the pill. He wanted to see a fertility specialist, so I had to pretend to be pregnant again. After so many "miscarriages," he didn't dare ask me to try again. The only reason I finally got pregnant for real was because he was ready to leave me for another woman. And now he's jeopardized everything.

After I found the paperwork Chase was hiding that showed that Lucas was not our biological son, I pretended that I had no idea about the switch. That I was just as devastated by the truth, after everything came out when he was arrested. I confronted him about why he did the test in the first place, and I was dumbfounded by his answer.

"I thought you had cheated on me. That you'd gotten pregnant by someone else," he said.

"That's a laugh! You're the one with the wandering eye. Why would you think I cheated?"

He told me about Lucas's blood type not matching ours. "I checked the box to be contacted by any genetic matches, because I wanted to know who his father was. But then it came back with a maternal match, and that's when I realized he wasn't related to either of us."

"Why couldn't you just leave well enough alone?" I screamed at him.

"I would have. But then Scarlett contacted me. I stalled, told her I needed time to think. She thought she was emailing Lucas. So I did some research. I asked someone good at hacking computers to see who else was at the hospital that night. And that's when I realized what had happened."

My blood is boiling. He's so stupid. "You should have just ignored her. She would have had no way to find you. And it doesn't matter that Lucas isn't ours biologically. He's old enough that the courts would never have taken him from us."

"But it's not right! All I could think about was how I'd feel if I'd been the one to have my child taken. His mother has a right to know. I had to see what she was like, if she was a good person. If she wasn't, then maybe I would have ignored Scarlett, left well enough alone. But Annabelle is a good person. I couldn't allow her to keep thinking her son was dead. And we owe the truth to Lucas too. He has siblings. When I got an email from Scarlett asking me to meet her, I was going there to ask her to give me time to tell Annabelle the truth, but then she ran from the coffee shop. I didn't hit her. I swear."

"Well, someone did. And they have a lot of evidence against you."

"You have to believe me, Tara. I didn't do it."

"Don't lie to me, Chase. You thought you and Annabelle would ride off into the sunset with my son? Make a new little family of your own?"

"No. I was just—"

"Save it. Doesn't matter now. But why did you have to hurt that poor girl?" I asked, relishing his pain, when I was the one who'd done it all along. The phone, the backpack. It was all me. I lured him to the coffee shop that day using the fake Gmail account in her name. Chase had never been texting that brat. I had been. Using a phone purchased with his credit card. I texted Scarlett and asked her to meet me there. I thought she would at least talk to him, listen to what he had to say. I was always planning to hit her and frame him. I was surprised that she came out so quickly. I followed her in the rental car. It was easy to hit her, grab the backpack, and drive off. Later that night, I damaged Chase's front bumper; I'd lied and said I was low on gas and borrowed it to go to the grocery store. I pretended someone had hit me in the parking lot. I promised to get repair estimates and work with the "woman" to have it fixed. Then I had everything I needed to teach my treacherous husband a lesson.

Chase had nothing to do with it. But no one will believe him; I made sure of that. And if that bitch, Annabelle, thinks she's ever going to see Lucas, she's sadly mistaken. I told Lucas that Annabelle had switched the babies because she never wanted him. That she had always wanted girls. It's a preposterous lie, but it's amazing what a vulnerable sixteen-year-old will believe. He probably *will* need therapy now. I was lying when I told Annabelle that he was seeing someone for anxiety. He's been a happy kid all his life. But I guess that will change. Now that his whole world has fallen apart. I have to make sure they never meet, that he sees Annabelle as the enemy. By the time I'm done, he'll have to depend on me even more. I can't lose him. I'll never lose him now. With Chase in prison, it will just be the two of us. I'll no longer be the outsider looking in. I should have never shown Annabelle my hand about leaving the country. There's no time now. We need to go. I'll gather up the passports, pull out the suitcases, and begin packing. Our flight leaves in two days, and then she'll never find us.

83

Annabelle

Annabelle couldn't stop apologizing to Chase. "I don't know what to say. Tara was so convincing. I'm so sorry I believed all those terrible things about you."

They'd met with his lawyer yesterday. Chase came by the house this morning. His attorney had filed an emergency motion for sole custody to preclude Tara from taking Lucas out of the country, based on the suspicion of her being involved in the hit-and-run. They were hoping to hear something today.

"Thank you for understanding why I didn't tell you who I was right away. Lucas already had one troubled mother. I needed to make sure I didn't throw him from the frying pan into the fire."

"I don't like being lied to, of course. But in your case, I do understand. Maybe if everything else hadn't happened, I'd be angry at you, but right now the only thing I care about is that Scarlett's okay, and that my son is alive. Let's hope the D.A. will drop the charges when your lawyer presents him with the rental car evidence. Tara's name is on that rental agreement." She rolled her eyes. "For once, I'm grateful for these dreams."

"Like he said, it will be important to see if the car was damaged, and if they have all those records."

"Try Lucas again," Annabelle said. Chase had been trying to reach him all morning.

Chase took out his phone and swiped, putting it to his ear. He looked at Annabelle. "Right to voicemail. He must have it turned off while he's in school. I'll send him a text." He did so and then put the phone down.

Annabelle couldn't shake the feeling that her son was going to slip through her fingers if they didn't do something fast. "Do you think the order will come through today? What if they've already left the country?"

"I called my attorney this morning, and he said they'll serve her either this afternoon or first thing tomorrow morning. She won't be able to leave."

"I think you should go to your house. I'm worried. What if she's taking him today?"

"My lawyer told me to keep my distance from her. I don't want to do anything to jeopardize her arrest. They have all the information from the rental car company, and he's meeting with the D.A. now." He looked at his watch. "Lucas isn't getting out of school for another half an hour. I'll go to the school and try to stop him before he gets on the bus."

84

The Wife—Tara

"Why did you pick me up early?" Lucas says as he gets in the car. "I have basketball practice."

"I have a surprise. We're going to see Gamma and Poppy. I've booked us a flight to Paris."

His mouth drops open. "I'm not going to Paris!"

This kid! Why can't he ever do what I ask? "Lucas, come on! Do you really want to be around for your father's trial? It's going to be a circus. This is for your own good. It's just for a little while."

"I'm not abandoning Dad. I don't care what you say. I believe him. There's no way he would hit someone and then take off. Besides, I've done some thinking. I want to meet her."

"But she didn't want you! Why do you want to meet her?"

Confusion fills his face. "How do you know that?"

I grab my phone and toss it to him. "Her number's in there, under Annabelle Reynolds. I've been to her house. We've met for coffee too. She said she wasn't going to file for custody. That she wants nothing to do with you. She has her perfect life with her two daughters and her husband, who had no idea she got knocked up before she was married. She doesn't want anyone to know. Call her if you don't believe me."

Lucas's face turns red. "I'm still not going to fucking Paris! I won't leave Dad."

I resist the urge to slap his face. My heart is beating so fast, it feels like it will erupt from my chest. This little shit. He's so ungrateful. I've sacrificed time and money raising him, and this is how he treats me. "You're still a minor. You have no say in the matter. Your father is going to prison for a long time. I'm your legal guardian, and you will do what I say, or I will take away your phone, your computer, and lock you up in this house until you're eighteen." I pull up to the house and slam on the brakes. "Now go pack. We're leaving here in an hour."

"I hate you!" he yells as he storms away.

"Join the club," I whisper under my breath.

85

Scarlett

"So now you know his real name," Avery said, scrolling on her phone. "Here's his real Instagram profile. I followed him, and he followed me right back."

She handed the phone to Scarlett. Scarlett studied Lucas's picture, looking for any similarity to herself. There was something familiar about him. His eyes, that was it. She glanced at his posts and saw that he had lots of friends—playing different sports, and then some pictures with some guys on the golf course. She clicked on a picture of him, Chase, and a woman. She looked kind of glamorous, all made up and in fancy clothes. Scarlett guessed that was his mom—the woman who'd been texting her. Her mom had told her who was really behind everything. It made Scarlett mad all over again.

"You should follow him too," Avery said. "Maybe you guys could meet up for real."

"I don't know. What if he doesn't want to talk to me?"

"Your mom said he knows, right? But he's not ready to meet her. It might be easier for him to meet you. Less pressure."

Scarlett thought about that. She was dying to meet her brother, but after everything that had happened, she didn't think she could take it if he rejected her. Even though she knew it wasn't him she'd been talking to, it still felt like the relationship had been real and then ripped away from her. Scarlett handed the phone back to her.

"Come on. What've you got to lose?" Avery persisted.

Scarlett picked up her phone, navigated to Instagram, and typed in "Lucas Sommers." She took a deep breath. *Here goes nothing,* she thought as she clicked the follow button. She looked at Avery. "Done." Seconds later her phone notifications lit up. "He accepted it!"

"See?" Avery said. "I bet he's as curious about you as you are about him. Send him a message and see if you can meet."

Scarlett began to type.

86

Annabelle

Annabelle paced as she waited to hear from Chase. She had wanted to go with him to pick up Lucas, but Chase was right; this wasn't the way to meet him for the first time. Her phone rang and she jumped. Chase.

"Hey! Did you pick him up?" she asked.

"He wasn't there. I'm heading to the house now. Tara picked him up early."

"Shit! I knew it. I have a bad feeling, Chase. Can the police call airports? Alert them?"

"She's not a fugitive. I don't have any legal recourse until they serve her. Hopefully, they're still at the house. I'll call you back."

Annabelle put down the phone and tried to take a deep breath. She was pumped full of adrenaline with no way to release it. She had to do something; she couldn't just sit here and wait. She was going crazy. She knew Chase's address. Before she could talk herself out of it, she grabbed her purse and ran to her car.

TWENTY MINUTES LATER, SHE PULLED up to the house and saw that Chase's car was parked in the driveway. He and Tara were in the front yard, and Tara was yelling. Annabelle flung her car door open and ran over to them.

"What's going on? Where's Lucas?"

Tara turned toward her, hatred in her eyes, then back to Chase. "What's she doing here?"

"I want to know where my son is!" Annabelle said.

"He's not your son. *I* raised him! You'll never get him!" She poked her finger into Chase's chest. "Tell your whore to get out of here, before I have her arrested for trespassing."

It took everything in Annabelle's power to hold herself back from striking the woman who had tried to kill her daughter. Tears of fury and helplessness spilled to her cheeks. "You're vile! What kind of a mother would do what you did!"

Tara sprang toward her, her fist reaching out to hit Annabelle, but Chase jumped in front of her. "Where's Lucas?" he yelled.

She looked at him with dead eyes. "He's gone."

87

The Wife—Tara

"What do you mean, he's gone?" Chase yells, his face inches from mine. I take my time answering, enjoying the look of fear in that bitch's eyes.

I give Chase a bored look. "He took off on his bike. He said he needed to get some air. He was upset about all this trial stuff. He'll be home later, and I'll have him call you. For now, get the hell out of here."

I don't tell them the truth. That the little sneak snuck out. I went to check on him half an hour ago, and he wasn't in his room. I went to the garage and saw that his bike was gone. I finished packing his suitcase, and I'll be picking him up as soon as these two get out of here. The air tag under his bike seat keeps me posted on his every move. He's at a park a few miles from here. Maybe he went there to cool off or to meet a friend. It doesn't matter. His ass is getting on that plane with me.

The two of them look at each other, and I see red. Already coconspirators? Let's see how long she waits for him once he's given a prison sentence.

"What are you waiting—"

My words are cut off by the sound of a police siren. What's going on? The car stops in front of the house, and two men get out and walk toward us.

"Mrs. Tara Sommers?"

"It's Tara Winters," I correct him.

"Winters," he corrects himself. "You're under arrest for the hit-and-run of Scarlett Reynolds."

What is this fool talking about? "My husband did that. Not me!"

"Also, for perjury and making a false report to law enforcement. Please put your hands behind your back."

He slaps handcuffs on me. Annabelle comes toward me, her eyes narrowed. "We know it was you. You tried to kill my child and then frame Chase. You're a psychopath!"

How did they know? Someone is going to pay.

88

Annabelle

Annabelle sat on a bench at the beach and gazed ahead at the water. It was unseasonably warm for late November, and she relished the feel of the sun on her face. She had suggested meeting here, somewhere neutral, somewhere with no walls, a space where neither of them would feel closed in. She was giddy with anticipation, and her pulse raced with anxiousness. She looked up as a figure in a white hoodie and blue jeans approached from the shoreline. She held her breath for a moment, waiting to see if it was him. As he got closer, she saw that it was Lucas. Her son. It took everything she had not to run toward him and pull him into her arms, but she held herself back. He stopped a few feet from where she sat.

"Are you Annabelle?" he asked.

That hurt, even though, of course, he wouldn't call her Mom. She nodded. "Hi, Lucas. Thank you for coming." She rose. "Shall we walk?"

He nodded, and together they moved closer to the water and strolled for a few moments in silence. Finally, she spoke. "I know this isn't easy for you. I'm so sorry for everything you're going through with your mother."

"It's not your fault. I still can't believe what she did. I'm just really glad my dad was cleared. She told me that you didn't want me. That you were the one who switched the babies. But Dad told me your husband did it."

What other lies had that hateful woman spun? "I would never have done that. I had no idea you were alive. I have missed you every day of my life, Lucas. Losing you was the worst thing that ever happened to me. I want you to know how much I love you."

He looked over at her and held her eyes. "Scarlett showed me the letter you wrote to me. I went to meet her the day Mom was trying to take me to Paris."

She was touched. Scarlett was doing everything in her power to make them a family. She had been the one to convince Lucas to finally agree to meet Annabelle.

"Can I be honest with you, Lucas?"

"Yeah."

"It's so hard for me not to give you a big hug. I know I'm a stranger to you, but I was the first person to ever hold you. And I loved you from the moment I saw you. When I look at you now, I see my mother in your eyes. And I feel such a pull."

They both stopped walking and stood looking at each other. Finally, he nodded. "Okay."

"Okay?" she asked.

"You can give me a hug."

She put her arms around him, but his hung by his side. Tears sprang to her eyes and she was filled with warmth. Slowly he lifted his arms and hugged her back. She held on until he let go, not wanting to be the first to pull away.

"Thank you," she said. They started to walk again.

"Are you going to take me from my dad?" he asked.

"No, sweetheart. I'm not going to do anything to make you unhappy. I would love, though, to be able to see you sometimes. And I'd love for you to get to know your sisters. Do you think that's possible?"

"Do you mean like partial custody?"

"No, nothing formal. I meant if you could come over and hang out sometimes. I mean, of course, you are welcome anytime and if you ever wanted to spend more time, we would love that." She didn't want him to think she didn't want him. "We want to see you as much as you want, and you don't have to decide anything right now."

Annabelle could see the relief on Lucas's face, and it pained her. The last thing she wanted was for him to dread her or be afraid of her. "It's going to take awhile for things to settle down. But your dad and I can work everything out between us."

"I love my dad. I'm sorry for all you've been through, but I want to keep living with him. I hope you get that. I'm not trying to be mean or anything, but I don't know you."

She realized it was unrealistic for her to have expected him to feel an immediate bond simply because of their genetic one. She had known about him. Had carried him, held him when he was born, thought about him over all these years. How would Scarlett or Olivia react if they were in his shoes? "I understand. I would never try to take you from your father. I'm only hoping you have room in your heart for more family."

"I need some time to figure it all out. I told Scarlett we could hang out sometimes, and I do want to meet Olivia. I've always wanted a brother or sister. So that's kinda cool." He smiled, and Annabelle's heart exploded. All she wanted was to see him keep smiling.

"I promise you, we'll go at your own pace."

"Okay."

They walked some more in silence, each lost in their own thoughts. Annabelle glanced over occasionally at the miracle walking beside her. She was grateful that at least he had been loved and cared for so well by Chase. The damage from Tara was unknown, but she would do her best to help him heal. It could be so much worse. And she knew in her heart that over time, Lucas would come to feel the connection between them. He would be her son again. There was nothing she could do to make up for the years they had lost, but she was grateful for the chance to fill the future with new memories.

89

The Wife—Tara

They don't want to give me bail. The judge said I was manipulative and cunning and couldn't be trusted. My parents are flying in tomorrow. I'm sure they'll get this sorted; they always do. The judge doesn't understand what true love is. To know that someone is the only one for you and that no matter what it takes, you have to be with them. I've made too many sacrifices for my marriage to let it all go up in smoke. I've been vigilant over the years, so careful, and one blood drive undid it all. If only Chase had come to me first instead of going all investigative journalist. I could have figured out some explanation. And now I've lost it all. My husband. My reputation. My family.

A guard comes to my cell and opens it. "Your pastor is here. I'll escort you to a private room."

I follow him down the hallway until we reach the tiny, windowless room and sit. He shuts the door and locks it while I wait. A few minutes later, the door opens and he escorts the man in, then withdraws.

"Nice of you to come visit," I say. "Are you the one who screwed me over?"

"Are we being monitored?" he asks.

I give him a cold smile. "No, *Pastor*. Meetings between pastor and congregant are confidential."

James leans forward and glares at me. "You bitch. You put my daughter in a coma! That wasn't what we agreed to."

I shrug. "I modified the plan."

He grabs me by the collar. "I should kill you." His face is red, and his breath comes in short gasps. "You know it wasn't supposed to go down this way. You were just supposed to make it look like Chase was a bad guy, so Annabelle would drop him and that would be the end of things. Make it seem like he was grooming Scarlett. She was never supposed to get hurt!"

I push his hands away from me. "Scarlett knew she had a brother. She wouldn't have believed me. I couldn't risk it. Getting rid of Chase wasn't enough."

"None of this would have been necessary at all if you had moved away like I asked you that night. Chase and Annabelle never would have met."

"What do you mean?" I ask, even though I know full well what he's talking about.

He shakes his head. "The night I switched the babies. You promised me that you'd move to another state. You lied to me."

"I like it here. I had a practice established. There was no reason for anyone to know that you changed my dead baby for Annabelle's live one. Everything would have been fine if Lucas hadn't given blood."

"Scarlett would have believed you if you had stuck to the lie we agreed on. That her brother was dead. She wouldn't have been a threat. Why did you have to hurt her?"

"Maybe she would have believed me or maybe not. But Saint Chase was going to spill the beans. He thinks it's a moral obligation to reunite Lucas and Annabelle. So the truth was going to come out eventually." I'm getting angry again just thinking about the two of them. I glare at James. "If your wife hadn't been trying to steal my husband, I could have let it go. But I knew eventually Chase would tell her the truth and then he and Lucas would leave me forever. I couldn't let that happen. I had to discredit Chase and how better than by setting him up to catfish Scarlett and then try to get rid of her. At least that way I could keep Lucas to myself. Why should I be left with nothing?"

"What makes you think Annabelle would ever leave me for Chase?"

"All their flirty little texts to each other. It was just a matter of time. But now she'll never have him. And she won't trust you anymore either. Not after my gift in the mail."

"You're the one who sent the motel receipt to Annabelle?"

I smile. "I wanted her to believe her husband was stepping out on her. To see what it feels like. I figured, What could you tell her? That you and I used it as a meeting place to put our plan together? Were you able to convince her of your fidelity?"

He glares at me. "Never mind that. You almost killed my daughter! How can you justify that?"

"I already told you. I wasn't going to lose everything. If I was going to lose Lucas, why shouldn't Annabelle lose one of her children? I wanted her to see what it was like to have your child snatched away! I didn't plan to hurt Scarlett at first, but when I saw the email from Scarlett to Chase, I knew I had to do something. So I pretended to be her brother and began texting her. I was going to frame Chase, then use that evidence to make him forget about ever telling anyone the truth about Lucas. I never intended for him to actually go to jail. I just wanted leverage to make him stay with me and keep our family intact. But then he hired Annabelle and they started going away together. And I could see from their texts that they were getting close. I had to stop him before he told her the truth. But then you tracked me down when you realized who Chase was and I only disclosed part of my plan to you. But Annabelle had to suffer. It wouldn't be fair for me to be the only one."

James gives me a withering look. "How did I not see what a psycho you are?"

"Oh please. Don't try to act so innocent. You were more than happy to go along with my plan to discredit Chase so you could hold on to your darling wife even though she was trying to steal my husband. Despite my best efforts, the truth came out because you couldn't keep your mouth shut." I watch as his face contorts into a mask of rage. I can see it's taking everything in him not to grab me.

"I didn't tell anyone what you did! I don't know how the police found out, but I'm glad they did. I hope you rot in here. I would never have given you Annabelle's baby if I'd known what a terrible person you truly are."

The door opens, and the original detective on the case walks in.

"James Reynolds, you are under arrest for the kidnapping of Lucas Sommers."

His eyes widen in shock. "I thought you said this was—"

I pull a wire from under my jumpsuit.

"Surprise."

90

Annabelle

One Year Later

It had been hard for Annabelle to overcome her desire to protect Scarlett and Olivia and try to sugarcoat what James had done, but in the end, she realized the truth was more important. She had been hiding from it for far too long. In time, maybe they would forgive their father for his actions, but that was between the three of them.

James was a broken man. Sentenced to twenty years in prison, his license revoked, the life he knew over. Tara had also been charged with kidnapping in addition to her other charges and received a twenty-five-year sentence. As for Annabelle, one day forgiveness would come, but it would take time. She had always known deep down that James wasn't the one for her, but she'd allowed herself to mistake feeling safe for feeling loved. Her instincts had been there all along. She wondered now if the reason that her mother had believed they were a couple was because James had been telling her so. His penchant for self-delusion was the only explanation she could think of, for how he could believe he'd done the right thing in giving her son away to Tara. It's possible that he had come to regret it over the years, especially seeing what the loss had done to Annabelle. But at any time, he could have come clean. Instead, he'd stolen sixteen years from her. And from Lucas. The only thing she couldn't regret was that he'd given her Scarlett and Olivia.

Annabelle sold the house, and they moved into a smaller one a few blocks from the beach. Her stock options had matured, and she invested the money from them as well as some of the house money. She wanted to make sure that her children's futures were financially secure. She'd been tempted to ask for a transfer to the California office, but she wouldn't separate the girls from their grandparents. They were heartbroken at what James had done and grateful that Annabelle placed no blame on them.

Now she stood on the deck, inhaling deeply, and watched as her children finished their cornhole game in the backyard and ran up to the house.

"Is dinner ready? I'm starving!" Olivia said, out of breath.

Following close behind her were Scarlett and Lucas.

"One point!" Scarlett said, shaking her head. "One of these days I'm gonna kick your butt."

"Good luck," Lucas said, laughing.

They went inside and sat around the kitchen table. "I made your favorite," she said to Lucas as she pulled the lasagna from the oven, the cheese bubbling over, and the noodles looking cooked, not crunchy. She smiled when she thought back to her first failed attempt all those years ago.

"Thanks. . . . Mmmom," he said, the word still not coming easily.

They were getting there, she thought. In the beginning, the only reason she saw him at all was thanks to Chase making plans with her. After a while, Lucas began to feel comfortable coming on his own. Annabelle and the girls started going to his sports events, and over time it became more natural for them to feel like a family. Then one night, about a month ago, he'd come to spend a Friday night for a movie marathon. Olivia, Scarlett, and Lucas each chose one film.

The girls fell asleep by the time the third movie came on, but Annabelle struggled to stay awake to keep Lucas company. She was surprised when he started talking, looking at the screen.

"I always felt like something was missing. I mean, I loved Mom and Dad, but deep down sometimes I felt like I didn't fit. Especially with Mom's mood swings. I never really knew how she would react to things." He finally looked over at her. "I didn't want to admit it, even to myself. It seemed so disloyal. But on some level, I wasn't completely shocked when I found out the truth."

Annabelle waited, not wanting to interrupt him in case he had more to say.

"Sometimes you say something, and it kind of reminds me of the way I feel about things. Thank you for not making me choose. I'm glad you found me . . . Mom."

She'd reached over and hugged Lucas to her and was surprised to feel his shoulders shaking with sobs. They stayed that way for a long time, and as she held him, she knew in her heart that her son had truly returned to her.

Now as they sat down to eat, she looked around the table and she was filled with an overwhelming sense of gratitude. Even though they'd only found each other a year ago, the gaps had been filled in more quickly than she could have ever imagined. The girls both adored Lucas, and he loved being a big brother. He still lived with Chase most of the time, but he had his own room in their new house, and he spent the occasional weekend here. Now that he was seventeen, though, his friends took up the majority of his time. Annabelle didn't mind. She was just happy to have him in her life and to see him thriving.

"Dad texted. He's on his way," Lucas said.

CHASE ARRIVED JUST AS THEY finished dinner.

"Time for some coffee and dessert?" Annabelle asked after he came in.

"Always," he said, smiling.

The kids cleaned up the dishes, while she and Chase went into the living room.

"How is Lucas dealing with Tara being in prison?" she asked.

"Honestly, I think he's just relieved that it wasn't me. Now that you've met her and know what she did, I'm sure you can understand that his relationship with her has been less than ideal. Still, I had no idea of what she was really capable of. The fact that she was complicit in the switch. And the other thing that's so unforgivable is that we never mourned the death of our son. Because, of course, I didn't know that he'd died. How she could exchange the babies like they were objects instead of people. It's inconceivable."

"Now I understand why James kept trying to get me to take a leave of absence. He didn't want me to find out the truth. He saw your picture on your website and recognized you from the hospital all those years ago. And Tara was so convincing. She had me believing you were this narcissistic monster, when she knew all along that she'd stolen my child. How did you live with her all those years?"

"It wasn't easy, but I couldn't leave Lucas with her. She was a fantastic lawyer; she would have gotten full custody, and then I wouldn't have been there to mitigate the emotional drama she loves to inflict."

"You must have been devastated to find out that she faked all those pregnancies. I can't fathom it."

"I believed she was a good person at heart. And that part of the reason why she would go into these dark moods was because of all she'd lost. But now, to know that she made a mockery out of everything . . . pretending to mourn losing those children and putting me through all that." Chase shook his head. "You'd think I'd be used to sociopathic behavior, with all the crime podcasts I've done. But you never think it's going to hit so close to home."

"That's totally normal. You wanted to see the best in her. She was your wife," Annabelle said.

"I know, but still. And she was always trying to make me feel like something was wrong with me. Saying I must be sick because I was fascinated with true crime. She actually accused me of being in those chat rooms so I could pick up tips on being a killer."

"You're kidding me. What kind of chat rooms?"

"Crime aficionados mostly, but there are, believe it or not, some support groups online for self-proclaimed sociopaths. I went to them in service of research, but Tara thought it meant something more. Probably because she's the sociopath."

"It's mind-boggling. It still freaks me out to think she could have succeeded in framing you and running off with Lucas."

"I know."

He took a sip from his mug. "How are things between James and the girls?"

"Olivia visits him in prison once a month, but Scarlett can't seem to forgive him, no matter what I say."

"Have you forgiven him?"

"I'm trying. Not for his sake so much, but for mine. I think of my mother and what she used to tell me about holding on to anger. I can either expend my energy railing against what he did and what he took from me, or I can be grateful for what I've been able to recover. I still can't believe what he was capable of. And it still seems unreal that he was choking me that day. I have to admit, I'm not sorry that he's in prison and can't be alone with the kids. The fact that he snapped like that . . . It was terrifying." Annabelle leaned back against the cushion. "It's strange. I've struggled all my life with the choice-versus-destiny question. Then I had all these dreams that I thought were about helping me to make the right choices."

"And now?"

"Now I realize that the dreams were trying to wake me up to what I knew all along. I was living a pseudolife: not making my own choices, ignoring my intuition, my gut. I guess this psychic ability turned out to be more of a gift than a curse."

"I would say so. I could be sitting in a prison cell, and Tara would be laughing at all of us. But your dreams saved me."

"That's terrifying. I still think about our choices. How we have no idea of the repercussions all these decisions have. If I'd taken the job instead of Riggs, then I wouldn't have gone away with you. Or maybe I would have. I don't know. Maybe things are going to happen one way or another." Annabelle smiled at him. "A good friend of mine told me a saying that really resonates. Her mother always said it."

"What is it?"

"If you're meant to drown, it won't do any good to move to the desert."

Chase laughed. "Yeah. I guess that's true. Any dreams lately?"

She shook her head. "No, I suppose everything's as it should be."

"Well, we still haven't taken that dip in the Pacific," he said with a mischievous grin. "What do you think?"

She smiled back at him. "Let me sleep on it."

Acknowledgments

I'm profoundly grateful to have such a wise, supportive, and passionate team whose diligence and excellence brought *Don't Open Your Eyes* to life. My deepest thanks go to the entire Bantam family: Jennifer Hershey and Kara Welsh, whose leadership makes it an honor to be part of this incredible publishing house. To my amazing editor, Jenny Chen—your uncanny ability to pinpoint exactly what needs to change and your brilliant edits never fail to leave me in awe. Jean Slaughter, your dedication keeps everything moving seamlessly toward publication—thank you for all you do. To the powerhouse marketing team—Emma Thomasch, Vanessa Duque, and Taylor Noel—your creativity and hard work are inspiring. And to Sarah Breivogel and Angie Campusano, publicists extraordinaire who tirelessly champion my work, I'm endlessly grateful for your commitment and expertise. A heartfelt thank you to Kara Cesare, Kim Hovey, Mark Maguire, Steve Messina, Saige Francis, Jo Anne Metsch, Fritz Metsch, Cindy Berman, and Paul Gilbert for your unwavering support. I'm absolutely in love with the stunning cover art from the immensely talented Scott Biel—thank you for bringing this book to life visually.

Jenny Bent, my steadfast and loyal agent, thank you for always being there—to listen, to strategize, and to encourage me to chase every literary ambition, even when it feels like we can barely keep track of it all! I'm so grateful to have you by my side on this incredible journey. Thanks to Emma Lagarde for your hard work managing foreign rights and thanks to Victoria Cappello for keeping everything on track.

To Dana Spector, my gratitude for your support and creative vision in bringing my work to the screen. Your guidance means the world to me.

I count myself blessed to have such a supportive and kind writing community. It is truly an honor to have made so many friends among this talented community. A special shout-out to Wendy Walker, Anthony Franze, Jean Kwok, Kim Howe, Jeneva Rose, Tosca Lee, and Lisa Unger for always being a quick text or phone call away.

No words are sufficient to express my love and appreciation for my sister and partner in crime, Valerie. You are my safe haven, always the first one I call in every circumstance, and I love you beyond measure.

Thank you to my family for your constant love and support. To Rick for letting me discuss characters as though they were people you know and for never getting tired of listening to me work out plot points (at least you don't show it)! And to Nick and Theo for being my biggest champions; you all mean everything to me.

Endless gratitude to my readers; your loyalty and support mean the world to me, and I'm deeply thankful. Heartfelt thanks to the librarians, booksellers, and book bloggers whose tireless dedication and generosity help bring my work to readers. It's a privilege to be part of this incredible community!

About the Author

LIV CONSTANTINE is the pseudonym of Lynne Constantine, an Edgar Award–nominated, *New York Times,* and internationally bestselling author. She is the co-author of *The Last Mrs. Parrish,* a Reese Witherspoon Book Club pick, and her critically acclaimed books have been praised by *The Washington Post, USA Today, The Sunday Times, People,* and *Good Morning America,* among many others, with more than two million copies sold worldwide. Her work has been translated into twenty-nine languages, is available in thirty-four countries, and is in development for both television and film. When she's not writing, you can find her curled up with her Labrador and golden retriever, reading a good book or binge-watching the latest limited series.

livconstantine.com
Instagram: @livconstantine2
X: @livconstantine2

About the Type

This book was set in Fairfield, the first typeface from the hand of the distinguished American artist and engraver Rudolph Ruzicka (1883–1978). Ruzicka was born in Bohemia (in the present-day Czech Republic) and came to America in 1894. He set up his own shop, devoted to wood engraving and printing, in New York in 1913 after a varied career working as a wood engraver, in photoengraving and banknote printing plants, and as an art director and freelance artist. He designed and illustrated many books, and was the creator of a considerable list of individual prints—wood engravings, line engravings on copper, and aquatints.